HUNGER'S DAUGHTERS

Nirmala Govindarajan

Om Books International

First published in 2019 by

Om Books International

Corporate & Editorial Office
A-12, Sector 64, Noida 201 301
Uttar Pradesh, India
Phone: +91 120 477 4100
Email: editorial@ombooks.com
Website: www.ombooksinternational.com

Sales Office
107, Ansari Road, Darya Ganj,
New Delhi 110 002, India
Phone: +91 11 4000 9000
Fax: +91 11 2327 8091
Email: sales@ombooks.com
Website: www.ombooks.com

ISBN: 978-93-52766-81-9

Printed in India

10 9 8 7 6 5 4 3 2 1

NIRMALA GOVINDARAJAN is a journalist, social sector documentarian and author. Her novel *The Community Catalyst*, is inspired by the life experiences of a civil servant, and is recommended reading for aspirants of the Indian Administrative Services. In 2010, she conceptualised and co-authored *Mind Blogs 1.0*, the first blog-to-book initiative. In 2014, she conceptualised and co-curated the debut edition of *The Times of India* Literary Carnival, Bangalore. She curates the Literary Lounge series at The British Council, and also introduces children to classics at the Library.

Her novel *Hunger's Daughters*, is born out of her experiences as a social sector documentarian. She dabbles in theatre, and also believes in harmonising with the elements through music—she plays the western classical piano, violin and guitar.

For

My mother Chandra Govindarajan

My guru Peter Colaco

The girls in the city—Yogita Dakshina and Mary Pascaline Radjou

All the little girls in the hamlets of Boudh, Balangir and Keonjhar districts in Orissa

And, the Man in a Blue Kurta.

I

I have always believed that the real history is made by ordinary people.

– Mahasweta Devi

Girls do not always have it easy. Even when they are thirteen. Susanthi Bodra is not thirteen yet. She became a businesswoman at age eight, when the village elders said her father had died. She started rearing ducks, and now has Rs 3,000 saved up at the State Bank of India's branch in the District Headquarters. In her forest hamlet, where there is neither electric pole nor pump to surface clear, drinking water, she is rich, especially for a girl of twelve, and a few months more.

I have a story to report, I wait in the lone classroom at the Bochagora Village School, Balangir District, Orissa, for over an hour to meet her. Time passes. I shift from my left foot to the right, and back. Some more time passes. They say she is on her way. I wait an hour longer, my attention drawn to little shirtless boys who have by now broken the language barrier between us with boisterous games of 'catch-me-if-you-can'. The village elders look on—women giggling behind their sari pallus, men staring, sometimes too probingly. Another hour passes. Susanthi still hasn't arrived.

Perplexed, perturbed, a group of social workers travelling from Bhubaneswar, the post-independence capital of Orissa, and I, decide to walk up the narrow path lined with frond-thatched hutments on one side, and rain-soaked fields of nodding paddy on the other.

A duck quacks, another joins in to form a quacking duet in the paddy pond. Two more ducks waddle in to form a quartet. I do not feel like hushing them—they are trying to tell me a secret. A secret which the Bochagora village elders have kept from us since the time the other social workers and I have arrived at the hamlet three hours ago.

The ducks quack louder, and I find a quartet running across the mud road, brushing my feet, and into a rugged brick-and-frond-thatched structure. I rush behind the quartet, enter a hut, and within it, another. In the darkest corner of this dwelling, a flash of pink moves, very slightly. So slightly, that I might have missed the movement had I chosen to blink at that precise moment. The village elders have followed me. They raise the dibri—that's what they call the kerosene lamp in these regions. This village can only be reached through meandering mud paths that have never felt the heat of tar before. A yellow light from the dibri draws attention to a face hiding a storm. It is a storm of tears which drench my pink kurta when I look into her eyes, and I take her into my arms, instinctively.

Today, Susanthi weeps until she has no voice left to speak. Her father has been pronounced dead. Her mother has abandoned her. She is alone. Very alone. She wraps her frail arms around me, and sobs until the tears will spill no more.

On the same evening, when we say goodbye, I know it is not for the last time. Susanthi too, knows it.

Goodbye isn't a kind word, I hope the Man in a Blue Kurta knows it. It indicates closure, a 'we-shall-never-meet-again' signal. The last time I said goodbye to him, I had enough salt from my tears to empty into the Great Arabian Ocean.

He has left me again, standing with his baby in my arms, steering the wheel of his rugged close-topped jeep in a direction I am not to know.

I refuse to say goodbye once more, the tears pour.

I run as fast as my feet will take me—the weight of his emotions and mine are weakening my pace. I am fortunate in my misery. I choose to not return home to Bangalore after my meeting with Susanthi Bodra. I board the only train from Bhubaneswar to the Union Territory which wears the Great Arabian Ocean like its own skin.

In the Union Territory of Goa, I cry some more.

As waves lash upon rocks, I watch my tears fighting for identity.

In my little reporter's notebook which travels with me everywhere I go, I address my sorrow:

Tear drops
Wet cheeks
Sweating hands
It's raining salt.
Perspiration
Inspiration
In what order?
Disorder.
Conscious beyond consciousness
Beneath the stone surface called skin
Oceans thrive on the salt of sorrow
Unresolved by you, me, humanity...

I close my notebook to watch the sun descend from the sky and sink into the Ocean as it turns into a big ball of orange fire, taking my identity with it. As I watch the fireball disappear into the Great Arabian Ocean, leaving its salted waters with a tinge of ethereal orange, a man in blue appears. This is the man I love. I stretch my arms out to embrace him, and melt into his lingering passion-arousing fold. The Great Arabian Ocean holds the promise of a scene from a tender moment at his front door. This door wears a curtain of Lantana flowers, and is patterned with freshly-drawn fish, ducks, and their relatives. The scene is emotion-perfect. I linger in the arms of the man I love and rest my head upon his bare chest until the orange fire has reached another shore, and a new night spreads its expanse over the Great Arabian Ocean. The distant stars in the deep of the night shine their tantalising light unto the Ocean and infuse me with a promise.

I stop crying.

I promise myself that I will never say goodbye again. Certainly not to the man I love. Certainly not to Susanthi Bodra—this little girl, almost thirteen, has forged a deeper than deep bond with me—we have both lost our fathers.

***

There is a storm in Balangir. The rains have been incessant—drowning the weeds, washing out the paddy fields. There is no other crop to talk of in these regions—people practise single cropping here because the elected leaders at the Centre and their representatives in the State have dismissed the need for water feeders in these 'insignificant-to-the-progress-of-the-Indian-nation' parts.

Progress has never visited these parts. I am in Bochagora one more time, I observe that Susanthi's home lies not many, but a few difficult kilometres into the forest. These are deep forests where there is Maoxal uprising, whisper the elders of Bochagora. The original agenda of this Left-wing group is to set right matters that the State and Centre have carelessly left out of their list of duties and responsibilities. This uprising is no surprise, considering that the Government does not know who Susanthi Bodra is. The elected democracy does not know of the existence of Domrudoru Baiga either—he is a little boy who lives in the same hamlet as Susanthi.

This hamlet in Balangir District is home to the Munda tribes of Orissa. They are as much creatures of the forest here, as are the elephants, the Neem trees, even the nature-endowed lakes serenaded by bunds. The inhabitants of this land use these bunds to reach the hand-etched stone steps that in turn take them to their source of life—the stagnant waterbody which is green with inedible moss. Here, the Mundas bathe, wash their clothes and cattle—mainly cows, the occasional buffalo, and a few goats. But in the recollectable past, as far as Domrudoru's parents and grandparents can remember, the inhabitants have been experiencing a constant sense of unease. Among the many reasons which subject them to fear, the wild animals are not the primary perpetrators, they are family. The animals largely mind their own businesses if humans keep out of their way. Being fellow creatures of the jungle, both Mundas and animals know the laws of nature to abide by. They follow these laws as strictly as they possibly can. Those who have chosen to go astride the law in these regions are the Maoxals, industrialists and some elected representatives of the country, sources say. These categories are groups of human beings who believe in taking shortcuts of a deviant kind, in their endeavour to amass fortunes befitting kings in a democracy. Some of this fortune is stacked away in banks, much of it is black as fertile soil—this soil is rich with imported worms to eat away the local 'pests'.

The 'pests' in these regions are the Mundas, as was Susanthi's father who refused to join force with a group of Maoxals when they stormed his home, guns and ration in hand, commanding his wife and their little daughter to cook an untimely meal for them.

Susanthi's father did not fare well with the industrialists either. He refused to take his children to the brick kiln, the owner of which in turn refused him and his wife work during the barren months. He wanted his children to go to the Bochagora Government School at the entrance to his village, instead. Susanthi's father did not turn up at the brick kiln when the industrialists most needed labour. Instead, he influenced fellow members of his tribe to leave their children back at school. They all stayed back at their Munda brother's beckoning, reveals Domrudoru's father.

I interview some more elders at the Bochagora Gram Panchayat, and learn that Susanthi's father had been influenced by the crusaders for rural equanimity from YUPAP. He chose to be a rebel by adopting a straightforward life of toil in a hamlet, which the elected democracy refused to acknowledge. On the days his family went to bed hungry, he told them to think of nothing but their books. Their books had rhymes, which Susanthi and Domrudoru—her best friend—sang for the other village children:

Hathi moi, hathi moi
Kothai jabo re
Hathi moi, hathi moi
Ekhane ashboo re...

This rhyme pervades the heartland of Orissa.

Susanthi Bodra, Domrudoru Baiga and the other children of the Bochagora Government School sing this native song of the forest hamlet, questioning mother elephant about where she was wandering off to, and pleading with her to return home.

Arriving at the Manipura Government School in the mining district of Keonjhar the following morning, I hear young voices sing the same song. The children of Manipura hamlet, Keonjhar District, belong to the Munda tribes of Orissa. *They are no different from the children of the Munda tribes of Balangir*, I write in my reporter's notebook when I meet them in flesh.

***

Susanthi plays a part in running her house. She brings her mother money to buy daal, salt and kerosene. The kerosene serves two purposes—her mother uses it to prepare a meal when she is able to sit up and cook, and Susanthi Bodra fills her dibri with it. Every day, she raises the burnt wick of the dibri to add more light to her dingy room. This is the only room in the house. This is where she sleeps, cooks and studies. This is where she changes her clothes. This is where her ducks waddle in after their evening walk to serenade her with a quacking refrain when she returns from school. This is where she reads and re-reads her textbooks word by word, line by line, one paragraph upon another, until it is time to lower the wick, and extinguish the dibri for a night of well-deserved sleep. Susanthi lies awake in the dark, until she comes to terms with the fact that her mother has left home. The hard truth has a strange way of knocking Susanthi to sleep. In her dingy hutment, she sleeps alone.

Susanthi does not dream when she falls asleep. She used to dream when she was a little girl. In her dream, she wore a bright red frock with white frills—the same dress which is dangling from a hangar at the store in the main market of Sambhalpur. In her dream, her father had bought the dress for her. When she woke up in the morning, her father was gone. Her mother released some bile, and lots of tears. Her mother told Susanthi it was time to stop dreaming. When her friend Domrudoru Baiga came to fetch Susanthi to school that day, she refused to go along.

Susanthi suddenly knows she cannot go on dreaming. She does not dream of the red frock she may never get to wear in her lifetime, anymore.

There is a certain Man in a Blue Kurta—he is a dreamer, he has known hunger, and he, with his unpredictable appearances and disappearances, intercedes my thoughts all the time. I have known him long before his baby was born. I have stood beside his bed, and seen his hunger burn him like a fire in the belly of a volcano, simmering, engulfing his capacity to think. His is no mean hunger—food cannot satisfy it. He has an unfulfilled passion, and that must be fed... I drift into another day... I touch his forehead, and feel him burning. I give him his blue kurta, the much-used khadi garment warmed by the coal iron. He wears it, and goes to sleep, I think. I cannot sleep because he burns. I shudder and remember how I want to play a part in every story. But this is not a story. I cannot tear away from the truth about love and its war against lust and my head is in a whir as I travel in and out of terrains I have tread before.

Truth is, the man I love has torn away from me to feed his hunger—his unfulfilled passion.

Truth is, I will not sell my soul to ease his burn. I will love him even when he scorches me. When I enter his room he spits fire, which by some aberration of logic, caresses me like the cooling droplets of sudden summer rain—my head is in a whir again—all past seems so present.

Summer has come and gone, but the Man in a Blue Kurta has not returned home to me.

Summer is a time for holidays. Susanthi has not attended her school for a year. But every day is not a holiday. She wakes up at 4 am to tend to her ducks. Cook a meal of light porridge. Go to her master's field to weed and tend to the freshly-sown crop of paddy. Return home to clean the bile her mother has extricated in the dark corners of their hutment—the stench of her excreta lingers days after she has left her daughter. It is 9 am. Susanthi's day has just begun. There's work to be done.

***

The search has just begun. Just like it began several years ago when I was eight, sitting alone in the balcony of my parents' home overlooking the paling BWSSB (Bangalore Water Supply and Sewerage Board) housing quarters.

I try to recall the emotions which had perturbed me then, and pen them in my reporter's notebook...

Hidden
Beneath the old mattress
Under the cot
In the laundry bag
Inside CD covers
Envelopes
Old books
Written in blue ink on inland letters
Within the heart
Knocking at the head
Cajoling the fingers
Words

Phrases
Strung together with emotion
Call themselves stories...

There are diverse stories that fight to be recalled in my search for the meaning of life. Somehow, they all seem to merge in a reclusive corner from where all this world seems a blatant lie.

My past is not a lie.

My past is not perfect.

My past is much like the moon's surface—smooth and glowing from a distance. In reality, scarred with craters.

In the depths of these craters, there are memories of oppression.

I visit a memory.

I am eight, and it is time to visit my friend Arti. She is also eight. Arti's house help is also eight. But she cannot play with us. Arti's mother must first beat her with the three-foot-long iron stick placed securely behind the groove of the bathroom door until there is a purplish-blue bruise on her right foot and on her knuckles. Then, the eight-year-old house help must work hard to scrub and clean utensils in which Arti's mother will cook for her biological daughters. The house help must then wash the utensils clean, sweep the floor, and eat two slices of dry bread to stay alive.

Each mid-morning, the eight-year-old house help dips the bread in weak coffee now gone cold, and puts her hunger to rest. I watch her from my balcony, and wonder: Who is she? She is Arti's household help, she is the same age as me, and she is hungry.

Do the hungry care about their identities?

The present is not perfect either.

I care about his baby's identity. I decide that I will never let the rotten hand of any living devil touch his baby. Never.

My work and personal life are indulgent of each other. Typing away at the notes I have gathered from my recent trip to Orissa, I am touched by Susanthi's story—my wavering gaze wanders from the computer screen, and lands on a blue allure lying crumpled on my bed. I pick up his blue kurta, still fresh from the scent of his body, and hold it close to my heart...

I feel his touch from a seemingly not-so-distant day in the past.

Touch is powerful. Each time the tip of my finger touches his, there is an awkward storm welling inside me. He has been careful not to let the touch happen. But it does when he throws the key to his rugged close-topped jeep into my palms and I shudder outwardly. He does not notice. I feel shunned like an untouchable—the storm wells, attacking my composure, and rises to gush out of its boundary to meet the world through my eyes. The world cannot see my tears. He cannot see my tears. He is my world. I blink several times to send the tears back into my eyes. I succeed just in time to smile, as though I have been enveloped by his arms and held in a passionate embrace once more.

In the present, he is gone.

He has left me warm.

***

I rock his baby until she decides I am her mother. I hold in my arms the labour of his love. She, a living reminiscence of his lost connections from a time when he had wandered far, far away from his home to seek new directions.

He now lives in another home hugged by Lantana shrubs, and an endless expanse of one thousand five hundred and thirty-three Sal trees encircling this forest shelter—all wood and leaf merging with their kith and kin in the lands disappearing into a dense mountain range. I have wandered through this forest hamlet, and into a Government health centre where a single hard bed and an ageing dibri draw attention to mediocre medical care. I later learnt that his mother had given birth to him on the same bed, and under the light of the very dibri which was around a little over thirty decades younger then. But I, Nainika Chandra, a reporter with an interest in art, distant cultures and tribal communities, have never visited his home during the many official trips I have made to the State of Orissa. He is not comfortable in my presence any more.

I feel a nascent tear run down my cheek, and tickle the baby's delicate frame resting in my arms. She holds my tears as they dance on her being like freshly harvested pearls.

I hear a knock. I place his baby upon a soft rug, wipe my tears, and open the door. My heart skips a beat. His eyes hold mine in a hot embrace that immediately melts the ice between his heart and mine. But only for a moment—he lowers his gaze, almost immediately. This is no time to embrace the woman who loves him.

I love this man. His favourite colour is blue. He always wears a blue kurta.

Today, I open the cupboard and my eyes settle on a new hole in his blue kurta. My heart races. I remember the day I had darned another hole in the same kurta…

That day, he sat bare-chested, playing a game of chess on his computer. I felt a nervous pleasure, and absent-mindedly let the needle engage the blue thread in a Hawaiian rumba to *Just the Way You Are*—a Bruno Mars classic tune playing on my tape recorder, until there was no hole left to see. My eyes glued to the kurta, I darned the hole mindfully, until I felt a gaze rest upon my near-bare shoulders. I looked askance to catch his eyes scrutinise my womanhood, watch his lips break into a smile, and my heart raced faster. I let the needle sleep on the kurta, and permitted my eyes to rest upon his bare chest. His chest, so sumptuously broad and warm to the touch… I abandoned the needle on the blue kurta, and laid my head to rest in his warmth, and dream.

This is no dream.

I hold the door open, my gaze now persistent on a brand-new hole in his much-worn blue kurta. I yearn for the warmth of his bare chest once more. I want to unbutton his kurta this very minute and darn the new hole. My eyes will then feast on his bare chest as he plays his game of chess, just the way he did the other day, nearly eighteen full moons ago on a day in the year 2015.

This is another day in the year 2017. The man at the door is not certain he wants to talk to me.

I hold back my words. It is not appropriate to tell him what I think. I think I must brew his favourite drink instead. Like the old days, he sips on his cup of chamomile tea, and I take him through the exciting day his baby has had. She is fast gathering admirers, I tell him. We will talk about them another day, he says. He must leave now. He has work to do.

As the blue vanishes inside the rugged close-topped jeep, I embrace the air. It is the same spot where he had stood and returned my hug hesitantly only a minute ago. I smell the warmth of his blue kurta flavoured with wild

Lantana flowers and Sal husk from the open yard filling into his home, upon my night-shirt. I hear the baritone of a bush lark which has left its nest on this rainy day to seek the truth about life.

Truth is, life is a long dash.

There are no full stops between long dashes. I haven't heard from the Man in a Blue Kurta in two months. I write his name, and then, draw a dash—a long one. He is constrained by his strong will. He will not write his surname. He is feeling abandoned.

His baby is feeling abandoned.

I will not abandon his baby. I take her in my arms and hold her tight.

The evening is young. I need to make a phone call...

'Good evening, Maestro Sridhar Haider D'Vaz, how is your painting shaping up?'

'Good evening, Madame Nainika Chandra!' replies the artist par excellence, spiritedly, as he always does. 'I think it has shaped up quite well—I gave it the final touches yesterday.'

'Wow! So soon? That's simply fantastic. From what I last saw of it, I'm certain the painting will dominate the frames at the Der Bundesrepublik Biennale!'

'Ha, ha, if you think so, Madame. I believe that an artist needs discipline even when his muse is undisciplined. You see, art is a personal calling, and the artist cannot afford to go haywire on the pretext of losing his muse for heaven's sake. You do know that my muse has been on the run!'

'True, true. I understand. By the way, you know his baby—she is such a becoming muse. And she's fast been drawing admirers, especially since you've made it known that you find her ravishing.'

'You better send her picture to me. I shall see what I can do for your special man's labour of love. The Blue Man's little girl, I say!'

'You are really very kind. Thank you so much, Maestro! Have a great day.'

I disconnect the phone, sit beside my baby, and stroke her slender frame. His baby is fragile and sensitive. I choose who I show her off to. She must not be seen in places that do not appreciate her father's ability to create a masterpiece born out of his breath, his pain.

...His breath is ever so intense and gentle, just like the stroke of a thrush-feathered brush, it fills my being with its alluring spell. I wear his breath like perfume, and it lingers long after he's gone...I think of him all the time... I see him stroke my hair in the mirror one minute. In a new minute, he is gone.

He has driven off in his rugged jeep, his silence louder than the sputter of the vehicle's macho engine...

I brush my hair, and hope that sometimes, he thinks of me. But that is not what he has bargained for.

I cannot help his bargain.

I still hope he thinks of me, at least sometimes... Often, actually every day, I shut my eyes to dream of that monsoon evening fourteen months ago when the sun shimmered, the Indian golden oriole twittered, and the Man in a Blue Kurta held my tiny palm tightly within the fold of his large and artistic hands. He was in Bangalore to show his fresh series of paintings, and I had dropped by to review his labour of love. His labour, a blatant culmination of subtle emotion and distant terrain that drew me into his world, and soon enough his embrace. Today, I look out of the window, and stare at the same spot where he had last hugged me—the night is leaning towards a fresh dawn, and I hope it will bring me close to the blue kurta one more time.

I close my eyes to dream of a happy ending.

But the story has only just begun.

It is futile to imagine that this day is just like every other twenty-four-hour stretch of sunrise and sunset that I have ever experienced. Each day brings a different story, so I ride into the sunset to look at the paintings in the Citizen's Art Gallery while his baby rests at home. But there is no sun on the horizon—the clouds have gathered for a shower even as the winds blow in disarray, and I ride into the imaginary sunset instead, like I have for the last ten years on the same 100 cc bike. Ten years ago, this bike belonged to my father. He never rode it. It still belongs to my father, a black Kinetic Honda, vintage variety.

When I ride my bike, all life is a blur, and I'm simply happy to hear the wind whistling through my skull. But there's no wind today. There are heavy clouds, and nostalgia.

Ten years ago, riding into the sunset on a November evening meant just that—slices of icy-cold breeze pregnant with rain, wind whistling through my skull. Somehow, riding the Kinetic Honda across town seemed to take away all the weight of uncontrollable emotion from inside my head. But the emotion rested in my heart. It beat heavily no matter how much wind whistled through my skull, and I rode faster to meet the reason for my heartbeat.

That was another time, another place, another era almost. Just graduated from university, the boy I crushed on loved blue of course, also orange, green, red and yellow. So, Sylvester Martin—yes that's the name of the boy I had fallen in love with—wore a red canvas shoe on one foot and a yellow one on the other. I giggled with the new-found identity of a girl who had just hit puberty, much in awe of my lover boy's creativity. His identity vibrant in his nonchalant dressing, colours mismatched in adorable haphazardness, subconsciously of course. I was barely out of college then and knew nothing of the complexities of romantic affection—that which means love to one partner, implies lust to the other.

So I rode my Honda with the wind, dubba of aloo parathas tucked into my jute embroidered bag—this, a meal I cooked for him every other weekend. He ate the parathas every other weekend, worked into the night, travelled the world, and came back with a girl from Croatia. He married her.

Years have passed since we last met, and I fondly think of Sylvester. I do not love him the way I do my baby's father. My baby's father—the Man in a Blue Kurta—yes, he has a name but I cannot write it for all to read, especially at this point when he isn't comfortable with his identity. I was only a girl when I cooked the lone dish I had mastered for Sylvester. I am a woman now, and have learnt to toss vegetables into sabjis, roll dough into palm-sized phulkas, and fill the tava with the batter of instant dosa. I have travelled the poorest regions of my country and visited terrains where little girls keep hearth—they know not the pleasures of a carefree childhood.

His child deserves a carefree life—and I have learnt to take good care of her. She, his girl child, is very precious to me.

***

Days have tumbled into weeks, and now a little over two months since the Man in a Blue Kurta drove away in a rugged close-topped jeep. Today, I sit in another close-topped jeep, driving through the Elephant Corridor with the YUPAP volunteers on a monsoon day which has not quite set according to season. Fresh and fresher raindrops topple over the closed windows, and we intersect through deep forests in the hinterlands of the steel city of Tatanagar. I notice that:

Dalma
Separates
Integrates
Consolidates
Misgivings
Between those who have land
And those who have wealth.
Money power.
Wild. Vivid. In the village called Thimri.
I realise...
Secret liaisons in the Dalma Ranges
Have been made public by perpetrators of change.
Change in the name of development and prosperity.
To what avail?

The Dalma Ranges separate the states of Jharkhand and West Bengal, and through their forest mountain paths, lead up to Orissa. This mountain territory nurtures life, secret to the occasional passing car and frequent heavy motor vehicles. You can call the four-legged inhabitants of these ranges animals, and their slithering comrades, reptiles—their habitats are lush and wild, they are truly blessed. Elephants, deer, leopards and jackals, a not-so-occasional snake slithering across the road, all traverse the Dalma Ranges by night, also by day.

As the day matures into another afternoon, I watch the road winding inside the bosom of the mountain ranges, until we arrive at Thimri. Squeals of laughter tumble from the lone cement building in Dalma's hamlet, and children at the Thimri Government School, Jharkhand State, display their milk teeth. It is time for their midday meal, and they rush out of the building, tumbling over each other, lighting up the rain-sloshed afternoon with flashlights of warm smiles. Their smiles are infectious. They appear on the lips of young adults who have learnt to harness solar power in a land where electricity is reality and myth, at once. These smiling young adults have been trained by YUPAP's volunteers to assemble solar lanterns to use at home, sell and service. They are all gathered at the Panchayat office to interact with me, and among them is Asha Paharia.

I watch the youth of Thimri, Asha included, assemble solar lanterns, all displaying their technical skills in an endeavour to make a respectable livelihood. We talk about their training, and their lives in the Dalma Ranges until tea break, when it's time to say goodbye.

Before I leave, Asha insists I visit her home. I take a walk through the hamlet of Thimri with the effervescent young lady. She shows me her hutment, and introduces me to her toothy grandmother sitting on a charpoy in the frontyard. We walk into her mud-walled hutment, and step out through the rear door, to the open backyard. This is where Asha and her family grow their vegetables, and dry their grain. This is also where Asha attend's nature's call in the thick of the night. This is where I smell the rustic warmth of Mother Earth, and watch her embrace those children closest to her heart. In this deep-set jungle hamlet, Mother Earth has a special place in her bosom for Asha, and the other two-hundred-odd inhabitants of Thimri.

***

No physical contact can get warmer than a hug which addresses you for the woman you are.

Like the woman I have just met in the hamlet of Poothotum, Mayavaram District, Tamil Nadu on a not-so-warm day...

30 kilometres from the main Shiva Temple
Is the abode of a Lesser Known Goddess
Albeit in a different avatar.
When the pilgrims,
After appeasing Lord Vishnu
To earn good karma,
Return to their Ambassador car—
A whispering wisp of grey-black hair, unkempt, emerges.
Immediately,
The combined sparkle of a million stars
Keepers of the universe,
Exude their brilliance in her eyes.
A face unhindered by loss, upholds this radiance
Supported by a body gone weak with age
Upon delivering ten sons.
All ten sons have found their way out of the hamlet
In which this never-worshipped human Goddess, who cares to love all creatures that meet her eye, lives.
Drawn towards her by an immediate connection from another lifetime
I hug her tight,
Give her some thayir sadam, this rice soaked in curd seasoned with mustard,

And find myself floating in an ocean of love, which only a selfless mother can inspire.

I do not know the selfless mother's name.
She does not know it herself.
What's in a name?
Shakespeare resounds.
It's all in the frame of this selfless woman
Fired with love,
Kindled with warmth in her bosom
For her long-lost children.
For you and for me.
What's in a name?
Shakespeare resounds.
For, she does not know her own.
So I simply call her the Lesser Known Goddess

And also document the name the temple priest has given her—Minnal, meaning lightning in the native Tamil language,

And promise to return.

When love comes full circle, there is no point of return. Minnal's selfless love steers me to the Man in a Blue Kurta. Stretching my lean and short body to its fullest length in the upper berth of the mail train from Mayavaram to Bangalore, I realise that I love him even when he throws the key to the rugged close-topped jeep into my palms, and leaves without further address. A storm inside me wells, and I steer my face away from the gaze of the blue bulb which lights the passage in the three-tier air-conditioned Indian railway bogie. I keep my eyes tightly shut, until I drift into a dream.

***

Minnal has not stopped dreaming, I write in my notebook. She is old, and definitely wise. Wise because she continues to love her ten sons although they have all deserted her, the people of her hamlet say. Last night, Minnal dreamt of her son. It is the same son who told her that he wanted to rule the world one day. 'A good ruler is well-informed. A good ruler ensures that people do not go hungry,' she had advised her son in return. To this day, Minnal's eldest son has not known hunger.

The people in the village of the Lesser Known Goddess know hunger, and they do not eat bread. They know the taste of puliodarai and thayir sadam prepared in the Brahmin kitchens by cooks of the same community. The Brahmin cooks dip five-foot long ladles into bronze vessels as the sour puliodarai and bland thayir sadam preparations are cooked over coal fire to delicious prasadam consistency. The prasadam is stirred under the strict supervision of the temple pujaris, until a distinct aroma of ground asafoetida creates rumbles in the hungry stomachs waiting outside the temple.

Journeying one more time through the State of Tamil Nadu, and into the hamlet where the flavour of the prasadam wafts, I note that Minnal is hungry. The temple has exhausted its prasadam—the edible blessing from the highest order who is said to reside in a world above Mother Earth.

Why pray is there no prasadam for a hungry old lady?

The Minister of Accounting Affairs—Thiru Venkataraman—elected representative of all Indian citizens with an office at the Centre, is visiting the temple with an entourage. The greedy members of the entourage have packed up all the prasadam in large steel containers.

They will carry the puliodarai and thayir sadam back to the Centre to distribute to their Cabinet comrades. After all, the man they pander to—Honourable Sri Thiru Venkataraman—hails from a district where the rains do not let its farmers down. Where, in addition to paddy, farmers grow daal, summer vegetables, winter carrots, and fruits of temperate weather.

When men fail to notice, monkeys intervene. In the village of Poothotum near main town Mayavaram, Minnal has found a banana. A greedy monkey has let it slip out of its furry hand, because he has way too many bananas vying for space in his not-so-big palm. This banana is the Goddess' food for the day.

Bless the monkey.

But this meal is an aberration from her daily lunch of rice which has kept her alive for a century and more—through the death of her parents, the birth of her ten sons, also the loss of her man. Minnal does not cook anymore. She does not have the strength to blow life into the coal fire. She also does not have the raw material for kunji—an indigenous meal of rice, salt and water. Sometimes, the kind woman next door fetches a pot of drinking water from the inundated well by the edge of the village. Minnal drinks it all up as an offering to her hungry stomach, and blesses her neighbour abundantly.

Today, the grand old lady sits outside the temple holding onto the banana as it turns from yellow to black, steadily ripening in the heat. Honourable Minister Venkataraman walks out of the temple with the air of God himself, and his entourage follows suit. In an attempt to earn punya, he takes notice of the beggars, and particularly observes the Lesser Known Goddess. He shouts out an instruction to his entourage, and they throw a few morsels of prasadam into the palms of the beggars to earn the Honourable Minister his share of goodwill. Minnal blesses the entourage, and Venkataraman in particular, who, in a fleeting moment, captures the blessed mother's eye. Minnal knows this gaze only too well—she extends her mouth into a toothless smile, and her near-century-old nose-ring captures Venkataraman's eye.

Susanthi Bodra too, wears a nose-ring—her father had saved one rupee every day, for an entire year, to bring his beloved baby girl the precious gift of bead and metal.

One fateful day in the year 2013, gazing at his once paddy, but now barren fields, Susanthi's father was in no hurry to go through with the official formalities, which would further enable him to get compensation from the Government of India in lieu of the untimely death of his son. The grief of paying seventy-five per cent of the compensation to the 'agent' who would 'guide' him through the otherwise impenetrable Government department to process the request, looked shallow in comparison to the amount his son might have earned in his lifetime.

Sons are assets. Daughters are not. That day, Susanthi, not quite nine years old, had to stop going to school, and start cleaning the dark corners of their small hutment. These corners, darker than the rest of their home, was filled with bile from her mother's stomach. Her mother had not been able to digest the loss of her elder born, her shirtless, half-toothed, and laughing ten-year-old son—Tilka Bodra.

Sons are precious. They carry forward the family name. In the city, families are small. Venkataraman has a small family in Pudupakkam, the Southern Capital with a Sea. He lives with his wife, and two legally-begotten sons in a bungalow that can house forty people, and more.

The Minister's wife wears a diamond nose ring. It resembles the nose ring of Goddess Mahalakshmi. The Minister, his wife and two sons, pay obeisance to Goddess Mahalakshmi every Friday. My reporter's notebook takes me back to that day, when the Minister and his family visited Bangalore to offer special prayers to the Goddess.

Goddess Mahalakshmi's diamond nose ring
A token of appreciation by 'upper class' minorities
I dare say.
Her double-bordered Kanchivaram sari
In resonance with the 'head up in the air' minorities
I dare say.
Her gold-bedecked frame
An interpretation of the 'well-fed' priestly minorities
I dare say.

Upon a rain-drenched evening in Sarakki Extension, Beantown

Goddess Mahalakshmi exuded supreme wisdom

As the Minister of Accounting Affairs, his wife, two sons, and an entourage of Brahmins clad in dhotis and silken saris, crowded around her in the inner sanctum

And the Shudras huddled in the outer yard

Soaking in the rain

Nudging each other to catch a glimpse of Goddess Mahalakshmi whose gold-plated figurine the Brahmins claimed to be theirs, and theirs alone.

Suddenly, the storm clouds retreated
To reveal the setting sun
And a diamond-speckled rainbow
Reflecting the nose ring of Goddess Mahalakshmi appeared

This, a heavenly blessing to the Shudras' delight.
As the Brahmins huddled together in the inner sanctum
Nudging each other to catch a mere glimpse of Goddess Mahalakshmi.
Who, lo and behold, appeared in the colours of the rainbow to her less fortunate Shudra children crowded outside the temple!
Warmed by the glow of the setting sun
Abundant with her blessing, the less fortunate children now know that all are equal in Goddess Mahalakshmi's eyes.
Now, the upper-class minorities clamour for her attention, instead.

The Minister of Accounting Affairs, on yet another religious sojourn, this time with his wife and two sons, remembered his mother, he told the press. She too, wore a nose ring. But it did not shine. The weathered red bead on her near-black nose was smooth to the touch. That day, I quoted the Honourable Minister—he remembered the texture of the bead and the fragrance of kaatu mallis… Venkataraman remembered the alluring forest jasmine tucked into her thick, wavy hair. But he did not mention his mother's name—he favoured greed over maternal love.

Love is a simple emotion. It is born out of gratitude towards what your heart melts for—I make my way back to Bochagora.

Your heart can pound at the sight of your four ducks which lay eggs all the time, and they turn into gold. Susanthi has golden ducks, and they are not for sale.

In Susanthi's hamlet, golden ducks are safe. The steel conglomerates do not care about ducks. They do not care about the way the waterfowl waddle—slowly, faster and faster into the paddy fields as shirtless little boys chase the ducks until they lose their balance, and topple into the wet slush, cascades of laughter tiding over each other, sending ripples of happiness into the distant mountains.

Susanthi's father's emotions tided over when the steel conglomerates threatened to ensure that his son, his first born would disappear shirtless, never to burst into cascades of laughter again.

Susanthi's father was left with two choices. They cannot be mentioned now.

A storm, a cyclone—a whirlpool of disdain is gathering over the paddy fields in Bochagora. Too much rain is not good news in this hamlet…

As my bandana slips off my head
On an unassuming windswept day at 4 pm
The gathering wet wind engulfs me in a hold
Tight, reassuring
From a day not so long ago
When the man I love, showed sudden affection.
Wait.
This storm is
Destruction
As it gathers momentum
Faster
Colder
Stinging my raw emotion.

I learn from the resident social worker riding the jeep with me

That on a similar day, many Pono Sankranthis ago, when the winds raged and a wild storm gathered during the native harvest festival

Water gushed like the mighty Ganges from the Himalaya, and filled the paddy fields

The people of Bochagora ran pell-mell

Maa Taarini, they chanted
And repeated the Goddess' name over and again
Louder
Shouting
Yelling over the storm
Until the paddy saplings in their fields
This paddy, their lone source of livelihood until the next monsoon arrives
Disappeared under a stream of water
Overflowing the bunds
Into the kutcha road
Separating their hutments from their fields
Taking with it the blood
Of ducks
Sheep
Mosquitoes
And Susanthi's older brother.
When the storm subsided
Susanthi's father had no one to thank for the pain of losing the next breadwinner of his family…

His biological son was dead. As dead as the steel conglomerates had threatened that his shirtless, laughing little Tilka would be.

When a son dies in Bochagora, his father morphs into the leopard of the jungle—the Kalarpatra Bagha. And an eminent artist finds his muse.

Sridhar Haider D'Vaz dyes his hair regularly. He is proud of his features—Indo-either Greeko/Arabico/Frencho or all aforementioned connections—the accurate biological combination is never well known in India. History has been documented here. Birth certificates have been created here. Both are accurate, one time in ten.

So what?

What is important is that D'Vaz and the Guru were born around the same year. The Guru is certain of his lineage—Saraswat Brahmin ascendants and Mangalorean Catholic descendants. What is more important is that the Guru spent his youth in a city which boasted English weather and honed all sorts of talent among the missionary school-educated Indian community in Bangalore, and otherwise. In his youth, D'Vaz sought his creative side, and painted wild animals which he often shot during his hunting expeditions. In his youth, the Guru nurtured people younger and older than him, from places near and far—they became established authors, filmmakers, artists, musicians and actors. D'Vaz created many wild pieces which have made him rich, famous, and a master painter to reckon with. The Guru created one masterpiece, a book on his city, which continues to keep him famous.

D'Vaz cares about his fame. The Guru does not. He did not care about who said what, even when his imagination kept him alive.

His baby is alive. She hears many stories—I narrate them to her every night. She wants to travel the world. She wants to travel in her father's world. I want her to travel the world. I need to make the right connections. I call him. I cannot reach him. I am afraid of calling him again. I do not want to sound like a nagging wife. He has not taken me as his wife. I have married him in my mind. I call him again. We talk. I sleep peacefully tonight because he sounds all right. I dream of places and people who will keep his child on a pedestal.

When the Guru was alive, he told me stories. I wanted to play a part in every one of them.

***

I have not said goodbye to the Guru. On his first death anniversary, as I sit in the lap of the Great Arabian Ocean, my Guru's favourite place on earth, I am moved to verse. I pour out my emotions in my notebook:

An ode to my Foster Father, Guide, Guru...
Where have all the good times gone?
They linger
Under the shade of the butter fruit tree.
The Guru, sipping on something hot
I on tea.
Sridhar Haider D'Vaz visits.
I make a call.
The Force SMSes.
Herr Hans Bauer brings more tea.
They call us the Guru's adopted family.
Today, there's the butter fruit tree
The shade
And your adopted family.
All lost without you, dear beloved Guru...

I know that despite his departure from earth, he has read this verse with critical attention to fact and detail. I connect with my Guru's philosophy. Meter and rhyme are of concern to the pedantic. Textbooks are masquerades worn by mediocre minds. Take a walk. Plant a sapling. Watch the Morning Glory blossom into a true purple at the crack of dawn. Hold this purple passion in your heart. Discover life as it blossoms...

Back home in Bangalore, I take a walk around my Guru's backyard, and feel his presence beside me. The Morning Glory is in blossom.

I understand life.

Life is overrated.

The meaning of life is understated.

I return to my computer, refreshed by the profusion of Morning Glories blossomed to purple passion in the Guru's garden. Susanthi Bodra has sent me a message. It has arrived in the form of an email from the YUPAP headquarters at Bhubaneswar.

YUPAP is a Non-Governmental Organisation, an NGO instituted to linger on matters of sustenance in areas where the democratically-elected machinery has failed.

I hear his baby cry.

I close my inbox.

My baby is at that tender age, which needs close attention. I watch her every minute movement. In time, her movements will either make or break her. I do not want her to suffer from a crisis—an identity crisis to be explicit. She cannot be broken.

What is the purpose of his baby's life?

It is time to go looking for the meaning of life. Her life.

***

My heart always has a way of winning contradictions put forth by my mind. I have not slept in a week because I have given in to the pressures of my murky mind. My mind says: 'Do not encroach upon his space, let him be.' My heart refuses to listen to my mind any longer. There is no point in arguing what the heart feels, so I call him. We talk about his baby, and what the future holds in store for her. As I speak, I realise how much I love his baby—she reflects his emotions, his attitude, and the depth of his connection with his roots. I wonder about his roots. I hold his baby close to my bosom, and rock her. She knows she is safe in her resting place.

But, the children of Balangir do not feel safe. Susanthi, the apple of her father's eye, is weak from the stress of running behind her own shadow. She also runs after her own shadow, depending on the time of day. She needs to watch her shadow because there are predators in the jungle. They resemble her father.

Fathers of the storybook variety create a happy world for their daughters—safe and comfortable, and free of predators.

My own foster father, the Guru died on his bed in 22002 Sunshine Apartment, Canterbury Town, Bangalore.

Between the pages of my reporter's notebook, is a tear-stained piece of paper from the day my foster father died in March 2010. It reads:

My foster father
My Guru
My guide
He was
Until
A minute ago
Home to a pounding heart
Beating
Faster and faster
Until it slowed down
To stop
Go cold
And become a corpse...
Still warm to the touch
As they take him away to the medical college

Where students will study his mortal organs to gain their medical degrees.

The world as I see it today, is the world the Guru painted for me through vivid words. In his company, I met people from worlds I had never been to. In the year 2005, we went to shoot a documentary in Kithapur Village, Gulbarga District, the hottest belt of Karnataka State, India. I was nineteen, and wrote what I experienced in my first reporter's notebook.

41.5 degrees centigrade
Gowravva's deep brown sari bordered with mango green imprint
Merges with the soil.
Meanwhile,
Beads of sweat
Cling to our skin
And the noon sun blazes menacingly.
We cringe
In discomfort
And eye the faraway Neem tree
Swaying in ecstatic rhythm
With the seemingly non-existent wind.
While,
Head bent
Gowravva tends to the land
Weaning out weeds of the natural
As well as humankind.
Fingers hardened by the coarseness of the land
Softened by the fruit her Mango trees bear
Moving with gentle finesse
Abruptly pausing to segregate
The good from the bad
And keep evil out of her home

And hearth.

Gowravva stops working

And beckons us towards the shade of the Neem tree

This arena, abundant with natural air conditioning…

Here, we relish Gowravva's bakri and shenga chutney with stuffed brinjal curry

This spread, her indigenous feast for 'special' guests.

As we relish the feast, Gowravva's children, except for her eldest daughter who has been long missing, rush into her arms

From the school yonder.

She feeds them pieces of dry coconut for lunch.

That is all the food there is.

She has fed the last morsel of the day

To her 'special' guests.

We cringe

In discomfort

And eye the faraway heavens

Seeking a solution to Gowravva's poverty.

We refrain from handing her a 100-rupee note

We hear from whispers in the air—still, outside the shade of the Neem tree

That Gowravva is the keeper of a well-guarded treasury

Called Self Respect.

We head home in the knowledge that

Her missing daughter is almost as old as I am

And that her blessed hands

Will always keep her children fed

And that to her touch,

Parched land will turn green.

Truth is, Gowravva knows hunger. The rains have failed, her lands are parched—she goes hungry to bed at least three times a week. But her stomach does not complain because her children are fed. She wants her children to dream. Even her daughters must dream. Gowravva does not have to go hungry to bed thrice a week. Recommended by a Gulbarga-based social worker who is a distant cousin to Minister Thiru Venkataraman's wife, Gowravva has been offered a house help's job in the city. It is at a minister's house, so the payment will be enough to feed her entire neighbourhood, they say. Gowravva knows that some ministers earn their money from the toil of people like her. Gowravva will not let her people down. Gowravva will not sell her soul.

The Guru's soul is loving—he does not physically accompany me on my official trips anymore—he makes his presence felt to his adopted children, and also to those who strive for a democratic land. I travel in and out of the hamlets abounding the districts of Keonjhar, Boudh and Balangir in Orissa—also, the deep-set villages bosomed in Jharkhand's mountain forests. Driving through the forest hamlets of Orissa on a sun-kissed afternoon, I remember Gowravva again...

Bochagora hamlet, Balangir District, Orissa...
Three nights and four days
After the floods have subsided
A little hamlet wakes up to the sound of a familiar jeep
Carrying unfamiliar faces.
Strangers are welcome
In this distant hamlet called Bochagora
Abundant with the sounds of squealing children
Running up and down
The only kutcha road which defines it.
This path creviced by incessant rain
Swallowing livestock
Foodgrain

Also the spirit of survival among its inhabitants—the men, the women, also the children of the Munda tribe.

But life must go on.

The hamlet readies its children
For a fresh day at school.
So, they all arrive
Some with shirts
None with shoes
And Susanthi Bodra is nowhere to be seen.

She, a girl nearing thirteen, now rearing ducks to feed her hungry stomach

Has recently been abandoned by her only living family.
Her mother has left her two nights ago
To return to the same man's bed...

Yes, the man who lusts after women from these parts, and he has already taken more than four.

I wish Susanthi Bodra's mother had another name—Gowravva.

Gowravva, the lady who wouldn't dream of deserting her children come what may.

I watch the forests merge into hamlets, and wonder what the names of these settlements are—there are no signboards.

What's in a name? Cliché.

He has a name, but no surname. I love his name too, and have learnt to repeat it over and again, because I cannot speak with him every day. I do not wish to disturb the Man in a Blue Kurta.

This disturbs me.

I have a name.

Susanthi has a name—it is fast becoming popular among the children of Sambhalpur District. She has recently visited the main town, two hours away from her hamlet to train children—some younger, others the same age as her in the art of rearing ducks. The workshop is a big hit among children who have been brought to the main town from their jungle-lodged hamlets. They are happy to learn a thing or two, even three, about ducks—this training is all about the art of multiplication.

Students multiply with ease when the teacher's knowledge of Math is sound.

In the hamlet of Manipura in Keonjhar, the mining district of Orissa, Naren Nayak is popular among his students. For no additional salary from the elected democracy nor additional fee from his pupils, he teaches Math, Music, and even Dance. In fact, he teaches any subject that will lure the children of that hamlet, and hopefully three more villages within the range of five kilometres, to the lone Manipura Government School.

Hereabouts, even one kilometre is a great distance—there are no roads to walk on. Where there are roads, they have caved in to resemble slush. Red slush, rich slush. Rich slush because the Kanjipani Mountains enveloping the district of Keonjhar, are abundant with gold—the Mankadia tribes of this region sift the slush with winnows for hours, sometimes days, until they find a shining speck of gold dust. It is red, because this rich soil is poor with the blood of its dead children. Some die hungry when there are no grains to grow their paddy and maize crops on. Others die because they own lands heaving with gold in the not-so-easy-to-access precincts of the Kanjipani Mountains, and when they mine the money-fetching metal, they must turn in most of the profits from its sale to middlemen from the city.

Naren does not want the men, women and children of the Mankadia tribe, also his own bloodline, the Munda people, to die of starvation. The Mankadias and Mundas of Keonjhar often lose their means of livelihood because they are separated from their lands forcefully.

Naren is employed by the Government of India to teach at the village school. So he teaches at the Manipura Government School. He also flattens the slush along the three-kilometre-long path to the school, at no extra salary. He wants the tribes of this land to increase. Increase in the knowledge that teaches them the alphabet and the number in an endeavour to train them to mind their own lands.

Naren is alone in his mission. Urmila and Manohar Mahapatra are his benchmarks of strength. The middle-aged Mahapatra couple who have spent their youth in Cuttack, have left their ten-year-old son in the care of his grandparents, and given up city life for the mountains... Mountains rich with gold, ridden with poverty, intense with wild animals, furious with Maoxals, ferocious with scavenging machines mining the ore out of the land, and with it, the livelihood of its inhabitants.

The Mundas are a farming community. They live off their lands. Over these lands, River Shammakoi's waters flow in abundance where the gorges are deep, and meander gently where the bunds check their flow. I have seen Switzerland, but only in pictures. I have seen the lands cradling in the arms of the Kanjipani Mountains time and again, I need no pictures. Deep in my heart, I know these lands in the dense interiors of the Indian Subcontinent are as beautiful as the sought-after snowy peaks in the Playground of Europe.

In his heart, Naren too, knows of the abundant beauty of his land. In his mind, he wants to preserve this beauty for generations after his own.

Back home, my maternal instinct takes over—I must preserve the beauty of his baby for generations after ours. She is meant to dazzle the world with untold stories from the hearts of men and women who have lived to give the Morning Glory a good name.

The Morning Glory—a flower by birth, a symbol of passion purpled to perfection by the first kiss of sunshine, and she dresses my windowpane.

I kiss my baby. She, a product of her father's passion to bring out the soul in resting beauty.

Today, I call her many mentors—in Delhi, in Bhubaneswar, in Calcutta, in Singapore, in Madras, in Der Bundesrepublik Deutschland, in Italy, and in the United States of America. Her mentors are all fine-tuning the raw diamond I have presented to them.

The stage is set for his daughter's debut. Our daughter's debut. But, the Man in a Blue Kurta has neither given me a ring, nor taken me as his legal wife.

I do not want a diamond ring from him. I like silver. White metal more. I like him in person most. There is more sheen to flesh and blood and the breath of a man with a tender heart, however distant he may seem from me at this point in time.

Distance is a relative term. I have chosen to stand by him, through the tenure of this distance. And I feel close, very close to his rock-solid chest where I place my head, and fall asleep. I wake up from a dream of love and caresses through the night. I sink into the dream by day, and wander about my duties—dazed and alert, at once.

I understand that the only way to live happily is to give happily. I close my eyes, and say a pray for his well-being—I give him all my love.

***

I visit 22002 Sunshine Apartment and recall how the days seemed longer when the Guru lay in his bed. His fingers were frail and tender, with blood continuously entering and re-entering his body. The blood flowed inside the purifying machine via a tube, and into his vein for over four hours. When he returned home from the dialysis unit, his fingers, slender and dexterous, hit a wholesome range of notes as he played his part for the duet score of *Eine Kliene Nachtmusik*.

Sitting at the 19th-century rosewood table in my Guru's home, I pick up my bleistift, scratch my head with its sharpened lead, and place it on the tisch. I love using the German words for pencil and table, ever since I started dreaming of one day, travelling to Mozart's homeland to listen to a million orchestras, keeping pace with the composer's connect to the tones and semitones, dividing melodic time between the breve, semi-breve, minim and crochet.

'Nainika,' Herr Hans Bauer calls out to me in his distinct baritone voice, and I'm awakened from my reverie. 'Sie have a case to present?' he asks.

'I, sie, me, have the entire project report printed and filed in a cloth folder. The folder has been made by trafficked women—they're hoping to make a comeback to "normalcy" as the watchdogs of society would have it,' I reply.

Normal is a word I relate to whenever I type out my Indian name—the 'international auto-correct dictionary' gives me the option of changing it to 'normally'.

The content in the folder presents carefully researched psychoanalyses of girls from troubled backgrounds. We need financial help to de-trouble them. We have tried hard and been unable to convince the Corporate Social Responsibility (CSR) wings of leading companies to sponsor the rehabilitation of these girls. One of the girls in question, is Gowravva's eldest daughter. She dreamed big. So, she took a bus to the big city. Standing under a bus shelter by midnight, she wondered where to go. A man drove right into the bus stand in a white Maruti Omni van, and asked her to get in. He would help, he said. She was mesmerised by this stroke of midnight luck, and got into the back seat. She felt safe because there were two more women in the car.

Years ago, Zeta Rani's NGO had rescued Gowravva's daughter from a brothel in Nagpur. She was being rehabilitated in Calcutta. She made fine jewellery, and had her own signature collection from otherwise unusable, snapped, piano strings. These pianos trace their birth to Germany. So does Sigmund Freud—Father of Psychoanalysis. The girl had been in rehabilitation, but was troubled. She was consumed by sudden spurts of sexual desire. She wanted to find her customers. She escaped from the rehabilitation centre in Calcutta, and riding in another Omni van, perhaps, found her way to Majuli in Assam.

Herr Bauer heads a funding NGO in Düsseldorf in Der Bundesrepublik Deutschland.

'Können sie diese maidchen helfen, bitte?' I ask him one more time.

Herr Bauer cannot help the girls in rehabilitation. Certainly not right now. He needs more evidence, more documentation, lots of paperwork.

He also wants an endorsement from the Minister of Accounting Affairs stating that the Indian Government is incapable of funding the rescue and rehabilitation of Gowravva's eldest daughter Nelli, and other girls with mental complications spurred by uncontrollable physical desire.

I call Zeta Rani to discuss this complicated matter.

***

Love is complicated. His dreams matter to me. My baby, his work of passion, looks resplendent at the gathering. She is the cynosure of all eyes. These eyes see that beauty is not skin deep. Their gestures show that she is a star in her simple attire—shades of light and dark hues bringing out the best in her. As she preens in their midst, I watch him break into a smile. I feel light and heavy as his smile extends into his heart. A ray of distinct light, hope for his baby's secure future, enters his pounding heart. In his trademark restraint, this hope hides under the fall of his blue kurta, and rests in his heart.

He has returned home for a few days. But for his daughter's sake, he says.

As I sew the broken button onto his blue kurta this morning, I feel revived in my heart. I realise how much I miss darning his well-worn clothes.

The clothes a woman darns, often belong to the people she loves most.

Gowravva misses darning her daughter's clothes. When she darns them, they look as good as new. But all the clothes are gone now. Her daughter took them in a spacious plastic bag on the day she left home to find attention in the city.

Cities are not always welcoming. Not even smaller towns. People do not know you in the big city. When they do not know you, they stare at you until you want to melt inconspicuously into the framework of the nearby blanket shop. It has saris too. I choose to retrace my steps, and scurry back to the hotel in main town Balangir. In the hotel, I have to remain in my room. There are men outside. These men are here to take back women with hope for a hunger-free life in the big city.

I am very near Susanthi Bodra's hamlet, and I fear for her safety.

Susanthi has never seen the big city. She hopes to first make a name in her own hamlet Bochagora. In the afternoon, when she has completed all her hut-hold chores and cleaned the bile in the corner, she opens Domrudoru's book. By the afternoon light, she reads all about Samrat Ashoka from the book for students of Grade 6. She reads until 3 pm, and goes back to her business. Her ducks need attention. They must be fed, allowed to flutter, and kept happy to produce more golden eggs.

Susanthi has learnt that life teaches every ruler a lesson, as it did to King Ashoka. She has heard that in the big city, King Ashoka's master, the Buddha, has stupas dedicated to him. Every day, people from far and wide visit the Stupa in Dhauli in the capital city of Bhubaneswar.

Dhauli is an important location—Herr Bauer visited the Stupa the other day.

I visit the hamlet by Mayavaram one more time.

Sitting outside the Vishnu Temple, the inner sanctum which the Lesser Known Goddess has never visited, the grand old lady prays for global peace. She is disturbed by a certain gaze, which reeks of greed. She saw this greed in the eyes of Venkataraman when he was visiting the inner sanctum of the temple last week.

Feeding birds is an everyday norm for Minnal. Every day, she buys grains worth two rupees from the kutti kadai on the main road—this small provision store is a landmark for devotees who turn off the main highway at its sighting to enter the hamlet with the much-visited temple. Every day, she sits by the lake at eventide, when the sparrows are ready to disperse into the trees for the night, and feeds them the grain she bought from the small shop on the main road. Minnal has two rupees left from her earnings of the day. Devotees throw coins into her palms as she waits her turn to receive the leftover prasadam from the temple priests. The Lesser Known Goddess secures the coins in a well-practised knot in her sari—these coins are her savings for a trip to the big city.

She now needs to see for herself whether her son, the self-proclaimed 'ruler of the world', indeed does justice unto the people who have voted him to power.

Thousands of kilometres away, Herr Bauer arrives at Kamalabari, the docking point to Majuli. He ascends a kerosene-fuelled motor boat to cross the deep waters of the River Brahmaputra, and arrive at the rustic island. In the boat, he finds himself amidst the usual travellers—men, women, children, fish, livestock, even cars. In the boat, he notices an unusual traveller—a young lady dressed in an orange sari. Her lips are painted orange to match the shade of her garment, her face is whitened with sandalwood-scented powder, her hair left loose, the tresses cascading over her slender shoulders. A bright pink rose is pinned onto her loose tresses. She moves close to Herr Hans Bauer. So close that he can hear her breath, and also the silent flutter of the heart within her bosom.

When Herr Bauer alights at Majuli and drives away in his chauffeured cab, he glimpses disappointment on the girl's face. The girl remains on the boat, which will take her back to Nemati Ghat in Jorhat.

But Herr Bauer cannot return to speak to the girl, he has a task at hand. He signals the chauffer to drive ahead, and into the island, until he arrives at the Vedic Vaishnav Ashram—it is the pride of the UNESCO heritage ethnic island of Majuli in the State of Assam, India.

A disciple, accoutred in a sacred thread and dhoti, meets and greets Herr Bauer with folded hands. Formalities in place, he leads the foreigner through a mud path, and into the backyard of the Ashram where all the bachelor students bathe in the man-made tank, then, wash and dry their dhotis. Here, Herr Bauer cleanses his hands and feet as the disciple weans the hand pump.

Herr Bauer is suitably clean—he is now free to wander the Ashram.

The Vedic Vaishnav Ashram is vast and clean, also serene. So, Herr Bauer decides to rest his head upon a wooden pillar and close his eyes in meditation. His mind wanders until it comes to rest in sync with the hum of the Vedic chants that the Ashram's disciples recite in synchronised baritone. The hum takes Herr Bauer's conscious mind to a proposal—my proposal with Zeta Rani's intent enclosed in the hand-made cloth folder.

***

No mission is impossible if the outcome is one's primary concern.

Gowravva's mission is to ensure that her children are well-fed and safe. Every day, she prays for her daughter's safety. Every day, she visits the police station to check whether there is news of her daughter. It has been over twenty years since the girl child who filled her womb, slept on her lap, and skipped in her hutment, has left her.

It has been over three years since Susanthi Bodra heard of her father's death. One evening after her brother died, he had ventured into the forests surrounding Bochagora. He did not return that night. Not the next day. Not three days later. On the fourth day, the Panchayat Mukhiya had news. An informant from the neighbouring hamlet gave the Mukhiya of Bochagora unscreened information that Susanthi's father was dead. The Mundas looked, and looked for seven days more, but did not find his body. In the absence of his dead body, the village elders made a mud replica of Susanthi's father, and performed his last rites, putting their fellow tribal's soul to rest.

Then, they brought out the Mahua—the people of Bochagora had to drink the local toddy to their brother's death. After all, death is another life. And all new life must be celebrated with Mahua.

I have visited the Mahua-brewing factory en route to Bochagora. It is surrounded by swaying Mahua branches, these tall trees inebriated by their own essence. This toddy is a blessing to the people of Balangir. It numbs their senses enough to have them forget that they are hungry and poor, also victims of land sharks. It makes them oblivious to the fact that the elected representatives of the democracy have forgotten to inundate their parched lands after the polls. The people of Balangir have not learnt the art of yoga, meditation, horse riding and golf to de-stress. Mahua is their only redemption.

As the toddy enters their throats, 'What on earth is stress?' they ask.

Stress is for people in the city who own two cars and three flats. Where there is no money, no roads, no vehicles, save the occasional Atlas cycle—this two wheel spoke and chain wonder's cousins dating back to the 1980s—there is also no stress. But there is hunger. One must kill this hunger with sleep. One must induce sleep with the magic elixir—Mahua.

Back home, sleep evades me. The man I love has left again. I need Mahua. I need the sea. I get on the night train one more time, to reach Goa, sit on a rock, and watch the Great Arabian Ocean perform her 'wave-upon-lashing-wave' symphony.

I am by the Ocean one more time. Towards eventide, the waters lash out at the rock I sit on, and drench my face, my neck, my thighs, my feet… I feel heady. Just the way I did after consuming the freshly-brewed Mahua in Keonjhar, while the people of Bochagora mourned their brother's death. The waves drench the rock once more, and whisper a message in my ear. I hear that the Man in a Blue Kurta is safe. Sitting on this rock, drenched over and again by the inebriated waves of the Great Arabian Ocean, I have met a deep sense of rest—they call it Nirvana.

Nirvana is known to meet a woman when her loved ones refuse to show up.

Under the Peepal tree in her hamlet, Minnal is in a constant state of Nirvana. When the wind rustles, the leaves shade her from the stark sun, and she knows that all her ten sons are safe.

This safety net does not extend to the forest lands.

Today, one of Susanthi's ducks has lingered into the forest. It has been consumed by a creature of the wild. Tonight, Susanthi, tired from weeping, falls asleep wondering whether this creature which has consumed her duck, has two legs, or four.

***

Gowravva's legs drag along the freshly-tarred road to the Gulbarga police station. She has never felt such weakness before. Not even when she ploughed her fields alone the morning after her husband died. A sudden illness—red fever they said—had consumed him. Gowravva did not have the privilege of mourning her husband's death in the silence of her hutment. It was harvest time, and the paddy fields needed attention. While she attended to the fields, Gowravva's eldest born, her daughter, felt that along with her father, her mother too, had deserted her. She was eight—an impressionable age which changes a girl's perception of relationships in inexplicable ways.

Susanthi Bodra is a breadwinner. She is still a girl. She is battling with a relationship that consumes all her waking hours.

Susanthi perceives her closest and only surviving family member as a 'matter of fact'. She lives with the woman who has given birth to her, although the latter had abandoned her child only weeks ago. This woman called Susanthi's mother, has returned home, and spews bile in the corners of their dark hutment. Susanthi feels consumed by the stench of the bile. But she does not complain. Not once.

I sleep. I dream. I am eight once again. Sitting alone in the large balcony one September evening, I see the silhouette of a little girl with short hair. She walks faster, breaks into a run, leaps over the gate, leaving a trail of fresh blood from her thigh and a piece of fabric from her cotton garment, the pavada, both of which have been ripped by the sharp edge of the rusted gate. The lights come on. Arti's mother emerges with a thick cane in hand—she has brought the 'disciplining' weapon from her village in the State of Andhra Pradesh, especially to keep her minor maidservant under control. 'Nelli,' she screams. There is no reply.

I quickly withdraw my dangling legs which had been making an attempt to reach the parapet wall, and rush to take my secret position behind the granite pillar supporting the high-ceilinged balcony. This evening, I have not turned the light on, and can watch without being found out.

The next morning, my mother found out that Nelli had fled her tormentor's home. Arti's mother had alerted the entire neighbourhood.

I am eight, I have a secret to keep. I bury it in the pages of my brown diary, where I write poems about all the men who have impacted my eight-year-long life—my Grandpa Jeeves, The Man in the Van, Perumal—the Rickshaw Puller and The Postman, all verses written with a blue ink pen in neat cursive.

***

I write out a note. Naren Nayak reads it, and dials a few digits on the telephone. It is a mechanical phone manufactured in the 1970s.

This pre monsoon, there are floods in Orissa. River Shammakoi's waters are overflowing, and the mud paths leading to Keonjhar's forest hamlets are nowhere in sight. It is neither possible to enter Naren's hamlet Manipura, nor exit it. The tribes of this region have not known free passage for a decade, maybe two. Nature's rage is not the only cause.

Love is a natural rage, it alters body temperatures to match the vicissitudes of a relationship.

I simmer.

There is a storm scurrying into the night sky. The Man in a Blue Kurta takes his seat. I scurry into a corner, far away from the chair he is sitting on, and tell him that his baby needs to travel on the night train to Bhubaneswar. We will travel second class, and I will take good care of her, I promise. He looks me in the eye. I feel a warm stream of passion flowing in my veins, and sink into his embrace from the far side of the room. He does not want me to touch him.

I shiver despite the rising heat in my body.

Susanthi shivers despite the rising temperatures in Bochagora. She waits until the break of dawn, and hops sure-footedly on the bunds separating the paddy crops growing across the kutcha road from her hutment, and all the way up to the base of the hill, where the boundaries of Bochagora merge into the forest. She has gone looking for her missing duck. Yes, her duck is not dead—Susanthi Bodra's sixth sense tells her so. Her sixth sense also tells the near thirteen-year-old that her duck is in the care of a two-legged creature. This creature, she now believes, is a monster who has disowned his own flesh and blood to find Nirvana.

When your own flesh and blood goes missing, the detachment that Nirvana brings with it, can well be blamed.

Minnal, too, knew that her eldest son had disowned his mother in his quest for Nirvana—instead, he sought salvation of the capitalist kind. Sitting under Poothotum's Peepal tree, eyes shut, Minnal remembers that fateful day when her eldest son boarded the white Ambassador car. He did not turn back once to bid his mother farewell. He was fourteen years old then, and had the features of a certain Brahmin lad, who, the temple priest said, was fairer than the Dalits, rounder than the Kshatriyas, eyes more piercing than his father's. His father, Minnal's handsome husband, belonged to the Katunayakan tribe, and was a brave hunter. That departing day, her eldest son travelled to the city in the company of bereaved parents who had lost their only son to a snake bite. Their own rascal son, almost a twin to Minnal's eldest child in age and looks, had, on a whim, grabbed a cobra right outside the holy temple. The chagrined cobra released its venom right into the boy's forehead. Minnal had wind that the lad from the city had grabbed the passing reptile to torture and slay it, and then take its skin back to school to show off to his city-bred friends. But he never made it back to the city, he was dead. Instead, Minnal's eldest son, whom the bereaved parents had lured with the promise of a good life in the big city, went.

With time, a big city tends to distort a child's connection with his roots in the village.

When Nelli arrived in the city, she had her long tresses to show off. When the Mentor, whose name she later learnt was Amrit Kumar, brought her to Arti's mother, Nelli's tresses were chopped off with an old and rusted knife. Within days, Arti's mother took her to the barber shop to have the girl's head shaved clean. Nelli's mistress certainly did not have time to comb and clean the tresses of a 'labourer, a slave, a mere maidservant'. She would give her food, shelter and two sets of old clothes from her own daughter's cupboard, and that would be enough.

Eight-year-old Nelli's journey in the big city of Bangalore had only just begun.

II

She wore flowers in her hair and
carried magic secrets in her eyes.

– Arundhati Roy, *The God of Small Things*

Multiple journeys have begun in the Southern Capital with a Sea, in Bochagora, in Manipura hamlet of Keonjhar District, in Gulbarga, in Kamalabari by Majuli, and in Bangalore—some journeys physical, others emotional, and all in quest of justice. In pursuit of justice, I document these journeys in the vacant pages of my reporter's notebook.

Naren Nayak has begun his journey to the big city in the southern part of India. He will travel second class, and has little money to spare for additional snacks on the three-day-long rail journey. His wife has packed breakfast, lunch and dinner to last him three days. For all three meals, he eats potato and rice soaked in yellow daal. By the third day, the sun blazes at forty degrees centigrade. The food begins to smell rancid, but Naren consumes it. He has no time for self-indulgence. He must focus on his mission alone.

Naren has the address of the ancestral home where Minister Thiru Venkataraman resides in the Southern Capital with a Sea. Venkataraman prefers the comfort of his ancestral bungalow to his fully air-conditioned official accommodation at the Centre. The Minister can be met between meals—10 am to noon or from 4 pm to 6 pm. Added clause: By Appointment Only. When Naren alights the train, the needles of the grandfather clock on

Platform No 1 read noon. There is time yet. Naren has an appointment with the Minister at 4.15 pm.

An appointment made with a person of authority, is often in the context of disappointment.

When she was eight, Nelli's appointment with her soon-to-be Mentor, Amrit Kumar had been fixed for 9 pm. She had managed to escape from her mistress' home with throbbing pain. Her wounded thigh had bled and bled, leaving a trail of red on the road, the dangerous colour visible all the way up to the park, where she was to meet the Mentor. Sitting on the park bench, wiping her wound with a dry leaf, Nelli thanked her good fortune unaware of her impending misfortune. The eight-year-old girl had managed to flee her tormentor. Just a few months ago, the very kind Amrit had brought her to Arti's mother in his Maruti Omni when he found her alone in the City Bus Stand on the night she arrived from Gulbarga to Bangalore. Three months later, on this night, he had promised to return, and take her to an 'exciting' place in Nagpur. Within two nights, Nelli found herself in a dingy tawaif ghar in Nagpur city, State of Maharashtra...

For over twenty years since, Nelli has been running away from rehabilitation. Over the years, she has been spotted in the Southern Capital with a Sea, in Delhi, in Bombay, in another tawaif ghar in Calcutta, and in another brothel in Guwahati. Nelli does not feel secure in the care of any other woman, save her mother, she goes wherever Amrit takes her. The same mother she cannot seem to live without, she has left behind in the hamlet of Kithapur, Gulbarga District, Karnataka State...

Just like the night when eight-year-old Nelli arrived at Bangalore, she has no money in her pink purse, save her precious two rupees—she saves her hard-earned money in a piggy bank. Nelli's gentle mother had thrust this much-folded pink currency note into her palm, when she had begun a new year at the Gulbarga Primary School. She had been promoted to the third standard, and her mother had been elated at her daughter's progress.

Mothers are inseparable from their daughters, even in their absence.

After scouring the bosom of the hill for her lost duck in vain, Susanthi returns to find her home empty. She runs from the hall to the kitchen, and back. She searches in all the eight dark corners of the two rooms over and again. Hoping against hope, 'Mayi', Susanthi calls out, gently first—then loudly, screaming, simpering and mellowing down in disdain until she falls asleep on the dung-washed floor. In the still of the night, Susanthi smells bile. She wakes up with hope, only to find it dashed. The stench is from another night, not this one—Susanthi's mother seems to have made a habit of deserting her only daughter every now and then. In a world where people appear and disappear as they please, the time is never ripe for remorse.

Naren's appointment with Venkataraman for this day is postponed to another. He must return two days later at 11.45 am, the Minister's moustached secretary has told him. This is a minor setback among the long list of disappointments which hinder Naren's mission. There is no time for remorse he believes, and takes the next bus to Beach Road. Naren will sit on the sand by the sea for five hours until his stomach grumbles for aloo, daal and bhath.

Self-respecting individuals face the sea when the tides turn against them.

Sitting by the sea on an empty stomach, Minnal feels stoned to death by grains of sand. She knows death is inevitable, especially when one reaches the ripe old age of one hundred and one, as she has. But grains of sand cannot kill her—every worry in the world is inconsequential when compared to the love she feels for her ten sons. She hopes to meet her eldest son in the Southern Capital with a Sea. She must stay alive to accomplish her mission. So, the Lesser Known Goddess decides to eat a pachai vazhapazham. She cuts into her savings, unknots the edge of her sari pallu which is thick with coins, and buys a spotted green plantain for two rupees from the Banana Vendor wandering Beach Road with a basket of fruits on his head, and a bag of peanuts slung over his upstretched and bony arms.

When a mother saves money, she is sure to find her lost child sooner or later. Gowravva's clay piggy bank is heavy with two-rupee coins. She breaks it to find enough money to visit the Southern Capital with a Sea. There are rumours that her eldest daughter was last seen in the metropolis. The kind policeman who has given her this news will help Gowravva board the correct train to the Southern Capital. Gowravva has never been on a train. In the forty-odd years that she has breathed the humid air of Gulbarga, Gowravva has only seen the railway station at the District Headquarters, which is a two-hour journey by passenger bus from her hamlet Kithapur.

I have been waiting two days and three nights for his call. Love is belief. I believe he is safe.

Susanthi believes her duck is safe. She does not know whether her mother is safe. Her mother has been missing for several days.

Herr Hans Bauer knows that there is a missing link. He has been pouring through the cloth folder word by word, over and again, intermittently pondering about his own roots. Gentle evening breeze over River Brahmaputra on the terrace of the motor boat, fisherman playing a card game for a win in the far corner, the contents of the cloth folder... all take Herr Hans Bauer to eine andere welt.

Herr Bauer has been in this other world, die andere welt, where poverty brings with it complex social change. This change does not bring with it any variation in the perception of women who have crossed the beaten path to overcome their poverty. Herr Bauer fondly thinks of die frauen in Deutschland—his wife and two daughters. The women in Herr Bauer's life are master controllers of their fate. Their decisions are not influenced by what the men think of them. In his short journey across the rippling Brahmaputra from Nemati Ghat in Jorhat to Kamalabari in Majuli, Herr Bauer has witnessed the suffering of a smiling woman. This woman, a fresh blossom from the ripe bud of childhood, is celebrated and chastised for the course of life she has chosen. But did she choose this life? Wind caresses Herr Bauer's pondering brow. The mighty Brahmaputra's waters refract the worry lines upon his deeply thinking, darker than Caucasian forehead.

Love is not a choice, it is a matter of fact that swells secretly in my heart, and panics visibly on my forehead when it throbs.

The rising tide of the Great Arabian Ocean cascades over the rock to reach and touch my forehead. The waves draw me into their ferocious fold by eventide, and dissolve my tears into their salted wetness. Rolling over the black sand which surrounds its banks, I writhe like a fish in and out of sea. I am a woman. I have made a choice to swim the vicissitudes of these unruly tides. The tides take me deeper, and deeper into the fold of love. I pour out my emotions on a fresh page in my reporter's notebook.

Love is
Just a four-letter word
Until
It begins to make you jump
At the sight of your own shadow
Because
You are no longer the centre of your universe.
He is.

It is best to let matters of love rest when little girls sleep hungry.

He has fixed up a meeting with Zeta Rani and me in the city with the Stupa. Herr Hans Bauer will join us. They call the man who has fixed up the meeting, Sridhar Haider D'Vaz. We agree to meet at the Art College en route to Dhauli.

Dhauli is not far from the city centre. The autorickshaw driver easily manoeuvres the bends along the upward inclination of the hill connecting the main town of Bhubaneswar to the Stupa on a meandering highland. The city below is green. The rains have nurtured green weeds. They have taken with them the paddy crops. In these parts, rain is good. Too much rain is not. I have taken a train from Balangir to Bhubaneswar, last night. I have left Susanthi and the people of Bochagora sitting on their heels, chests buried between their knees, heads wagging in disbelief at the edge of their paddy fields. There is enough food for tomorrow. But what will the people of Bochagora eat next week? What will Susanthi Bodra eat?

Sitting on the stone bench in the canteen at the Art College, I find D'Vaz eating from a plate of potato bondas—

he describes them as dumplings to the people he meets at international destinations. It is difficult to miss him, accoutred as he is in his multi-hued shirt. I remember his shirt from a party at the Guru's apartment. Sridhar Haider D'Vaz pouring his creative angst over glasses of Scotch whiskey, Herr Hans Bauer nodding animatedly at first, slower over a glass of rotwein, slowest after a shot of tequila, placid after the glass of brandy seasoned with clove and cardamom—this heady cocktail brewed fresh by the Guru.

Zeta Rani taps my shoulder, bringing my mind back to the canteen—she is enticed by the aroma of freshly brewed coffee. She has travelled on the night bus from the mining town of Keonjhar, and arrived at the Bhubaneswar Bus Stand to join me on our trip to Dhauli this morning. D'Vaz orders a cup of coffee and lemonade. Herr Bauer sips on the lemonade, and rubs his slightly bulging stomach. He is feeling sick from the meal on the flight. The flight from Guwahati to Bhubaneswar had been turbulent with monsoon winds.

The Southern Capital with a Sea is turbulent with riots. The Anti Democracy Party revolutionaries have made their point. The citizens of Pearl Island, the neighbouring country, cannot enter or exit the State, of which the Southern Capital with a Sea is the headquarters. Minnal, oblivious to burning vehicles, seethes in the wisdom of her own discovery. She has discovered that her eldest son will meet her only by appointment.

A meeting is only possible by divine intervention. That too, when the time is right. Naren's appointment with the Minister of Accounting Affairs has been furthered to another time, another uncertain date. Across the road from Venkataraman's residence, Naren enters a public telephone booth, and places a call. On the other side of the connection, I advise Naren to return home to Manipura the same night.

Gowravva boards the train that night. She will arrive at the Southern Capital with a Sea in about thirty-two hours. She has packed joladda rotti and shenga chutney for breakfast, lunch and dinner. There has been a good yield of corn and groundnut in her district this year. When Nelli learns of the golden yield, she will be happy to return home, Gowravva feels. Her eyes tear up as she remembers how Nelli ran through the corn fields by sunset every evening, soaking in the soothing rays of the setting star of all life forms. Every day, Gowravva called out to Nelli, telling her to watch out for the irate haavus. Nelli was not afraid of the haavus that the city people referred to as snakes—not when they were irate, and certainly not at all when the reptiles were placid. She knew by instinct, how to let them slither past without minding her intrusion into their territory. Once, when Nelli was bitten by a venomous viper, she ripped the red nylon ribbon which Gowravva had fastened her braid with, and tied it unto her ankle. The ribbon held tight enough to stop the flow of venom to the rest of her body. Nelli had saved herself from the snake's venom.

The human mind functions in mysterious ways.

Venom flows in mysterious ways amongst the human race, says Minnal to her new friend in the Southern Capital with a Sea—the Banana Vendor.

She peels a banana, and before taking a bite, continues to spell out the venomous nature of self-destructive emotions:

'Also,
Jealousy
Greed
Pride
Anger.'

Minnal has often told her ten sons that they must stay free of these varieties of venom. The Banana Vendor listens to the Lesser Known Goddess' discourse until an uproar on Beach Road yonder, fills the Southern Capital with venom. From their conversation spot on the sand by the sea, Minnal and the Banana Vendor look on as a furious mob of priests—their foreheads smeared with ash and their right hands brandishing lethal weapons—swords, knives, even trishuls—chase a frightened mob of construction workers out of their temple premises. These labourers are all from the State of Orissa, working in Tamil Nadu. 'These lowly tribes from Orissa pollute the land of the blessed,' bellow the priests, swearing by Mariatha, the Goddess they worship, until an angry siren, accompanied by five more, see the arrival of khaki-clad men with lathis. These lathi-bearing men are here to upstage the persecutors.

When the persecuted flee, all roads leading home are blocked.

The labourers from Orissa have nowhere to go—the ticket collector on the only weekly train to Bhubaneswar from the Southern Capital with a Sea, is not about to let them board without reservations. He is a man of principles, after all. Hundreds, maybe a few thousand people board the train despite the perspiring ticket collector's plea, and latch themselves unto the windows and doors of the train's bogies, all bruised and petrified labourers set to travel home to their families, ticketless.

The train chugs to life with ticketless labourers et al, and Naren watches the people from his State—men, women and their children—their hands, legs, heads—bobbing out of the doors and iron-grilled windows of the exploding bogies. The persecuted are going home to barren lands, brick kilns and mining companies—to a land where all their means of livelihood are exploding with wrath for the elected democracy.

Naren does not board the train. He is a man of principles, he will not travel ticketless.

Principles tend to evade the elected representatives of this democracy. Thiru Venkataraman explodes in a fit of anger, and smacks his driver's jaw. The Uncrowned Head, yes, Prime Minister Prasad Bharathi stationed at the Centre, has summoned him to his air-conditioned chambers in the Capital. Venkataraman's wife reminds her husband that he is a Brahmin, and cannot use physical prowess to outsmart the weak and the meek in body and brain—let alone his squiggly pan-chewing driver. The Minister remembers his roots, and his mother, who has on dark nights sung him songs of the land, where might is not right all the time.

Right time, wrong place
Wrong time, right place
The saga goes on
And on
Until you discover
That there is no fault
With either time or place.
Just that right and wrong
Refuse to co-exist
Although they are fraternal twins
Born of the same parents

Called Prejudice and Ego.
Dare to go against them?
No one dares the Minister of Accounting Affairs—he is a Brahmin, his wife reminds him every single day.

***

Dare to love a man whom you have not heard from for two hours, two days, two weeks, two months? I have not spoken with him in two months. I spend much of my savings on frequent personal journeys to Goa. Here, the waters of the Great Arabian Ocean enter my eyes, nose, mouth… My ears too, until I feel a wave of passion gushing inside me. I want to see his gentle smile, feel his tentative touch, and grow warm and red to the hot brush of a kiss planted by his lips upon the corner of my cheek, his passionate breath heaving inside my right ear.

Reluctantly steering away from his passion, I kiss the fragile frame of his dazzling daughter, and tell her about her journey to Bhubaneswar. I have word from the capital city of Orissa. D'Vaz was in Bhubaneswar last night, and the weather was suitably pleasant, he said.

I learn that the atmosphere is not pleasant at the canteen in the Art College in Bhubaneswar, though. Students of art are up in arms against the Government for banning a psychedelic 3D water-colour painting of a certain Indian God depicted in an intimate pose with his lover. 'Radha and Krishna are known for their intimacy. They have been depicted as lovers in the scriptures too,' rues D'Vaz, a great devotee of Lord Krishna, and more so of his innumerable gopikas.

The young artist in question, rues the loss of creative freedom. God is a liberated artist, he feels. Creative license is for us humans to take—we can only please some, and definitely displease the rest.

Sheltered from rain under a frond-thatched enclosure in the hamlet of Manipura, three young lads bask in their creative freedom. They mould nature-fresh clay into Lord Ganesha in his myriad avatars as cricketer, policeman and political leader. The three young lads are joined by their neighbour Nominta Debury. This little girl of the Mankadia tribe, they learn, will soon visit Sambhalpur to meet another child called Susanthi Bodra, and learn a thing or two about rearing ducks which lay golden eggs. You cannot put all your eggs in one basket. Especially if the basket is made of sticks and leaves and is tearing apart.

Susanthi's frond basket is sagging under the weight of the eggs she has collected this morning, and is threatening to give way. Among the many traditional skills which are passed down generations of Munda tribes, making baskets from dried leaves is one. Susanthi has not acquired this skill as yet. And her mother, a skilled basket weaver, has left home one more time. Staying away from home is not as easy as leaving it for good.

When Nelli left home, she put two sets of langas to wear in a plastic butti woven by her mother. Gowravva has been missing the basket too, since Nelli left with two sets of floral patterned long skirts. It was the only basket in the house, and, over the years, she has not had the heart to make another. Neither does Gowravva have the spare money to buy plastic wire from the Gulbarga Main Market, and weave it into a butti. She has saved every currency coin she can spare to travel to the Southern Capital with a Sea.

Minnal sits facing the sea by twilight. She has been told that it is futile to attempt to walk to the railway station where she can rest on the platform for the night. Minnal has an insatiable affinity to the natural elements—she finds solace under the open sky, as she has on many dark nights back home in her hamlet, for many long years after her ten sons have left her.

When sons leave home, parents do not worry that their bodies will be used for business; sex trade in particular. When Nelli left home, Gowravva worried about her first-born child's body. That body, which she had massaged with Neem oil when Nelli was just born. This homemade traditional Neem oil when kneaded into a baby's flesh, wards off diseases, increases immunity, cures wounds, and till date, enhances Nelli's natural beauty. The healing qualities of Neem are concrete.

Zeta Rani loves the indigenous tribes of Orissa—she keeps her appointment in Orissa's deepest villages despite her autoimmune reactions—she massages her newly-acquired infection with Neem oil. This natural extract's ingredients numb the pain externally and internally, and prevent the spread of bacteria.

During the course of her social work, Zeta has found that the tribes of Keonjhar—Gound, Santal, Mankadia, Juang and Munda—all believe in the magical healing nature of Neem oil. Neem trees grow in abundance in arid regions. These tribes feel Mother Nature-blessed by the regular occurrence of Neem trees in the forest lands that surround their homes. Farmers, children, cattle, even reptiles rest under the shade of these Neem trees.

Uphill from main town Bhubaneswar in Dhauli, the sun's rays gently file through interceding gaps between the adolescent Neem tree's tiny medicinal leaves, and blazes at forty degrees centigrade on the stark ground outside its envelope.

In this seemingly quiet environ
The ground
Is cracking
Simmering
Burning
Exploding
With anger
Retaliation
Inner vengeance
Outer vehemence
Eyes, nose, mouth, entire faces
Contorting

To establish that students of art will not be subdued by unnatural laws against freedom of expression.

D'Vaz reads these expressions. He leaves Herr Bauer, Zeta and me to deal with the situation at hand, and heads out to understand the depth of dissent among the students of art. Dissent inevitably disrupts progress.

Progress among people in the Southern Capital with a Sea translates into money. If you do not have money, you cannot sleep under the stars for free. The public beach is not a resort. Minnal cannot sleep under the blanket of the star-speckled night sky and in the air-conditioning of breeze blowing from the sea. 'This is a "public" place,' the moustached khaki-clad policeman tells her. Minnal does not have the means to bribe the 'law keeper' and buy fresh air. She begins her walk towards the Central Railway

Station—the public place with a roof. She is frugal with her coins. But she will buy a platform ticket for five rupees at the railway travel counter to gain access to her resting place for the night.

Naren spreads his cotton towel on the railway platform where he will rest for the night. There is no point in leaving the Central Railway Station to look for accommodation. The Southern Capital with a Sea has no tolerance for coins. Naren's rupee notes are fast depleting into coins.

Gowravva fastens her coin pouch as the train arrives at the Central Railway Station. She tucks the pouch along with her sari into her petticoat, and adjusts her pallu to cover her oiled and neatly-combed head securely.

***

Seated in the canteen at the Art College, Herr Bauer feels secure in the company of Zeta—she is to explain her mission to him. 'I am wirklich flabbergasted by what I read in diese cloth folder,' he says.

'Although there is one explicit case study, and several briefer ones represented in this cloth folder, it is not the story of Nelli alone,' Zeta explains. 'Many little girls have an urge to go missing when they become breadwinners by default,' she goes on to explain.

The fault can be with destiny, they, say. It often rests with the man, the 'documented' breadwinner of the family, who chooses to drink 'wine' instead.

Zeta uses the word 'wine' for the benefit of Herr Bauer. In Indian rural parlance it is Mahua, Baby—the popular brand of country liquor—also Arrack, and Neera.

In Indian urban parlance it is rum, brandy with Coke or Thums Up for 'good' measure. Wine, in these rural parts is unaffordable. Wine does not take the man on a high, higher than society permits him to rise. Or higher than where his ego would imagine him to be.

Imagination is therapeutic. I feel free to imagine. I imagine him dressed in blue standing on a podium, plaque in hand, letting a smile slide shyly across his face as it does when his heart is touched. He doesn't smile at me often. On the seldom occasions that he does, my heart skips a beat. When he does not smile, I feel restful in the knowledge that I have a dream for him. I have a dream for his baby. Although her father doesn't trust me enough, she knows only too well that her mother loves her.

A child in need is a child indeed.

Susanthi Bodra knows that her mother has left her to seek another child. This child, she had borne nearly twenty years before Susanthi, or even her older and now dead brother Tilka, were seeded in her womb. Susanthi cannot join her mother, she is told by the elders of Bochagora. Susanthi must accept that every now and then, she will be alone in her dingy little hut.

Sitting alone on the charpoy that night, Susanthi cries softly. She does not want to be alone in the dark hutment. She cannot keep the dibri burning all night—she has no spare money for more kerosene. Susanthi's fear increases. She is also insecure. She chokes on her own tears, and wants to cry louder. But she brings her hand to her mouth, stifling her torrential grief. She cannot be weak, she has been told by her mother many paurnima's ago. On this full moon night, as the tribes of Bochagora hamlet pay obeisance to the wholesome paurnima in the distant sky, Susanthi remembers that she is the breadwinner of her family.

But, where is her family?

Gowravva's family waits by the tea stall in the hamlet. Her second, third and fourth born wait for the telephone to ring. Standing by a tea stall on Platform No. 7 at the Central Railway Station, Gowravva looks for a telephone to call her children. But there is no telephone at the tea stall. The Southern Capital with a Sea is different from her hamlet, there are no telephones in the city's tea stalls.

There is a public telephone booth at the Central Railway Station, and Naren has found it.

Naren Nayak's telephone bill reads eleven rupees and fifty paisa. The vendor at the telephone booth on Platform No. 1 at the Central Railway Station returns three rupees to Naren. The vendor owes him fifty paisa more, but keeps the change.

Naren remembers Asha Paharia at Village Thimri, Jharkhand State. She minds the telephone in the Panchayat office, sometimes. Once on an official visit, Naren has used the phone, and duly paid for his call. Asha had returned a change of fifty paisa, when all she owed Naren was twenty-five. Naren owes Asha twenty-five paisa. He must meet her soon.

D'Vaz owes us a treat. He has just met us.

Sridhar Haider D'Vaz has just been nominated Honorary Consultant of the Student's Union at the Art College. He owns many titles, all honourably acquired for being a proficient painter of animals, both of the domestic and wild variety. He is also honourable for 'his ability to heartily mingle with the crowd and become one with its sentiment' as the press once wrote. He mainly mingles with various groups of people to understand his subjects better. Humans are his subjects because they interfere with animals. Animals are his claim to fame. D'Vaz travels the world to give talks on his natural connect with wild creatures in the jungles of India, Africa and in art-supporting cities around the world. He has become acquainted with Herr Bauer while on an honourable trip to Düsseldorf. There, he mingles with the German literati who have grown fond of him. They invite him home for Christmas every year. D'Vaz was with Herr Hans Bauer, his Frau and zwei töchter last Weihnachten. He had spent the rest of his Christmas break visiting museums around Deutschland, and regales us with his escapades.

I escape from the conversation mentally, and wander into a day in my past... '*Last Christmas, I gave you my heart, by the very next day, you gave it away...*' I hummed and looked at the life-size poster of George Michael. In school, I found George Michael's music soulful. I listened to his songs on the double-decked tape recorder which occupied most of the space in my room, and my heart surged with emotion for the boy who liked to wear a red canvas shoe on one foot, and yellow on another. Sylvester, my girlhood love, wore his hair a little below his shoulder, just the way George Michael did.

'Nainika,' D'Vaz calls out to me. I snap out of my trip down memory lane to learn from a Source who has come to meet me at Dhauli that Susanthi has been forced by the village elders to cut her waist-long hair short. She loves her long hair. But with her mother's constant appearances and disappearances, the task of braiding it herself is daunting. It comes tangled in knots each time she attempts to divide her locks into three equal parts, and then overlap them to make a braid.

***

No two people are equal. The Lesser Known Goddess is emotionally strong. The Minister of Accounting Affairs is emotionally weak. His fits of rage are known to unsettle his driver, his watchman, even his Burly Secretary who sports a thick moustache. On the day the Minister has been summoned to the Capital, his fury has rendered his driver nervous. Losing control of the steering, the driver of the Government sedan mowed down a physically-handicapped beggar, two sleeping dogs, also a pregnant cow with the Minister spewing abuses from the comfort of his rear seat.

All mowed 'parties' have survived, except for the two sleeping dogs and the cow's unborn calf, reveals a news report. There are two eye witnesses to the incident, which occurred at half-past eleven, a respectably late-night hour yawning into midnight. Fortunately for Venkataraman, the two eye witnesses were inebriated at that respectably late hour. They had spent their day's wages on the inebriating elixir, Baby.

Baby is the most potent, well-received brand of local toddy. It has been certified to wipe the body clear off its senses. It numbs the stinging physical pain one feels from a hard day's work at the construction site or spends removing the metal man-hole cover to enter and scrape the sewage pit. It also numbs the emotional pain caused by the loss of a child, parent or sibling who has not been able to survive terminal illness; minor injuries from road accidents, and 'unintended' mowing down by Government vehicles.

Venkataraman's wife has confiscated her husband's Government sedan. It bears evidence of the accident, there is a dent on the front bumper, and the paint has been scraped off the bonnet by the bronzed bell hanging around the pregnant cow's neck. The Minister's wife is chagrined that the calf is dead. There is no crime more unforgivable in a Brahmin's fate metre than the murder of an unborn calf. It does not matter that the curs are dead—they are not worshipped by the upper-class minorities. The beggars have been taken care of—they have been threatened at sickle point to leave the Southern Capital with a Sea before the blaze of noon, when the khaki-clad policeman will officially look into near-midnight deaths by 'accident'. Venkataraman's wife, on her part, has been kind enough to send the probing policemen a grand sum of rupees ten thousand each.

In penance of the death of the unborn calf and injured cow, Mrs Thiru Venkataraman has organised a Maha Yagna—a grand ritual to be performed by one thousand Brahmin priests. In consultation with the Burly Secretary, who has in turn sounded out Venkataraman, she has ordered the disbursement of a small sum of rupees, 'one crore only', from the Ministry's coiffeurs for this holy affair.

Venkataraman cannot be present at the Maha Yagna, Prime Minister Prasad Bharathi will not tolerate his absence from the upcoming Cabinet meeting at the Centre. Venkataraman is suitably chagrined, his fury scorches his Burly Secretary's cool disposition. The Secretary vows for the first time in his career as underling to the Minister of Accounting Affairs, that he will set his master's life ablaze. Only, the right moment must present itself.

Minnal will wait for the right moment to seek attendance with Venkataraman. For now, she will continue to rest her frail and tired limbs on Platform No. 1, at the helm of the Central Railway Station.

Frailty, thy name is not Gowravva. Gowravva is a woman, but she will not rest until she finds the telephone booth that 'they'—passengers, coolies, vendors and policemen on duty are guiding her to. She follows the gestures of the direction givers, not their words. She has just set foot in the neighbouring state. The language here is understandably different from what she speaks back home in Kithapur hamlet.

Languages
Dislodge identity
Unearth frailties
Known to the human race.
They call these frailties
Inebriations of the vacant mind
Where words are greater than actions.

Unable to speak the tongue of her neighbouring state, Gowravva begins to assimilate the fact that there is no unity in diversity.

Nelli is a child blossomed into a woman of diverse cultures. She speaks her mother tongue as well as she does the dialects of Deori and Mising, both languages of the aboriginal Assamese Mising tribes in the UNESCO heritage island of Majuli.

I am ahead of the mission at hand. Zeta has requested me to go on a reconnaissance to gather leads on the missing girl who has mastered the art of fashion jewellery making, but fled the training centre run by Zeta to return to her independent life as a sex worker.

This afternoon, I drink rice toddy, and sway with the Mising in Majuli. A baby is born, the island's women preen in their bright cotton saris. The Mising men praise their women as they sing louder, their baritone voices splicing the air, rising above the Vedic chants in the not-so-distant Vaishnav monastery.

Herr Bauer has arrived in Majuli ahead of me.

Resting his head on the pillar in the monastery, Bauer listens to the rhythmic sound of Vedic chants rising over Mising ditties and chronicles of daily life, these healing mantras colliding, conforming, and merging into the natural sounds of the aboriginal heritage island. Herr Bauer is in a trance.

We, Herr Bauer and I, meet.

We drink freshly brewed rice toddy with the tribes of the land.

We dance with the Mising.

Alarmed, the new-born Mising baby in whose name the tribes of Majuli and we celebrate, cries aloud.

I am high, I wonder whether it's my baby's cry. The other day, when his baby rested in my arms, I saw in her eyes her father's reflection. I fell in love with the Man in a Blue Kurta all over again. That day, I decided to walk two steps behind him, watching him reach his milestones. Today, I am inebriated by the Mising tribes' exotic elixir, rice toddy. I fall in love with the Man in Blue all over again.

***

Herr Bauer has scaled many milestones in his career as a development professional. To begin with, he chose this noble profession to better the lives of artists and musicians abounding the parks and streets of Der Bundesrepublik Deutschland, and people who have never been able to present their works in the country's rustic museums and acoustic-controlled auditoriums, have benefitted. Secretly, since his boyhood, Herr Bauer desired to pick up the violin and play symphonies on its slender frame. But the career he has chosen will not permit him time to explore his hidden musical talent. During his travels around the world, Herr Bauer finds himself lost to reality in rhythmic surroundings. These rhythms range from Vedic chants in religious ashrams, and especially the Vaishnav Temple in Majuli to a capella renditions of Gregorian chants rendered by religiously well-versed school boys in Nigeria.

Zeta sings hymns a capella style with the conscience of an activist leading the world to light, freedom, and acceptance. During a recent visit to Nigeria, she has learnt that her activism in India will no longer be supported by European nations. The focus of these European nations is now Africa, and all funds for development will be directed to that nation. Zeta must now seek funds from corporates within India for her developmental activities.

Susanthi's focus is now on her remaining ducks. She has no bile to clean. She has no mother. She is the only official orphan of the hamlet of Bochagora. The Panchayat Mukhiya has ordered the village parents to jointly look after Susanthi, bring her up as a little girl of the Munda tribe, as people of their kind have done for generations before them.

Looking after a girl of twelve plus, does not involve toilet training. Toilets in Bochagora are non-existent. During the late hours of the night, when Susanthi wanted to attend nature's call, her mother, despite her frail condition, would accompany her to the backyard. She would stand in watch while Susanthi emptied her bladder, some days under the stars, on others, under a moonlit sky, and on yet others, in the midst of a storm raging in the night sky. Bochagora is abundant with Susanthi's foster parents. But which of these mothers will accompany her on her mid-nightly nature's call? Her newly acquired adolescent demeanour will not permit her to ask her neighbour. Or even Domrudoru's mother who lives two hutments yonder, in a frond-thatched shelter by the entrance to the dense forest.

Asha Paharia wanders into the forest by night to answer nature's call. She does not walk far from home to reach the thicket of trees. The hamlet of Thimri itself is a clearing in a thicket—resting between a natural enclosure of age-old Sal trees. Here, a cluster of hutments, a school and a hand-pump hint human civilisation. Asha's hutment is part of this settlement, and her backyard is the forest. She has been to school and passed Inter, which equals Grade 12 in the Western world. She has never used a toilet which is enclosed by four walls. There are no sanitation pipes, underground or otherwise in Thimri because the elected democracy has not mapped this hamlet on its development chart.

Not so far away, across the border from Jharkhand to Orissa, there are no sanitation pipes in Manipura. In this hamlet, by the hour of midnight, Nominta Debury visits her backyard to answer nature's call. Tonight, her mother does not accompany her. She is preoccupied with her fifth born, Nominta's baby sister. Tonight, Nominta comes tearing into the house, wetting her skirt along the way. She is petrified. She has seen a shadow sprint across the makeshift wooden fence with barbed wire meant to keep leopards and tigers at bay. Snakes and men are able to wean the wire's spiked overcurrent, untouched. Nominta is shocked by an undercurrent, which numbs her down to a fever, her body temperature steadily rising above the 101-degree centigrade mark.

The Vedic chants gather momentum and steadily rise above the dome of the Vaishnav Ashram. Herr Bauer meets his 'still centre' amidst the variations in the chanting. He closes his eyes, and meets the Guru, my mentor, right where he is sitting.

The Guru defines the still centre as the core point central to every human—this is the point where the true you, resides—it is where you are happy to be you.

Herr Bauer is not happy to be who he is. He is not happy about being a moneyed developmental professional from Der Bundesrepublik Deutschland. He believes that his true self is not attached to wealth. But he has a Frau und zwei töchter who will decorate the Christmas tree and put up the mistletoe, under which his wife will kiss him when he returns home for Weihnachten.

Back home, the Man in Blue visits me briefly to resolve pending matters, and I want to kiss his pain away. The man I love is in pain. But I cannot kiss him because I need to maintain distance, preferably a long and silent one. He has drawn a very strict boundary, which I dare not trespass. I wish his pain away instead, and in the silence of the night, say a fervent prayer to the heavens. His baby shines in the dark of the night. I have not attended to her needs today. I kiss her loneliness away, and call D'Vaz. 'While in Bhubaneswar, show her around. Let the stunning little maiden get acquainted with the city's quirky circuits of creative people. I have mailed you their addresses,' instructs Maestro D'Vaz.

***

I have word from a Source—addresses are not easy to locate in Thimri. There are no door numbers. There are huts within hamlets invisible to the passing car in the Dalma Ranges. To a stranger to these regions, all hutments look alike. When the frond-thatched roofs and the unseasoned mud disintegrate in the floods that the monsoon rains bring along with it, these huts disappear. They reappear in another location nearby. Until then, the people of Thimri sleep in the rectangular school building with a single classroom built by the State Government. They sleep between puddles of water which have filtered into the classroom through the inept ceiling. The Department for Land and Buildings will not repair the ceiling because it has exhausted its 'ample' funds for the construction of schools in not-so-easy-to-access hamlets. But the Government's expenditure does not tally with the outcome—public schools in Dalma's hamlets are in a dismal state. Despite the damaged ceiling, this is the only building built of brick and stone in the hamlet of Thimri.

The people of Thimri belong to the Sauria Paharia tribes of Jharkhand—they do not have the money to build homes of brick and stone. Their small savings are not sufficient to build homes of mud either. While the mud is abundant in their natural surroundings, the rains bring down their rebuilt shelters each time they construct them.

Asha Paharia wants to save the people of her hamlet from the precipice of poverty. Last night, when she went to attend nature's call, a man and a woman from the hills, both dressed in khaki and brandishing country-made guns, have met her. They have spoken to her about a way to save the people of Thimri from poverty. They claimed their allegiance to the Maoxal Society, and will pay Asha a grand fee of six-thousand rupees every month, they said. Promising to return two moons later, they disappeared into the surrounding Dalma Ranges.

Tonight, Asha falls asleep between puddles of rain water, and dreams of her hamlet Thimri abundant with sturdy homes, all made of brick and stone.

Brick and stone do not make a home. Susanthi does not feel at home in the village school. But she has started going to school again. Soon after her father died, when her mother too, left Susanthi, Domrudoru told the other children of the Bal Panchayat of Bochagora that she must be convinced to go back to school. So the children of the Bal Panchayat, ranging from gurgling, crying new born babies to fifteen-year-olds, marched to the Peepal tree under which Bochagora's Mukhiya sat. Here, they told the Mukhiya and the other members of the ruling body of their hamlet about their concern, and presented a petition for Susanthi to be enabled to return to school. In his turn, Bochagora's Panchayat Mukhiya instructed all the parents in the hamlet to jointly convince Susanthi to go back to school. The parents in turn went to Susanthi's home, one with a satchel, another with a notebook, and a third with a hairband, to convince the near-orphan to go back to school.

Susanthi is back in school, but she is not happy to be the only near-orphan among her friends. She cannot show off her ability to read all about Samrat Ashoka in the English language to her long-gone father, and her recently disappeared mother. After all, Samrat Ashoka embraced the ways of Gautama Buddha because he could not bear the gore and bloodshed of war.

Not so far away from Buddha's Stupa in Dhauli, there is sudden uprising in the Art College. D'Vaz, Zeta, Herr Bauer and I duck for cover as the students do, when the policemen in khaki let their guns do the talking. One student has been seriously injured, another dead. He is dead because this is a democratic country. Democracy does not translate as freedom of creative expression. Herr Bauer's still centre is roused with the fervour of what he first set out to do in Der Bundesrepublik Deutschland.

'First, calm down,' booms a baritone. It is a distinct voice. It is D'Vaz's voice. He has emerged from his cover to calm down the policemen in khaki. D'Vaz will not tolerate the confinement of creativity behind the bars of 'unbending' norms. He will fight his war against the democratic 'kings', but calmly. D'Vaz is deeply influenced by the Buddha, and the ascetic's gentle ways of checking bloody dreams which lead kings to war. The policemen retreat when they spot D'Vaz—the award-winning artist has connections in high places, he can take anyone to task—even these so-called law enforcers.

Silence prevails.

Students retreat in a scuffle to mourn the death of their recently shot friend.

Friends are
A pocket full of roses
Thorns and fragrances

Pain and pleasure
Lingering on
And on
And on
And on...

***

Lingering on the pleasures of motherhood, Minnal is transported to a time when all her ten sons fought for a place on her bony lap. Back then, the fields were always green because dams did not stop the flow of water. Neighbours did not dig borewells. They shared yours. Interstate boundaries were not taken seriously. People were proud to be Indian.

Minnal is proud to be an Indian. She remembers Mahatma Gandhi, and weeps profusely. The killings in the burning Southern Capital with a Sea catch up to torment her well-nurtured will to remain strong against all odds.

There is strength in emotion. There is strength in being able to tell the person you love, that you do. I have written a mail to the Man in Blue, and stated that I love him. He is silent.

Herr Bauer is silent in the knowledge that democracy is dead in the Art College. Students are divided in the opinion that the 'protectors of law' and 'normative morals' must be questioned for the sake of our fundamental right to live as we please, so long as one person's nose does not physically touch the other's without mutual consent.

The Centre is shaken by the double blow in the Southern Capital and the Art College by Dhauli.

Venkataraman is relieved that the chagrin of the ruling forces at the Centre will be divided between him and the law-keepers who have taken a student's life in Bhubaneswar.

Minnal is relieved. After fifty years, her tears have flowed like the River Cauvery which was born in the Western Ghat Ranges of the neighbouring State, and irrigates her land. Today, the Lesser Known Goddess has wept for the dead, and for her disappearing sons. Today, Minnal will leave no stone unturned to gain an appointment with the Minister of Accounting Affairs.

At the appointed time, Naren's wife dials the interstate code followed by the eight-digit number of the telephone booth on Platform No. 1. Naren learns that his student Nominta is burning with fever, the sudden quivering illness brought on by a lurking shadow. Naren wants to rush home, but the Southern Capital has been cut off from the rest of the country. The Centre will restrict the movement of railway and air passengers travelling to and from the Southern Capital for two days and three nights.

Gowravva's movement is not restricted within the Central Railway Station. She has, by trial and error, walked up to Platform No. 1 to find the telephone booth. She smiles for the first time since she has arrived in the Southern Capital. She has found a telephone booth!

The first time Minnal held a telephone to her ear, she had felt a shudder down her sprightly spine. She was being told by a nurse at the Tuberculosis Hospital in the Southern Capital that her husband had died. Only a week earlier, she had gathered all her savings to bring her ailing husband from the hamlet of Poothotum to the Southern Capital. They had made the 278 km-long journey on a bullock cart. With a whip in her right hand, Minnal had goaded the bullock to move faster, and with moistened cloth in her left hand, she had wiped unending perspiration from her husband's boiling head... Minnal had left her husband at the Government run Tuberculosis Hospital in the Southern Capital to return to Poothotum, and tend to their fields. She had ten hungry sons to feed, and an ailing husband to save... She had left the phone number of the village headman with a kind and caring nurse who had offered to look after Minnal's husband... Minnal has not spoken into a phone since that call fifty-three years ago.

***

Years pass unintentionally into decades in Majuli. Nelli has crossed the waters of the Brahmaputra over 900 times until now to accompany her guests to Majuli. Across these waters, she wears her favourite colours—sparkling red, arousing orange, startling purple, and raging pink. In her steel trunk, there are four saris with matching sequenced blouses and petticoats. There are two more not-so-bright saris meant to be worn when there are no guests to accompany.

The guests alight at Nemati Ghat in Jorhat, the docking point which connects Majuli with the highway leading to Kaziranga, and further down its winding terrain serenaded by tea gardens all the way to the capital city of Guwahati. Nelli has travelled the highway to Jorhat just once in her approximately three-decade long life. She remembers snatches of her mother tongue Kannada from her childhood. 'Hege iddira?' she enquires after the well-being of those guests who she suspects have travelled to the island from the State of Karnataka, South India.

Nearly thirty years ago, when Herr Bauer visited India as a twenty-year-old adult, he travelled along the coastline from Bhubaneswar to Goa, and thereon to Mangalore in the South of India. The Guru lived in Bangalore and kept returning to his roots in Mangalore where fish and rice are as staple as vinegar and meat missang which flavours pomphret, butter fruit and brinjal with a tangy essence. This 'vinegared' essence clings to your taste buds, and leaves you yearning for more food, long after you have downed your meal. Herr Bauer fell in liebe with Indian cuisine in Mangalore, Karnataka's harbour city. He also fell in love with the Guru, who introduced him to the tangy 'Mangy' taste on this coastal visit to Mangalore.

Herr Bauer remembers the pomphret, Mangalore's exotic fish from the sea.

Herr Bauer also remembers the rohu, Majuli's fish for those who cannot afford the hilsa from the mighty Brahmaputra.

Nelli's favourite dish is deep-fried rohu flavoured with mustard and cooked with ridge gourd. There is always the bhut jholokia to accompany the rohu. Nelli loves these dangerously spicy chillies—they remind her of the menshinkais back home in the fields of Kithapur. That home, where the small green chillies are left to redden on their mother plant, and are about quarter the pungency level of the hottest chillies in the world—the bhut jholokias of Assam.

Nelli does not know that Majuli, the heritage island of the aboriginal Mising tribes belongs to the State of

Assam. She does not know that the hamlet she was born in belongs to the State of Karnataka. Over the years, Nelli has forgotten the lessons she has learnt in Grades 1 and 2. She stopped going to school when she ran away from home at the end of her first term, while still in Grade 2.

Yengeyo, yeppovo pona pullaigal thiruppi varamathangal. Minnal has been told by the people of her hamlet in the native Tamil tongue that her long-lost sons will never return. If they will not return, the Lesser Known Goddess will go find them.

Gowravva will not return home until she has news of her daughter, Nelli. Returning home is no longer an option for Nelli.

Home
A place
Not so far away
From the rhythm of Nelli's beating heart.
It is where she learnt to breathe
And let her heart beat in tandem with the sounds of clanging steel plates
And steel tumblers.
Her petite nose etched with soft curves on her octagon-shaped face,
Inhaling
The jasmine-coated perfume of incense that Gowravva lit up in the hutment's puja corner.

***

Minnal watered her Jasmine Creeper every day, she nurtured her like her own child. This Creeper was the only daughter among her ten sons. The Lesser Known Goddess has done well by her daughter. The Jasmine Creeper still clings to her maternal home in the hamlet where she took root, blossomed, grew winsomely, and wound herself around the wooden pillar which supports the thatched roof of Minnal's humble abode. From here, she spreads her fragrance to nearby homes by day. By night, Minnal and her neighbours dream of paradise in the mesmerising totality of the Jasmine Creeper's nocturnal fragrance.

The rains bring the nocturnal fragrance of Jasmine tonight. With head on my pillow, I recite.

Rathri Malli
Rath ki Rani
The scented flower of the night
Gentle in her fragrance
Which spreads far into the world
And upwards into the sky
Reaching out to a million stars
Which return to touch the dreams of the poor
With songs of hope
Love and reunion.

I sleep restfully, and dream of the Man in a Blue Kurta. Within my dream, I open my cupboard to touch his kurta, and hold it close to my bosom.

Will I wake up to be united with the man I love?

At the break of dawn, a gentle ray of sunlight throws sparkle on his daughter's well-etched features. I stroke her octagon-shaped face, and begin the day with phone calls. I begin to make arrangements to unite her with her destiny. She is destined to embark on a journey which can only bring her close to fame. His baby and I are now linked to the circuit, all thanks to Maestro D'Vaz. Linkages are essential where roots matter.

Susanthi is linked to her ancestral tribe by virtue of her pure Munda-blooded birth. When Susanthi was born, her father invoked the spirit of the land to bless his wide-eyed baby girl with all the virtues of Maa Taarini herself. Susanthi Bodra believed that the little girl in the mirror with button-like eyes and silken tresses falling loosely over her distinctly-round face, was a Devi. Only Devis, Goddesses, had straight silky hair like Susanthi, believed a tribe which wore its curls and waves with unrestrained pride. The women of Bochagora wore their wavy, curly hair in braids and buns according to what the occasion demanded.

Minnal wore her hair in a bun until she lost most of it when she turned ninety-eight. Until she was seventy-eight years old, she had adorned her hair with flowers from the Jasmine Creeper, and proudly flaunted her daughter's fragrance to neighbours and visitors to the temple, especially those who came from the big city.

Alone in the Southern Capital with a Sea, Gowravva feels surprisingly brave. She is in the abundant company of travellers from all over the country, many of whom do not speak the language of the State. Gowravva has spoken with her children. They are happy to know that she has a roof over her head for the night. In the Central Railway Station, night is brighter than day. Tubelights shine their brightest, each vying to outdo the other's whiteness. Each time Gowravva tries to count, there are a hundred other blinking shades of white, as tubelights most certainly should. And she loses count. There is certainly no dearth of electric supply in the Southern Capital with a Sea, Gowravva concludes, and thinks of her life at home…

In her own hutment, Gowravva burns the midnight lamp. There is no electricity to light up the lone bulb in the hall where she and her four children sleep. Gowravva must keep the lamp burning because scorpions and snakes find their way inside her hutment, often in the deep hours of the night when she and her children are sound asleep.

These days, Susanthi keeps the dibri burning in low flame all night. She is afraid of the dark. She is afraid of the shadows cast by the light of the dibri on the ceiling and the walls as she struggles to find sleep by night. Susanthi Bodra misses the comfort that her mother's constant presence gave her all these years. She wonders why her mother has left her again.

It is not easy for a mother to leave her children and face the chagrin of destiny.

A mother intervenes when destiny rankles the innocence of her child. The Lesser Known Goddess must intervene and battle with destiny to find and save her eldest son from the shackles of self-destruction.

Minister Thiru Venkataraman does not believe in the chagrin of destiny. He believes that destiny is large-hearted—it saves the rich from destruction. On board the Indian Airlines aircraft flying to the Centre, he is treated like a Maharajah in his business-class seat. He is waited upon with dried fruit and special beverages by hostesses who know him by face. Thiru's face appears intermittently on news channels as the hostesses surf the menu for desi films, news and serials, especially during international stopovers. Today, the news channels have not shown the

Minister in kind light. Venkataraman is being accused of murder, riot and unrest between communities speaking the same language across two nations. The Minister will not waste his precious waking time on matters that need to be dealt with at the Centre. He sips on his special beverage, and lets his Political Advisor aka Burly Secretary aka Aandavan Kangal worry about the impact of the news being relayed on the twenty plus English channels in India, and in many countries across the globe.

Aandavan Kangal is of the opinion that all coverage is important to catapult the Minister of Accounting Affairs to fame. Good news or bad, being in the limelight is essential for a Minister who aspires to take on the additional responsibility of Prime Minister-ship, sooner or later in his career as a politician.

Politics is a lucrative career. Politics was once considered a vocation like teaching, journalism, medicine and motherhood. Venkataraman does not think highly of the vocation of motherhood.

Minnal is only a mother in name. The people of her hamlet are aghast that she thinks of her ten sons even seventy years after her eldest born has left home, never to glance back at the mother who birthed and bred him with unconditional love. His nine younger siblings followed their big brother to the Southern Capital with a Sea. They have been lost to Minnal's world as they merge into the framework of a city where the common man is not celebrated.

In the big city, the common man is used as an icon to base news stories on, create reality shows, and as fillers between advertisements which speak of how the human race must strive to be uncommon by investing in products which make them unique.

Each of Minnal's sons is unique. She would simply know them by looking into their eyes amidst a hundred, thousand, million other pairs.

Blue silk sari-clad hostesses walk down the aisle in pairs to serve the Minister of Accounting Affairs his mid-flight snack of hot idlis with chinna vengaya sambhar and piping hot filter coffee. The aroma of baby onions fills the aircraft, and has many passengers who have sworn that they will not touch the desi meal of rice dumplings and South Indian sauce on their posh trip to the Capital, salivating.

Trips on aircrafts are still considered posh in India. The marginal few who can afford to fly are born with silver spoons; others sweat it out in air-conditioned corporate firms to earn their 'I am posh, I only fly' titles.

***

Herr Hans Bauer has chosen to travel by rail, many times in the nature-conditioned bogies, sitting on rexine seats alongside the working classes.

Women of the working class do the double shift—they work in offices which have no air-conditioning, and in meagre homes with scalding kitchens that are not fitted with exhaust fans. Herr Bauer feels the need to associate with die frauen who carry baskets of home-cooked food to serve the large families accompanying them on the train journey. These women from Indian hamlets, tier-two cities, also towns and District Headquarters are naturally conditioned to serve their children, their men, near relatives, and distant cousins especially from their husband's family line.

Women serve men everywhere—this is considered to be the will of nature. The word of God. Is God a man?

Nelli serves rice toddy to the men who visit Majuli. This batch of rice toddy has been prepared by the Mising tribe for the special festival of Holi. Nelli's male guests love the potency of the indigenous rice-brewed spirit. On a full-moon night which coincides with this festival of colours, the male guests at Majuli feel one with nature. The natural surroundings are light with laughter and song, men and women swaying together in a group dance. This dance is a form of meditation, diverse from the rhythmic chants steadily rising in tempo to counter the hum of mantras in the Vedic Vaishnav Ashram.

Upon this moonlit Holi—the Indian festival of colours—Herr Bauer sways with the Mising who tanz away the muscular pain caused by physical labour. The rice toddy which has by now filtered into every cell of his body all the way from his dark-haired head to his short big toe, brings him back to the distant reality of his frau und töchter back home in Der Bundesrepublik Deutschland.

Home may be distant, but it is still a reality.

Lounging by the side of passengers from hamlets, tier two cities and District Headquarters, Naren's home seems a distant reality. From a distance, he remembers the news about Nominta's shock and ensuing fever. Naren must return home to Keonjhar and get close to the scene of shock. He must save Keonjhar's children from the raw abuse of money power on people who have lived without it, built thatched-roof homes, tended to fields, mined gold, and grown their families from two to four and manifold.

Money cannot buy happiness.

Nelli does not know what to do with the money she earns every day. 'Put it away for your retirement, for your old age,' the people of Majuli say. Nelli puts her money away, and her piggy bank feels heavier by the day.

Minnal has no use for money in her old age. She did not have money to put away when she was younger. Feeding twelve mouths, including hers, did not leave her with any savings.

Venkataraman has saved enough money for three generations to come. His two sons wake up at 5 am every morning to go out to work. They workout in the gym for two hours, and spend the rest of the day pampering their bodies with food, drink, branded clothes, fancy gadgets, also heady aftershave lotions to camouflage their rough interiors, and attract the feminine gender with suave smoothness.

Zeta Rani pampers her mind with a song. Also, thoughts for a nation which will hold every woman in her arms for her innate abilities.

***

I have the innate ability to love him. I can go on loving him if I let go of the innate desire for him to look at me, and smile. I smile at the thought of the journey I will be making with his baby.

Susanthi Bodra is getting ready for her journey to Sambhalpur. It is her first journey outside the boundaries of Bochagora, into the forests, driving past neighbouring hamlets, across kutcha roads, pukka roads, streams and bridges over the rivers Telnadi and Mahanadi.

Susanthi's journey is not easy. But there is excitement in the heart of the near thirteen-year-old as she crosses the Neem tree, the landmark which separates Bochagora from the forest, driving through the kutcha roads in the rear seat of the close-topped jeep with YUPAP's social workers. Headed in the direction of the Sambhalpur Rozgaar Kendra, Susanthi waves back at her foster parents, who are by this time, nearly out of sight. The people who wave back at her include all the parents in the hamlet, the Mukhiya, her friends from the Bochagora Bal Panchayat, and of course, her best pal Domrudoru. This is not a final goodbye. Susanthi will return to Bochagora in fifteen days, once she completes her training on the intricacies of rearing ducks which will perpetually produce golden eggs.

Nominta Debury wants to travel to Sambhalpur to attend the workshop on duck rearing at the Rozgaar Kendra. She must ensure that her fever subsides by the time the night disappears into a new morning. Otherwise, her mother will not allow her to travel with social workers Urmila and Manohar Mahapatra to the Sambhalpur Rozgaar Kendra.

***

Tonight, Nominta Debury sits upright, shuts her eyes, tightens her muscles from head to toe, loosens hold over her body, and allows her thoughts to come to rest in the middle of her forehead. Her teacher Naren Nayak calls this region on the forehead the third eye. It is that part of the human body which is not visible to any other eye from near or far, and must be used from time to time to heal oneself, he has told his students. Nominta concentrates hard to let the shock caused by the stealthy stranger out of her small frame. It is an important ability for eleven-year olds, especially girls in Keonjhar District, to possess. These little girls often see strangers who shock them into a fever.

Strangers often become friends at railway stations. Especially when they spend the night communicating with each other in sign language on Platform No. 1 of the Central Railway Station in the Southern Capital with a Sea.

Gowravva has spread her slim green cotton towel beside an old lady who wears a divine aura about her. This divinity, Gowravva recognises in the lady's toothless smile. It is a smile, which immediately draws Gowravva into the arms of a mother. Mother, a notion, which became part of her subconscious mind when the woman who gave birth to Gowravva was carried away on a wooden stretcher by her father and his three brothers, her amma's body, never to return. That night, the rains refused to stop. Gowravva was eleven years old when her mother died, and she swore never to let her children witness her being taken away on a wooden stretcher to be buried alongside her ancestors. Not on a rainy night, not otherwise. Gowravva's mother had died of starvation.

When her children are fed, a mother does not starve, although she goes to bed without a meal.

Minnal has not known starvation. It does not take more than one tumbler of rice kunji to fill her concave stomach. The Lesser Known Goddess has kept healthy for over a century on one tumbler of rice porridge, every day. The eggs, the daal, the greens, the pulses, the occasional chicken and goat, she fed her man and her ten sons. She fed her daughter the Jasmine Creeper two pots of clear water every day—once at sunrise, and again after sunset.

Well-fed sons leave as they please, they seldom return home to their mothers.

Thiru Venkataraman arrives at the Centre well after sunset. The meeting at Prasad Bharathi's office has been adjourned for the next day. Venkataraman is happy to sleep soundly for one more night. Aandavan Kangal, the watchful Political Advisor, keeps awake all night while the Minister of Accounting Affairs snores at intermittent intervals through the dark night, and into the wee hours. Aandavan must strategically move the pawns in favour of Venkataraman. In a duel of politics, words are not as important as silence.

Silence is a mark of endurance.

Silently
She whimpers
As the guests pay
For the attention
She bestows upon them.
Nelli is bestowed with the gift of endurance.

Nominta Debury endures the cold night air wafting through small gaps and big holes in the frond-thatched ceiling of her one-roomed home. She sits by the low flame of the dibri, and rubs her palms together, her trembling lips saying a prayer in earnest to Maa Taarini for her fever to subside.

Naren Nayak rubs his palms together, looks at the lines defining his destiny, and says his nightly prayer to Maa Taarini. Every night, ever since the time he can remember, Naren has prayed for the safety of the tribes of Keonjhar. Santals, Juangs, Gonds, Mankadias and Mundas, all included.

The Mundas and Mankadias are distinctly different from each other. They have similarities too. Both tribes live off the land. These lands spread far into the forests, under the cover of the Kanjipani Mountains where elephants and snakes appear, disappear and re-appear through the day, into the night.

As the forest lies still, the song of her children resounds, and I wonder:

Kothai jabo hathi moi?

Woher gehst die weiblicher elefant?

Where did the mother elephant go?

She went to comfort her calves hidden from the sight of prying eyes. Eyes have a way of believing what they see.

Asha Paharia's father is at the door of their hutment in the far corner of the hamlet, overlooking the dense forests yonder. A village youth has been sent by the Panchayat Mukhiya to summon him, he follows the messenger. On instinct, Asha breaks into a slow run, scaling the dry and hot muddied path, barefooted, until she sees her father drawn into a crowd by the Peepal tree. All the village elders have gathered by the eighty-nine-year old Peepal tree casting its shadow over Thimri's Government School. Asha's heart races fast. Her bare feet race faster. Her hands part the crowd until she finds herself tumbling, her head now flat on the ground, her eyes meeting another pair of pupil she knows from her childhood. Asha stares into her brother's open eyes, unblinking, until a tear trickles down, wets her lips, and triggers her vocal chords into a loud wail. This wail louder than her father's cry, rising high above the astonished village elders' sighs, tears the silence in the not-so-distant jungles, and stirs the cuckoo from its nest. Asha's brother, Ravi Paharia, has been shot dead by the Jharkhand Police in the wee hours of the morning, at 4 am. The bullet has entered his brain—the killer device has torn right through his ear...

Asha will never hear her brother knock on her back door in the dark of the night every other Tuesday. Asha's nights will never be the same again. She will now be the breadwinner of her family...

Asha's mother, father, paternal grandmother, elder sister and two younger brothers do not know that their new and automatically appointed breadwinner will leave their hutment forever next Tuesday, at the stroke of midnight.

Time alters temperament, especially where little girls are concerned. Nominta Debury fears the clock when it's big needle and small hand confluence to settle on the midnight hour. She has spent many nights evading the whistle from the forest, which with its tall trees, Lantana shrubs and wild vegetation, embraces the backyard of her hutment. This nightly forest sight enchants Nominta until she hears the distinct whistle. Even as she crouches by the dibri, praying fervently, wishing her fever away, the whistle, she knows, heralds the appearance of the dreaded stranger.

***

Susanthi Bodra whistles a tune for the first time since her brother Tilka died. This tune takes her back to her childhood, when her father went to work in the fields and her mother cooked daal and bhath over the coal fire in their dingy, rectangular hutment with no windows and a single door. On special occasions, there was maach, fish from the stagnant lake on the highway. This occasional maach, the family relished heartily with more than generous helpings of daal and rice. Today, the same highway takes Susanthi away from Bochagora, towards the town of Sambhalpur.

Highways are intervened by kutcha roads winding along the natural inclines of mountains and valleys. Human settlements merge with the natural accoutrement of trees, wood, grass and dry fronds which defy these inclines to hold their own.

Holding her own, Nominta Debury has defied her rising fever to travel on the old Atlas cycle with her school teacher's sari-clad wife Parbothi Nayak, both feminine forms journeying the natural vicissitudes of the Kanjipani Mountains all the way to the main Keonjhar highway. From here, she will be driven by social workers Urmila and Manohar Mahapatra, through the descending highway between the mining town of Keonjhar and the Sambhalpur Rozgaar Kendra for vocational training.

Nominta feels more than a surge of excitement as she enters National Highway 6. Over the next five hours, she will travel the 250-kilometre stretch from the mining town of Keonjhar to Sambhalpur in a closed jeep with Urmila and Manohar Mahapatra. This is Nominta's first journey in a vehicle which consumes the non-renewable resource, petrol.

On Nelli's last journey, she travelled in a closed jeep along National Highway 37 all the way from Guwahati to Jorhat. Nelli has on occasions seen signboards which read Nagaon, Sibsagar, Dinjan, Dibrugarh and Tinsukia. All these indigenous towns are smaller than the big city of Guwahati, and larger than the hamlets defining its forest cover. They appear along National Highway 37, running right through the width of the State of Assam, and aside the southern flow of the bounteous River Brahmaputra. Nelli's guests tell her stories of how they have crossed National Highways 31, and or 31B travelling across the Brahmaputra at Goalpara to meet National Highway 37. Nelli's fascination for River Brahmaputra supersedes her desire to someday visit the Kaziranga National Park which branches off from National Highway 37, diverging into dense forests, and onwards to the Karbi Anlong Ranges between big city Guwahati and small town Nagaon.

I prefer to not cross the highway to Bhubaneswar with his baby. It is too dangerous to expose his labour of love to the stark elements. Maestro D'Vaz suggests that I travel by train with the fragile maiden who knows that her mother wants to keep her safe. To love, is to see your beloved safe. I pray that he is safe. I worry that the holes in his blue kurta have reappeared. I have not seen him in what seems like a lifetime...

D'Vaz has made an agreement to meet Zeta, Herr Bauer and me in a few weeks. There are more urgent matters to be set right. D'Vaz is working with the Student's Union in the Art College by Dhauli to lead matters related to creative expression towards democratic inclusion. Democratic politicians do not operate at the Centre, they work with a conscience wherever they are. But, do they exist?

Thiru Venkataraman must appease the capitalist sentiments of the governing authority at the Centre. Aandavan has worked all night to arrive at a formula to appease the speaker of the governing authority—they fondly call this man Prasad Bharathi. The formula outlines a lucrative land deal in the Southern Capital with a Sea.

Land is plenty in India's hamlets. Land is precious in India's cities. Land is identity in every corner of India.

Minnal has a piece of land with a hutment and her daughter, the Jasmine Creeper thriving at the edge of her hamlet, to call her own. Many years ago, her ten sons played the Indian rural national sport—Kabaddi, on this very land. Their friends from the school occupying the heart of the hamlet joined them. Minnal always found a few mangoes, especially during the months of April, May, June and July, to cut, salt and feed the band of rambunctious boys, their numbers adding up to seventeen on an average day. If the Lesser Known Goddess had had seven more sons, she will have ensured that they were also fed sumptuously, as rambunctious boys would have it.

Where there is a mother's will, no son goes unfed.

What about their hungry daughters?

The monsoon winds grumble at the sight of a hungry daughter on the highway. Nominta's stomach is grumbling—she feels low despite the excitement of her impending highway travel to Sambhalpur. She has gone hungry to bed last night. Her mother and her father have five more mouths to feed. When it rains too heavily, their paddy fields lose their potency. When it does not rain, there is no plan to grow paddy. Few vegetables—gourds and chillies grow in their backyard, despite the pouring rain or in its absence. Fish surface in the stagnant waters of their drowned paddy fields when it has poured all night. Nominta's father and her two brothers set up their fishing hooks to bring home their meal for the day. The meal does not hook itself to the fisherman's bait always. There are many fishermen from many hamlets in Keonjhar District, all angling at the same fishing pond. Luck favours few.

***

The Guru favours those who do not depend on luck alone, but turn every stone to live by their passion—all those who have chosen the Guru to be their guide, know this for certain.

Herr Bauer's eyes are shut—he watches the Guru's fingers run with certainty over the keyboard of his upright Euterpe piano, first in legato, then staccato, sounding the treble range of the *Eine Kleine Nachtmusik* duet, phrase by melodic phrase. Herr Bauer is drawn towards a distant night in his teenage past to the Hohensalzburg Fortress. Here, he held his beloved Greta Meier's hand on a Saturday night as a violin ensemble consumed the teen couple with Wolfgang Amadeus Mozart's Serenade No. 13, a composition for strings in G Major. Smitten by the serenade, Herr Hans Bauer und Fraulein Greta Meier feasted on salmon filet dripping in white wine sauce, alongside parsley, potato and vegetables, the dish mostly orange from the large portion of winter carrots in the recipe. That night in Salzburg ended in a hand-in-hand view of the Hohensalzburg Fortress from the cozy comfort of the restaurant with the triple bonanza of music, wine, and an illustrious view for romancing couples…

Over goblets of homemade wine quelled from the gregarious grape variety Bangalore Blues, Herr Bauer and the Guru remember the many romantic wonders of Austria. They go on to talk about the intricacies of duets. Herr Bauer is amazed that his passion for the violin has been rekindled so far away from Der Bundesrepublik Deutschland in a southern Indian cosmopolitan city. Tonight, Herr Bauer decides to give the queen of instruments a go. The Guru favours Herr Bauer's inclination for the violin, and other sentiments which uphold root, fruit, and all that belongs to the Indian soil.

Exchanging favours is common between the Mundas and the Mankadias. They exchange maize for pulses, especially when the rains have been kind enough to wet their lands in adequate measure. During such months, both tribes sleep soundly, having feasted on wholesome meals.

A meal is never the same during the drought-prone months in Keonjhar.

Tonight, Naren Nayak dreams of the empty plate occupying the space between his hand and his beloved wife Parbothi's dainty fingers, on a distant night in his teenage years. That year, when Naren turned nineteen, Keonjhar received no rain. That year, when Naren was married off to Parbothi, he lost his father to starvation. That year, his mother breathed her last to disappear beneath a pile of bones, which were her own. On many starlit nights, Naren and Parbothi disappeared into the forests, dibri in hand, searching violently, playfully, earnestly for wild berries to fill their grieving stomachs. When the crickets sang at their feasting points over decaying plants in the thick of the forest, Naren and Parbothi swayed to the buzz, hoping that with this music of the jungle, the rains would arrive.

The Maoxals arrived instead, hoping to convert the unfavoured tribes into rebels for fortune. Naren knew even when he was a teenager that fortune favours those who stand rooted to their passion in the face of adversity. Naren was passionate about becoming a crusader for rootedness and so, chose to be a teacher.

The Guru is a teacher in name, he never shies from sharing his knowledge.

My foster parent, the Guru, met his still centre by instinct, and demystified the complexity of recognising one's deepest passion. He inadvertently helped you to explore your innermost talent. You in turn worked hard to manifest this talent to yourself and eventually, put it out there for the whole wide world to witness.

I remember that day when the world witnessed my Guru being taken away in an ambulance. That day, I stood alone in my writing. Writing is the lonely foil of a mind which aspires to create a contrast between the uttered word and the unuttered sound.

I am distracted by the sound of his voice whispering in my ear. What? Did he say he loves me? The man who loves blue? It does not matter what he said, he is not even near me.

I have work to do. The date for the journey with his daughter, the precious baby I hold close to my bosom, has been decided.

***

Nominta Debury has decided to give poverty the slip. She will follow in the footsteps of her master, her guide, Naren Nayak, she tells Parbothi as they wait on the highway for Urmila and Manohar Mahapatra to arrive in their closed jeep. For every meal that Nominta has gone to bed without, she will harvest an acre of paddy, she has told Parbothi in the wee hours of the morning even as her empty stomach rumbles the sleep out of her eyes.

Naren Nayak is indeed Nominta's role model—he works through the wee hours to upgrade his knowledge on the politics and sociology of his motherland, the heartland of Keonjhar. He has read about Samrat Ashoka many times over. The life story of the great ruler, whose emotions went to ruin over the unconscious spilling of blood during the Great Kalinga War, teaches Naren that earning good karma points furthers more stability than scoring over one's enemy with unprecedented assaults. Naren draws up a Moral Progress Chart for each of his students. Here, Nominta Debury, Priti Moi Nayak, Lipin Hati, and other children who burn the midnight dibri in their distant hutments encased in the valleys of the Kanjipani Mountains, maintain their karmic scorecards.

Walking away from the Art College en route to the Stupa of the Buddha rooted sedately in a location uphill Dhauli, D'Vaz is keen on gathering his good karma points. He will lead the students of the Art College to the Centre in a wild attempt to convince Prime Minister Prasad Bharathi and his Cabinet of ministers that police and politics must be kept out of the purview of art. The students forming the Union Committee of the Art College have unanimously agreed to disagree with the police and the politicians. Especially those 'ps', who refuse to ascribe democracy to art and expressionists of the all-consuming medium, as it were.

Zeta cannot come to terms with all this democratic fuss about art, especially when her cloth folder still remains unread by the powers at the Centre. If they do not act in time, they cannot save even nine. Most recently, nineteen girls have gone missing from one hamlet in Balangir District of Orissa, alone.

My heart goes out to the missing children, I hold my little girl, his baby tight. I do not want her to succumb to the inevitability of failure due to any lack of understanding between her parents.

Parents in Balangir District have never been to school. They have known hunger since they have stopped suckling their mothers' bosoms. The parents of each of the nineteen missing girls have been promised a steady monthly income of six thousand rupees per household.

The Honourable Venkataraman does not know or care about how much it costs to run a hutment in a jungle-nestled hamlet surrounded by thick mountains inhabited by wild animals and leopards, tigers, and the wild boar included.

***

Sridhar Haider D'Vaz has often captured the feline features of the indigenous leopard of the Kanjipani Mountains. This leopard has won him international accolades on two occasions. One auction in Der Bundesrepublik Deutschland alone, had enabled him an income of one million Deutsche Mark. Today, the sum equals one million Euro, as Deutschland is joined by the fellow institutions of the European Union alongside Austria, Belgium, Cyprus, Estonia, Finland, France, Germany, Greece, Ireland, Italy, Latvia, Luxembourg, Malta, the Netherlands, Portugal, Slovakia, Slovenia, Spain and Lithuania, to embrace this united currency. Britain has just voted an exit from the Union.

Working in unity is the best solution for financial woes. The Bal Panchayat members of Bochagora are holders of a united currency. They have put all their savings together in a steel piggy bank with a key, and made a duplicate of it. They have meticulously kept count of which member has contributed, and how much. All the members of the Bochagora Bal Panchayat, aged five to fifteen years, have sacrificed the urge to buy chocolates and butter biscuits at the highway tea stall to create this joint saving of one thousand and two hundred rupees. This saving will rescue the members of the Bochagora Bal Panchayat in time of dire need. The Bal Panchayat will together decide whether the need is dire. Right now, Domrudoru's sister is ill. She has been vomiting a green gooey liquid for eight days. Members of the Bal Panchayat acknowledge Domrudoru's need as dire. The treasurer of the Panchayat unlocks the steel piggy bank in the presence of its members, and loans the boy of nine, a grand sum of one hundred and fifty rupees. With this money, Domrudoru Baiga's mother and father will take his younger sister, who turned three, four months ago, to the one-doctored clinic on the highway. While his sister gets treated, Domrudoru must work hard to repay the sum of one hundred and fifty rupees along with an additional five rupees, which will serve as an interest to the loan.

In the interest of the indigenous tribes of Majuli, Nelli tucks twenty rupees into her personal tortoise-shaped terracotta piggy bank every day. Nelli brought home this delicately-manicured tortoise from a rare trip to Manipura in Keonjhar District. She had accompanied a guest on this working trip, and her Mentor Amrit Kumar had travelled with them. Amrit always travels with Nelli when she has work to perform outside the perimeter of Majuli. Nelli keeps this piggy bank safely inside her steel trunk nestled between the generous folds of her glittering saris. Amrit must not know that she has a piggy bank, and that there is steadily accumulating money in its belly.

Money breaks relationships when the desire for it precedes the will to love minus the perks of reward. I find my reward resting in my arms. I see his passion in her. I am happy to connect with the soul of the man I love while he goes about his business, unmindful of my existence.

***

Sridhar Haider D'Vaz searches for soul in art. He finds soul in the young artist's psychedelic 3D water-colour rendition of Lord Krishna. D'Vaz finds that somehow, love seems more concrete in the psychedelic hues that fill the frame. The range of the artist's palette filling the vicissitudes of emotions that go haywire, vivaciously confluence to add up to the density of the 3D water-colour.

In the young artist's frame, Radha and Krishna are novices and seasoned lovers, at once. Such is the soul of love—ageless, boundless and ever dynamic between the rise and fall of passion.

Nelli has felt the passion of romantic love rise once in her body. She visits this emotion every night in the darkness of her room. Her room in Majuli has a small window. It overlooks the mighty Brahmaputra. Every night, from the confines of her room, she migrates into its heaving waters to seek out her love. Only, she does not know the name of the man she loves. She does not know where he lives. Majuli has the distinction of playing host to visitors who have chosen to transgress the norms of the city. One transgressor has left Nelli in raptures over his deviance.

Tonight, Nelli takes a gulp of toddy from the earthen cup placed in a room overlooking the seemingly serene Brahmaputra in the north-eastern region of India.

In the southern region of India, Herr Bauer is in raptures over the tangy, bitter-sweet taste of the Guru's homemade wine. He permits the potion to ride over his tongue, and ponders over the disruption at the Art College by Dhauli. Herr Bauer arrests his desire to call D'Vaz. He will discuss the predicament of the subdued student on another day. Herr Bauer must visit more immediate matters now. These matters are close to his heart. Tonight, the texture of the Bangalore Blues will accompany him through the report in the cloth folder, phrase by word, emotion by intent.

In the same city, sitting in another home, Zeta Rani has poured over every word in the cloth folder, a glass of Port Wine from Goa keeping her company. Zeta is not one to rest after a task is done, no matter the sweet red wine in the glass waiting to be relished, sip by slow sip. Zeta is running against time, she stumbles out of her easy-chair to fetch her mobile phone. It has been ringing incessantly at this midnight hour, and she answers the caller on the fifth ring. 'There is no time to let asunder,' Herr Bauer heaves melancholically under the genteel influence of the Bangalore Blues crushed to intoxicating perfection.

Zeta nods, and talks to Bauer about their next step.

It is strange
How wine
Brings the bold-hearted together
To deal
With the death of virginity

By force…

The midnight discussion with Zeta has brought Herr Bauer's focus to Majuli. But he must go back to the Art College by Dhauli to resume the interrupted meeting with D'Vaz, Zeta Rani and me.

In the same city, in yet another home, I sip on a glass of Sula, fine wine made from Nagpur's green grapes. I wander into that night when he and I melted into the gaze of ardour. I linger by that night in his balcony, each of us sipping on our own glasses of wine, gazing for a long moment into each other's eyes. I fall in love with the Man in a Blue Kurta one more time.

Reluctantly, I detach myself from that night, and attach myself to its memory.

In memory of that night, I kiss my baby's forehead, it is so well-defined, warm and easy on the eye.

***

Minister Thiru Venkataraman is pinned in the eye of a political storm. The Centre resembles a cyclone. The Uncrowned Head is supremely unreachable—no minister is allowed within ten metres of Prasad Bharathi's pedestal. The lower ranking ministers must stand thirty metres away. Today, the Minister of Accounting Affairs remembers that evening, months ago, when the rains divided the 'touchables' from the untouchables in Goddess Mahalakshmi's temple. Venkataraman stands thirty metres away from the Prime Minister's pedestal—he is an untouchable. This is a new distance from the closer, ten-metre range that he had happily maintained with Prasad Bharathi until a few moons ago. Now, his luck has run out.

Venkataraman is unable to predict whether luck will return in his favour.

Aandavan, his clever advisor, has a plan.

Naren Nayak has a plan. Before he fell asleep on Platform No. 1 in the Southern Capital with a Sea, he had made a phone call. His wife Parbothi does not know about this phone call. Parbothi is concerned about her husband's safety. Naren chooses to keep this phone call a secret. He wants Parbothi to close her eyes, and dream of a carefree world for children like Nominta Debury and other little girls who are not quite thirteen years old, living in Keonjhar District.

The world can only be as carefree as a mother creates it for her child.

Minnal has created a carefree world for her ten sons. Yet, they have left her, one by one, to join their other brother in the city. Minnal is not concerned that her sons have left her. She has learnt that her ten sons do not believe in a carefree world for other boys and girls, men and women, all of whom have spent their childhood years under the caress of a Neem tree, and the wisdom of a Peepal tree. Minnal is concerned that her ten sons do not believe in a carefree world the way she does.

A rock
Against the tide of troubled waters
Stands alone in the face of adversity.

The Lesser Known Goddess is alone in the pursuit of her ten sons.

These sons will need to return to their roots, learn to live.

Also let live.

Zeta Rani lives in a terrain which brings her face-to-face with young women who have been forced to give up their virginity. This, at a time when they were not quite aware of the meaning of virginity.

What is virginity?

Nominta Debury has just discovered the meaning of virginity, she feels shy and hungry at once on the highway. The previous night, as she packed her cloth bag for her first journey in a petrol-driven vehicle to Sambhalpur, Nominta's mother told her all about becoming a woman. Nominta was on the verge of menstruating—she will soon be ready for procreation and motherhood, in that order. But would the menstrual bleeding turn this near thirteen-year-old into a woman? Pondering about her recently acquired insights on womanhood, she had packed long, haphazardly cut strips of her mother's oldest sari along with her frocks—one pale green, the other blazing orange. Both frocks are hand-me-downs from her older sister, now nineteen, and a mother of two girls and one boy.

Nominta is shocked to know that she will bleed. Nominta is elated that her mother has consented to let her travel to the Sambhalpur Rozgaar Kendra with Urmila and Manohar Mahapatra despite her impending biological transition into womanhood. But Nominta is not emotionally prepared for womanhood and its impending consequences of marriage and motherhood, in that order. Nominta knows that her mother will face the ire of the entire hamlet for allowing her daughter to travel at this delicate transitional time. Urmila and Manohar Mahapatra are aware of Nominta's impending biological transition. After all, they are no strangers to the inhabitants of the hamlet of Manipura in Keonjhar District.

Asha Paharia has met several strangers after her brother has been shot through his ear by a member of the Jharkhand Police Force. These khaki-clad officers have taken Asha along to the Special Court chaired by Inspector General Tuffwinder Singh Bawa in the main city of Tatanagar. Asha has been told that silence is golden in the Special Court.

Silence is platinum in the presence of the police.

Parallelly, the police in the Southern Capital with a Sea has been scouring Platform No. 1 for possible miscreants. Platform No. 1 in the Central Railway Station looks placid with heaps of sleeping passengers snoring at varying levels of baritone, ranging two scales on the base cleft, music of an uncertain kind. Certainly, miscreants do not snore so rhythmically in public, the police know from experience.

Simultaneously, in the city of Bangalore Blues, Herr Bauer watches the Guru's slender fingers resting on the tones and semitones of the base cleft of his Euterpe, an early 20th century dual tone, German upright piano, practising his range of the *Eine Kleine Nachtmusik* score. It's raining ice-pellets outside. Inside, droplets of rain are turning into a steady heavy drizzle of notes as the Guru rustles up a downpour with the base keys.

The Southwest Monsoon rains in India travel northwards, in the direction of Sambhalpur.

Susanthi Bodra swallows the incessant droplets of September rain, sticking her neck out of the window of the closed jeep, mouth wide open, her senses in tune with nature. Susanthi has been singing the folklore of the forest about birds and ducks, bees, peahen and mayouro preening, priming her senses with the joys of the jungle. Her joy is short-lived. The last time Susanthi saw a mayouro in the jungle, the peacock, with its fan of multi-hued feathers spread wide during a dance in the September rain, was dead.

Further north, in the thick forests of Jharkhand, it is raining fire.

The jungle rests after 4 pm every day. From what seems like the deepest pocket of the Dalma Ranges, a volley of gunshots lays the tranquillity of these dense forests to rest. Bats lie in wait, downside up as they are wont to, and birds of the day flutter in zigzag randomness between tree, shrub, and the occasional lamp post which never glows. The electricity line in the Dalma Ranges keeps the jungle and the hutments in the hamlets within, alight for fifteen minutes every morning. By night, it is the turn of the dibris to light up homes.

Tonight, Asha Paharia's home is dark. The strangers are here to take her back with them. These strangers do not belong to the Jharkhand Police Force. Asha's ageing parents are perplexed and nonchalant, at once. Strangers often visit their hamlet. Nobody knows which force they belong to, the Jharkhand Police or the Maoxal Society. Both factions of strangers are dressed in khaki attire.

In these regions, khaki is the colour of law.

Khaki is also the colour of dissent against law.

Khaki is the colour which bridges the gap between lawfulness and lawlessness.

And khaki renders the poorest of the poor helpless in their forest homes.

Thiru Venkataraman hobnobs with both these khaki-wearing parties. Prasad Bharathi is disappointed that the Minister of Accounting Affairs is not discreet about his simultaneous involvement with either of these khaki-wearing parties. After all, khaki is a noble colour.

Colour brings harmony.
Colour causes disharmony.
Colour, colour, which colour do you wear?

Nelli recognises the colour of a flower by its fragrance. Tonight, she smells Marigold. When Nelli was a girl of five, her mother pinned a string of Marigolds which bloomed the previous night, unto her waist-long braid. The fragrance lasted through her day at school. Nelli's classmates treated her like a princess. 'You smell like a Marigold,' they giggled. Nelli liked being a princess, and everybody followed her everywhere. One day, all her classmates followed Nelli to her hutment by the edge of the hamlet overlooking the highway. Nelli's mother fed the trail of eight-year-olds pieces of mango from the tree which was once the source for her livelihood. From that day on, Nelli's entourage followed her mother Gowravva, instead. Nelli choked with tears when she learnt she was no longer their princess. 'You are still my little princess,' Gowravva told her first-born. 'But you are not an entourage. You have stolen my followers—all of them,' retorted eight-year-old Nelli.

***

The Lesser Known Goddess has many followers. They follow her home to pluck the flowers off her lissome Jasmine Creeper. Minnal's daughter takes pride in her flowers—they are delicate and small, but carry her fame far and wide. Minnal's Creeper has been a homebound daughter—she has spread her mesmerising fragrance far, despite her rootedness. People from the hamlet and visitors to the temple have worn the fragrance of her flowers to the main towns and big cities in her home state, and other regions too. This Jasmine Creeper has wandered far beyond her boundaries, but her roots remain firmly attached to the woman who has nurtured her.

For mothers who are sole breadwinners, it is easier to keep a daughter from wandering, especially when she wears the distinction of being a Jasmine Creeper.

I know that his daughter will not forget her roots. Even if she does, her features will talk of where she belongs. She belongs to a certain dimension of his mind which shows that he cares about his roots although he vehemently denies it. I, her mother, nurture her with care in her father's absence. I hope that when my daughter becomes a big star, both she and her father will remember me.

Hope always lingers in the air, it is for the human mind to access it.

Riding on the highway with the YUPAP volunteers, feasting on fresh rain splashing across her face, Susanthi Bodra hopes to one day make Bochagora rich, and have its people afford two meals even when the monsoons have decided to play truant. Ever since her mother last left, all the parents of Bochagora are hers as well. In her little over twelve-year-old mind, Susanthi knows that she is the daughter of all these parents. She must not fail any one of them.

Failure is the mark of a self-obsessed politician. The Minister of Accounting Affairs has failed everybody. The Uncrowned Head is disappointed that the bungled accounts of the nation are now in public view, thanks to Thiru Venkataraman's foolish and drunken statements to the Press. Prasad Bharathi, together with his Cabinet of ministers, has siphoned off funds from resources allocated to all sectors pertinent to the development of life, amenities and livelihood of the country's taxpayers, by misrepresenting income versus expenditure statements. The brain behind the bungled accounts is of course, Thiru Venkataraman. The drain behind the secret of the bungled accounts, is also Thiru Venkataraman!

The irate Prasad Bharathi has given Thiru Venkataraman three months to 'un-bungle' the accounts, and remedy public impression.

Aandavan, the brain behind Venkataraman, has made extensive notes of the Prime Minister's requirement.

Herr Bauer notes that the Guru's doorbell is ringing. The Guru's musical spirit continues to strike the tones and semitones of the Euterpe in accurate symmetry with Wolfgang Amadeus Mozart's composition. Herr Bauer removes himself from this rapturous rendition with restrain, and answers the doorbell.

Alarm bells go off in varying levels of crescendo on Platform No. 1 at the Central Railway Station in the Southern Capital. Gowravva awakens with a start, and rubs her tear-soiled eyes. The Lesser Known Goddess calmly opens her eyes, wide and all perceiving. Naren, who is accustomed to staying asleep amidst strange sounds ranging from the eerie howl of the midnight owl, to gunshots in the not-so-distant Kanjipani Mountains, and his neighbour's boar-like snore, continues to shut eye oblivious to the unmelodic bells.

Nelli's forehead is in a sweat, she opens her eyes in panic at the midnight hour, to escape her dream. She has a vivid vision of a man chasing her into the chilli fields of Kithapur.

He has smelt her out of her hiding place through the scent of Marigold on her hair. Running, hiding, escaping the man's pudgy grip, Nelli becomes invisible behind the lone Neem tree in this shadow-bereft chilli field. There is something about this dream which Nelli cannot decipher. She breaks into a shiver.

Nominta Debury shivers as the rain splatters through the open window of the closed jeep along the highway from Keonjhar to Sambhalpur. She has not quite recovered from the fever. Urmila Mahapatra digs into her seasoned jute bag to retrieve a paracetamol for Nominta. Manohar Mahapatra is confident that this brave little girl from the hamlet of Manipura will have given her fever a miss before she arrives at the Sambhalpur Rozgaar Kendra. Such are the reviving powers of the paracetamol, he believes—this medicine is not easily available to the citizens of Manipura. The only provision store on the highway by Manipura also stocks medicines—it is located in a two-storeyed building eight-kilometres from her hutment. Nominta is overwhelmed by Urmila and Manohar's kindness, she suddenly feels like bursting into a song…

'Jhumur Jhumur
Jhumur Jhumur
Kothai jabo re?
Jhumur Jhumur
Jhumur Jhumur
Nominta Debury Samabhalpuro jabo re…'

In this folksong of her native land, Nominta wonders where she is going. The jhumur has its answer—Sambhalpur.

Such is the reviving power of this refrain, Nominta sings the jhumur to the passing truck, and to the incessant rain.

Wenn es regnet in Der Bundesrepublik Deutschland, Herr Hans Bauer möchte tanzen mit die Frauen und singen mit den Herrn. When it last rained at home in Der Bundesrepublik Deutschland, Herr Bauer danced with the ladies, and sang with the men. Herr Bauer has much to learn in the company of the Guru and the visitor for whom he has just opened the door.

Greeting Herr Bauer with a smile, D'Vaz leaves a puddle of melting ice-pellets at the Guru's door. He must wash and change before the trio shuts door to the outside world, and formulates its strategic plan.

The Guru's eternal touch stimulates the final phrase of *Eine Kleine Nachtmusik*—this sprightly melody to render hope. Herr Bauer brings out the cloth folder, and places all the allied paper documents on the expansive late 19th-century rosewood table by the French windows in the Guru's airy living room.

***

Inspector General Tuffwinder Singh Bawa stands with his back to the French window at the Tatanagar Police Headquarters. Asha Paharia looks through him, past the window, and two kilometres beyond at the smoke emanating from the Steel Plant which defines the city of Tatanagar. Smoke emanating from his once cool ears, the Inspector General raps his baton gently on the glass-topped table to capture Asha's gaze, and bring it to focus with his.

The constables on Platform No. 1 at the Central Railway Station rap their batons randomly, hitting sleeping passengers in their unmindful frenzy. All is silent except for a lone baritone encompassing the entire octave of the A Major scale. The constabulary panic as Naren continues to snore to the scale of A Major—it is music to few ears, and cacophony to the rest. And the rest are majority.

Khaki-clad law enforcers in the Southern Capital with a Sea cannot imagine how a man can be lost in the restfulness of sleep amidst all this pandemonium.

Who says sleep is restful? This moonlit night, Nominta's mother does not sleep. Her eyes are shut to the world. Her body does not know that this mother is awake in her subconscious mind. In her subconscious mind, she sees Nominta shivering in the closed jeep with an open window. Has she made the right decision by sending her daughter on this distant journey to Sambhalpur? It is difficult to come to terms with one's personal choice in a mining industry-invaded agricultural region where neither the elected democracy nor the Maoxal Society have assured this mother that her children will continue to live by their lands and use their ancestral skills of farming, grazing, fishing and duck rearing to meet their basic food, clothing and shelter needs. That too, Nominta Debury is a girl on the verge of puberty.

Tonight, Nominta's mother sleeps in unrest.

Unrest is often the outcome of panicked perception. The Lesser Known Goddess hails the unrest on Platform No. 1 at the Central Railway Station as a matter of little concern. 'This is a velayattu of the Government,' she tells her neighbour on Platform No. 1. Gowravva has somehow understood from Minnal's expression that she believes this is 'game play' by the Government. 'Howdu, Sarakarada hudugaata,' replies Gowravva, beaming at Minnal.

Yes, this is a child's game, as Gowravva says. The Government is juvenile, it is playing this game.

The Minister of Accounting Affairs indulges in a game of chess with the Political Advisor. This game is in celebration of their momentary victory at the Centre. Venkataraman has chosen the white pawns to match the colour of his freshly washed and starched dhoti. As the white rook checkmates the black queen, there is pandemonium on the chessboard.

The pandemonium at the Central Railway Station subsides as Minnal breaks into a shrill refrain.

'Thandane thaane naane naa
Maata Pitha Guru Daivam
Aanaal pasangalikku vore kovum…
Thandane thaane naane naa
Aaa…hahahahhahahaa…'

Minnal grunts out a shrill series of laughs in conclusion to her folk ditty about parents and gurus being Gods, and children being chagrined over this status.

The constables in khaki, chagrined by the toothless old lady's rapturous rendition, decide to take Minnal into their custody. Minnal enjoys visiting new places—she is only too happy to go with the constables to the police station by the Central Railway line.

Mothers are often the butt of their children's chagrin—they just don't seem to mind their temper tantrums. Nelli remained chagrined with her mother for months after her followers had abandoned her. The chagrin died as time passed. But the deeply-ingrained wound did not.

How was Princess Nelli to live without her entourage of followers?

His baby has gathered her entourage of followers. They call me every other day to say they find her physical composition alluring. When can they see her next?

When will I see the man I love next? I am dying to tell him about his daughter's increasing entourage of followers, but there's pandemonium in my heart. The man I love is distant and withdrawn.

***

Minnal's daughter misses her. The water travelling up her stem, down to her roots, into her buds, leaves and flowers does not have the same sweet taste she has grown accustomed to when her mother fed her. The people of the hamlet with the famous Vishnu Temple take turns to water Minnal's Jasmine Creeper every single day. They miss the Creeper's mother, and her rapturous song. If she does not return soon, they will all give up two meals each in prayer to their indigenous deity Mariatha, and prepare to visit their own Lesser Known Goddess in the Southern Capital with a Sea. They miss the warmth of her toothless smile. She has been gone for over a week now. They begin to wonder when Minnal will return to her hamlet to her adopted children, and to her daughter, the lissome Jasmine Creeper bursting with a profusion of fragrant white flowers.

A woman who leaves on a mission, is seldom known to return on time. Asha Paharia's hutment is fragrant with incense. The incense will burn for one month by the newly blown-up photograph of her dead brother. In this photograph, Asha's brother looks years younger than he did the day he died. This is an old photograph taken when her brother was admitted to the Thimri Government School. He was ten years old then.

When Asha's brother died, he, by the joint recollections of his grandmother, mother and father, might have completed twenty-four years around the time of the Vishwakarma celebrations this year, if only he had been alive.

In some parts of India, staying alive is perhaps more traumatic than being dead.

There was no incense when the Guru died.

They lit a candle, and said a prayer

For the Guru's soul to rest in peace.

Only the Guru's soul can rest in peace.

His body was donated to the Medical College in the Garden City.

The city, which is still home to the Bangalore Blues

And the Guru's early 20th century Euterpe piano.

The Guru cannot be dead.

It continues to rain outside. The Guru continues to play the *Eine Kleine Nachtmusik*, phrase by intense phrase on the Euterpe. The rains subside, and patter to a drip on the windowsill.

D'Vaz, changed into the Guru's silk kurta, sits on the rocking chair by the windowsill, and lights his English pipe. Herr Bauer sits on the stool by the near-century-old wooden table overlooking the Guru's window. The Guru looks outside the window, something, someone, has caught his eyes. From several 'being told off by the Guru' experiences, Sridhar Haider D'Vaz and Herr Hans Bauer know better than to ask the impressive presence on the chair, what or who has caught his all-pervading eye.

III

Getting a man to love you is easy. Only be honest about your wants as a woman.

– Kamala Das

By this time, everyone's attention at the Central Railway Station has turned towards Minnal. While the constables in khaki wave their batons to hush the encroaching mob of passengers-turned-bulldozers, Minnal continues to sing aloud. Naren continues to sleep. 'Bidrayyo,' Gowravva continues to admonish the khaki-clad brigade in her own tongue, cajoling the keepers of law to leave the Lesser Known Goddess alone.

The khaki-clad mob will have none of Gowravva's native tongue in the Southern Capital with a Sea. She too, must be handcuffed.

Gowravva is handcuffed.

The men in khaki now have two victories in hand. An old woman, and an older woman, who have both chosen to speak their own tongues.

Tongues untied.
Hands tied.
Bodies tide over each other
To untie
The old woman
And the older woman
Who have chosen to speak in their respective tongues.

The men in khaki pat their respective backs. They have found the old and the older woman—these mothers, the noise-making 'miscreants' they had come looking for.

Or, have they?

Thiru Venkataraman and Aandavan pat their respective backs. The pandemonium in the Central Railway Station will keep Prasad Bharathi satisfied for a while. Aandavan is satisfied with his counter move. It is not checkmate for the Minister of Accounting Affairs yet.

Affairs of the heart are unlike the counter moves on the chessboard. There are no moves to counter when love is lost in pursuit of its victory. Love is not war.

I am at war with my emotions. I am fragile. I shatter a million times to the second. Shards of emotions, born out of love, buried out of dissent, melt into the Great Arabian Ocean to become salted tears. The tears, now waves at eventide, linger on the rock by the shores of the blue-green Arabian Ocean. I see blue. He loves his blue kurta despite the increasing holes rendered by Lantana thorns in the hand-woven fabric of his motherland. He does not look me in the eye anymore. His baby beckons. I have miles to go with her. Inner wars must be put to sleep.

Nelli fights a war with her heart as night gives way to another dawn. At the crack of dawn, she must travel with Amrit Kumar to another town, Nagaon. There is important work to be done in this small big town. Work does not drive Nelli anymore. Love drives her. Amrit tells Nelli that love is not greater than work. 'Worship your work, and you will always want to give your best,' the Mentor advises her.

Nelli takes pleasure in looking her best. This morning, she chooses to wear her startling purple sari. Last week, the Mentor gave her a cardboard box full of glittering purple bangles with gold inlay work in recognition of her commendable performance. Nelli finds herself in the mirror—she looks fresh as a Morning Glory, succulently purple at the hour of dew in her passion-driven ensemble—sari, bangles, bindi embellished with a pearl droplet, nail-polish, a fake leather bag, and even lipstick, all adornments in varying shades of the signature hue for the day.

Miles away in the city of Bangalore Blues, Zeta sinks in the comfort of her bean-bag, and examines the signature in the Form of Consent. She knows from the incline in the tail of the 'N', that the signature is not Nelli's.

In the same city, and in another home, Herr Bauer examines the photocopy of the Form of Consent. He studies the signatures of girls who have been enrolled at various vocational training institutes with branches in Majuli, Nimdi and Sambhalpur. Herr Bauer looks closely, and observes that the signature of the girl consenting to be adopted as a trainee at the local Rozgaar Kendra does not belong to Nelli. The Guru studies the signature. Maestro D'Vaz reclines in the near-century old easy chair, and studies the Guru's expressions. All solutions to issues that D'Vaz has ever found, are buried in the Guru's expressions.

The Guru has buried many solutions in the bosom of the Great Arabian Ocean. I believe that his soul rides the ebb and flow of the Arabian Ocean. I capture the solutions he has provided me when the tide rides high.

***

Swami Vishnu Prem Anand, the recently initiated head priest of the Vedic Vaishnav Ashram in Majuli has solutions to all matters concerning identity and crisis. The grieving sail the moody tide of the Brahmaputra every day, often every other night to seek audience with the newly appointed

Swami. He will meet only those who have been screened by his inner circle of shishyas at the Vaishnav Gurukul. These shishyas, nine in number, are called the Eclectic Disciples—they have access to a library of documents, which together contain numbers that outnumber the 'legal' income versus expenditure statements in the office of the Minister of Accounting Affairs. These shishyas have access to the bungled accounts which have been kept safely amidst Vedic texts in the Vaishnav Gurukul. Thiru Venkataraman has sneaked them into the Ashram through the well-known Mentor, Amrit Kumar.

Amrit Kumar is a distinct shishya, but he does not belong to the inner circle. He holds high office in Swami Vishnu Prem Anand's Vaishnav Gurukul where Vedic hymns resonate long after they have been chanted—this acoustic phenomenon, a result of the temple's high-domed architecture. Amrit chants Vedic hymns at the break of dawn, and basks in the texture of his own voice when it returns as an echo.

Nelli has learnt to chant in rhythm with Amrit. But Nelli must chant only in private, she is not a man. She can only satisfy the man who is allowed by religious law to chant the indigenous hymns of the Vedic Vaishnav Ashram in public.

Amrit Kumar is a man.

He is permitted to chant hymns in public.

Nelli must satisfy Amrit time and again.

Thiru Venkataraman will make a public appearance soon. He must communicate to the masses in the Southern Capital with a Sea that he is harmless. In fact, he is incapable of harming anything, not even an 'ee'. The Minister has made a public announcement to the citizens at the Southern Capital.

Through the din in the Central Railway Station, Minnal guffaws at how frightened her first-born is of flies, these irksome creatures they call 'ee' in her hamlet as well as in the tongue spoken in the Southern Capital with a Sea.

'He cannot harm an ee,' she gloats, loud and clear for all to hear. The men in khaki cannot be bothered by the toothless old woman's rant anymore. She is a prime catch—guffaw et al.

And then, there is another khaki-clad man who must be feared—he holds the law in high esteem, they call him Inspector General Tuffwinder Singh Bawa.

Inspector General Bawa has a list of prime suspects. He keeps the list in his head, and tears up the evidence.

Before she leaves with the strangers, Asha Paharia has a long list of people to meet. Toping her list are members of the Dalma Mahila Sangh. This women's group is hyperactive, and meets every Saturday by noon, at the hamlet's school. Women from all across Nimdi and Rukdoo blocks, which lie distinctly outside the boundaries of Tatanagar in secret terrains of the Dalma Ranges, assemble at the Thimri Jan Sanstha every week.

Susanthi Bodra will spend an entire week at the Sambhalpur Rozgaar Kendra. She could spend an entire month, if she wished to. Susanthi has no mother waiting for her, worrying about her little girl child's safety when she is far away from home in Sambhalpur, a town which the people of Bochagora know as popular, but unknown territory.

Domrudoru Baiga is worried. His nine-year-old ears have been hearing rumours about the Rozgaar Kendra. The trade which his intelligent friend Susanthi will learn, is not meant for girls from respectable homes, say the rumour specialists of Bochagora. Domrudoru has seen nine Vishwakarma festivals over nine Septembers, and knows a thing or two about respectable trades.

What is so vile about the trade Susanthi Bodra will learn at the Sambhalpur Rozgaar Kendra? Will Domrudoru's friend turn a thief by trade?

There is a thief in Naren Nayak's dream. Armed with a lathi and masked with a black cloth over his mouth and nose, leaving only his eyes and forehead naked to view, the thief is making his way into Naren's hutment by the backyard connected to the rest of the forest range. The hutment is dark, except for the shine of a nose ring. It is the lone gold jewel in Naren's hutment. The gold for the nose ring has been sieved from the wet, red soil by Parbothi's brother. Parbothi is a proud lady of the Mankadia tribe, and wears this jewel all the time. This nose ring is testimony that she is Naren's ardhangini. Parbothi as Naren's wife, shares his dream of a home that will not slip away from their hands. The homes of the Gonds, Santals, Mankadias, Mundas and Juang tribes of Keonjhar too, must not slip away.

Nominta Debury's home is a hutment with a backyard. It quacks with ducks and sways with vegetables, mostly green. This backyard must not slip away from the hands of her mother and father, and the rest of her family. Nominta is not an ardhangini as yet. But she is already a brave nari, a bahadur lady who will learn a trade at the Sambhalpur Rozgaar Kendra. She will then earn to keep her home from slipping away and merging into the dense forests to be swallowed by bulldozers, and then, annexed by ministers for their private use.

Jhumur Jhumur
Jhumur Jhumur
Nariyon ka jhonda
Sada uporo re

Let the flag, which catapults the woman and places her amidst the celestial stars in the firmament, better still above the firmament alongside the Gods, always fly high.

I feel the firmament beneath my feet slipping away. Have I forgotten my place? After all, I am a woman. I am fired by love for a man who seems to have forgotten me. I am unhindered by compromise. I have chosen to be a mother. The mother of his gorgeous baby. This baby, a true treasure.

***

When Minnal first became a mother, she was still a child. When the child she birthed died, she wept with joy. When her mother-in-law learnt of her joy, she took her to the hamlet's most powerful and feared man, the Maha Yogi, and beseeched him to remove the rakshasi which had made a home in a prime part of her daughter-in-law's body—the womb. In a tearing hurry to drive the devil out of Minnal's womb and back to its place on the Neem tree, the Maha Yogi plucked a chicken feather out of his 'not-washed-for-at-least-twenty-years-pungent-with-grime-and-sweat-matted' grey hair, and rubbed it over his forehead. He then grunted to Minnal's mother-in-law, and instructed her to soak the veebhooti-smeared chicken feather into a bowl of freshly drawn blood. This was sacred blood drawn from a pregnant goat, and the flow of red more powerful when touched by the chicken feather. The confluence of the chicken feather and the goat's blood was potent, the Maha Yogi had said. 'It is certain to remove the rakshasi from your irate daughter-in-law's womb.' In turn, Minnal's mother-in-law fed the potion to the not-quite-fourteen-year-old girl with the 'possessed' womb.

The Lesser Known Goddess
could be stirred
by neither ee
nor Maha Yogi.

So when her mother-in-law forced her to swallow the potion,

Minnal,
she, held the semi fluid in her mouth
until she reached the age-old Mango tree
under which the anti-Godman sat
and spat the potion straight into his face.

The blood so wholesomely red was visible for all his disciples to see...

Red wine. Rotwein. Elixir of love in city territory.

Tonight, his goblet of wine touches everybody's but mine. My goblet is shattered. The shards pierce my heart. My heart beats for his baby. I gulp down the pain trapped in my bubbly, and return home to her slender frame.

Home beckons Nelli. Riding in the closed jeep with Amrit, deep green sloping gardens of export variety tea waiting to be pruned, race past, blurring, merging into golden paddy fields which beckon Nelli.

Paddy is seldom cultivated between Nagaon and Nemati Ghat in Jorhat. It is cultivated in Nelli's hamlet, on the highway between Gulbarga District and her hometown Kithapur when the monsoons are friendly. During one monsoon shower, Nelli made the paddy field by her hutment her kingdom, and called herself the Princess of Kithapur.

Her entourage, which had not changed factions yet, walked in front of Nelli with flowers from the Lantana shrubs lining the edges of the paddy fields. Nelli wore a crown of flaming orange and glowing yellow Lantana flowers to match the floral carpet her entourage strewed along her walking path.

Walking at breakneck pace, Inspector General Bawa looks placid despite the blood rush.

Inspector General Tuffwinder Singh Bawa is of pure blood

And an irrevocable will

To trace every fine needle

In the haystack of evidence.

There are two inferences so far, and Inspector General Bawa has made them both. According to one evidence in the haystack, there is a brand-new recruit to the Maoxal faction. As per another evidence in the land records, the Centre is swarming with criminals.

Inspector General Bawa is a smart and meticulous officer. He works in tandem with a Special Task Force.

Holy men are always smooth, they lead by muted force.

In Swami Vishnu Prem Anand's mind, Eclectic Disciples, all men in sacred thread trained to military perfection, march in tandem with the psychedelic Vedic chants of the Vaishnav Ashram. These Eclectic Disciples, nine of them in all, tell Swami Prem Anand exactly what is going on, and where.

Well

This much I will tell.

Beware of Swami Vishnu Prem Anand!

***

Beware of the Minister's wife. It is imperative for Thiru Venkataraman to visit the prophetic Vishnu Temple in the little hamlet off the highway serenading big town Mayavaram. His money-wise wife will not take a 'no' from her husband—the interfering snakes Rahu and Kethu are playing havoc, wreaking tsunamis in Venkataraman's planetary charts, they are destroying her man's career. All the bad karma visiting their fate is a matter of supreme blunder, disrespect to the God of Gods by her husband, the man they call the Minister of Accounting Affairs. Bah!

Aandavan is in agreement with Venkataraman's wife. He seconds her thoughts that the God of Gods must be appeased.

By the way, the Uncrowned Head, yes, Sri Prasad Bharathi is no lesser than the God of Gods.

Asha Paharia is not concerned about how God will judge her. She is ready to meet the khaki-wearing strangers who have promised friendship. Their khaki attire is a few shades darker than that of Inspector General Bawa.

Shades
Shadows
Khaki
People
With lands
Now without
Melt into the Dalma Ranges
By night.

Tonight, Asha is leaving home to earn her family daal and bhath, she melts into the thickness of the Dalma Ranges with the khaki-clad strangers who beckon her into their hidden world.

En route to Samphalpur, Susanthi Bodra closes her eyes and travels to a distant day in the future. She is distanced from her home by khaki-clad strangers. She is a prisoner. Susanthi will not allow distance to dictate her future. She will define her own future.

The future is not quite here.

Opening her eyes, back in the present, Susanthi realises she has not seen her father's dead body. Nor have the elders of Bochagora. Nor have the Panchayat Mukhiyas. Definitely not the knowledgeable members of the Bal Panchayat.

Members of minority communities...
Strange
And not so strange
Village Panchayats
Bal Panchayats
Herds of elephants
Shoals of fish
Schools of sheep
Flurry of birds
Dancing mayouros
Dead mayouros
All whisper a secret from the jungles beyond the highway
Into which Susanthi migrates
From her window seat
In the closed jeep.

Suddenly, Susanthi is in the future. The future brings her eye-to-eye with human flesh and emotions that have been dead to her for nearly three years.

***

Sridhar Haider D'Vaz needs a break—he takes off on an artistic sojourn, and sees eye-to-eye with the leopards of

Keonjhar. Among their leap is the Kalarpatra Bagha. He is the majestic leopard of the same region, and has the same agility as a human. In fact, he is human.

How did D'Vaz come eye-to-eye with the Kalarpatra Bagha in the first place?

When he first visited Keonjhar fifteen years ago, Naren Nayak, the young school teacher who taught the children of three hamlets, led the visiting artist D'Vaz into the forests of Manipura. The school teacher scaled the depth of these forests, walking across the slim tributaries of River Shammakoi, trekking over the lower, gently inclining peaks of the Kanjipani Mountains on his fours, plunging into the jungle's darkness, and following the Kalarpatra's footsteps to a patch of land where the sun lit the handsome leopard's human features.

Years later, when D'Vaz received his award, the accolades spoke of how the leopard resembled a young man. The artist par repute had created an image which seemed to overtly merge the undefined line between man and animal.

There is an animal in every man. Susanthi's father has turned into an animal. His small, piercing eyes are bloodshot. He wears a shotgun harnessed by a green-yellow odhni. This odhni draped Susanthi's mother on her wedding night. It was the only sheer length of nylon material which draped her womb on the day Susanthi's brother Tilka was born. Nine years later, her mother wore the same odhni on the day she heard that Susanthi's father was gone. Susanthi has since, remained strong. Very strong.

Or, is she?

Am I strong?

My weakness is my strength.

What is the purpose of being strong when all that you care for is gone?

I care for his baby. She is not gone. I am strong.

Susanthi remains strong.

The closed jeep stops on the highway by a thicket in view of a cluster of Mahua trees. Susanthi leaps out of the vehicle and wanders into the jungle to answer nature's call. As she sits behind the Lantana shrub which is bursting unawares into pleasant blisters of purple flowers, a leopard springs. Or so Susanthi thinks, until her gaze wanders into the piercing eyes of a man she knows from the day she was born. Susanthi stares into her father's eyes—she is unable to answer nature's call. Her father lowers his shotgun, and unveils his mouth and upper nose. Susanthi lets out a near shriek which has risen from her stomach but stops short at her throat.

Silence!

Susanthi Bodra knows better than to yell out loud when she meets a khaki-clad man who masks his face and carries a shotgun. It does not matter that the man behind the mask was her father once. A man remains a father until he becomes dead to his family.

Susanthi Bodra does not have a family to go back home to.

She returns to the closed jeep to seek solace in her new family—the volunteers of YUPAP are her foster parents for the duration of her journey and thereafter, during their stay at the Sambhalpur Rozgaar Kendra. This is the duration of 'suitably arranged family bonding' that the Panchayat Mukhiya and her foster parents in Bochagora have specified for Susanthi.

How will Susanthi tell her foster parents that she is feeling uneasy because she has not been able to answer nature's call?

Irrespective of one's gender, journeys must be broken at the beckoning of nature's call.

Both vehicles, one ferrying Susanthi Bodra and the other Nominta Debury, are on the same highway. Minutes after Susanthi has fled the patch of land aound the Lantana shrub, Nominta's foster parents, Urmila and Manohar Mahapatra tell the driver to pull their closed jeep to a side. Nominta springs out of the vehicle, and hops her way into the jungle to answer nature's call. As she sits by the same Lantana shrubs, most of its leaves hidden by clusters of adolescent purple flowers, a Kalarpatra Bagha appears. Or so Nominta Debury feels, until the leopard begins to resemble a lean-framed man with a shotgun harnessed by a sheer odhni. As the man leans forward to grasp her, Nominta lets out a 'highway-din-ripping' shriek, which has risen from her stomach and escaped through her mouth within a matter of three seconds. Nominta's mouth remains wide open under the firm grasp of the odhni. The lean man has cupped her mouth with the odhni to muffle her might-have-been-loud-enough-to-be-heard shriek.

***

Herr Hans Bauer gasps at the sheer illegitimacy of the Form of Consent. This Form has been designed by a certain authority who calls himself the Mentor, Amrit Kumar.

By Indian law, which girl under the age of eighteen has the right to sign the Form of Consent?

Zeta Rani has found an access point—there was a girl who was in rehabilitation in Calcutta when she was not quite eighteen. According to sources, she is a tad over thirty now, and has been spotted in Majuli. She has signed the Form of Consent, and follows Amrit to places where there is supposed to be work.

Herr Hans Bauer's nostrils smell fische. Diese fische heisen rohu. Im Majuli, die leute essen rohu am Sonntag.

Die leute von Majuli, the people of the Mising tribe, do not have bank accounts. They do not need bank accounts to buy rohu. This river fish is abundant in the voluminous River Brahmaputra.

Robibaar

Sonntag

Sunday

Fish day

For the Mising of Majuli.

For Herr Hans Bauer von Der Bundesrepublik Deutschland.

For Zeta Rani from Thirunelvelli.

For the Guru from Mangalore.

For Sridhar Haider D'Vaz from all over India.

For Inspector General Tuffwinder Singh Bawa from Punjab on posting in Tatanagar—the premier city of Jharkhand.

Also, for Swami Vishnu Prem Anand from nobody knows where. But Swami Prem Anand has abstained from his favourite food—fish—ever since he has taken on the holy post as head priest of the Vaishnav Ashram in Majuli.

***

Ever since Minnal has been taken into custody by the khaki-clad men, the people of her hamlet have been counting their saved-up coins to visit the Southern Capital with a Sea. Thanks to Minnal's city friend the Banana Vendor who, riding on a rice laden lorry, appeared at Poothotum in person to inform its people of their Goddess's plight. Ever since the Banana Vendor has returned to the Southern Capital with a Sea, Poothotum's people sit at the entrance to the Vishnu Temple every morning, noon, twilight and night. They crouch and open their palms to receive coins from the devotees of the big city. These moneyed devotees arrive in cars, tempos and other types of road hogs which consume petrol to transport people to their place of worship in ultimate luxury. The devotees from the city ask Lord Sri Ranganathar, one of the myriad forms of God Vishnu, ensconced by his two wives Bhudevi and Nila Devi for wealth, which will enable them further luxury of road hogs, a few plots in the Southern Capital with a Sea, stakes in acres of agricultural land taken over for mining purposes in the metal rich regions of Orissa and Jharkhand, and also other lifestyle encumbrances.

Gowravva is an encumbrance to the khaki-clad cops who have taken her into custody along with Minnal. Gowravva belongs to the state neighbouring the Southern Capital. She does not speak the tongue of the khaki-clad men here. But Gowravva understands Minnal's tongue with the same clarity as she does her own language of loss. Gowravva's heart beats for her lost daughter. Minnal has a beating heart. The emotions in her heart cannot be described in words. The Lesser Known Goddess's words are smitten with 'not-so-directly-obvious' love for her ten sons. Buried under Minnal's mirth-filled abuse, is the kind of love that only a mother who has lost her sons to lifestyle encumbrances might have.

Nelli has life encumbrances. She must work hard to satisfy the Mentor. Nelli must receive her payment of twenty rupees to tuck into her tortoise-shaped terracotta piggy bank every day. Nelli will abide by Amrit's instructions, and perform well at her newly designated work spot in Nagaon.

It breaks Nelli's heart to perform at work. To perform well implies that her heart must remain calm in the face of brokenness. Nelli remembers the face of the transgressor from almost eighteen months ago—he has not touched her, but left her in awe of his artistic demeanour. Left with the memory of that 'just gaze into each other's eyes' romantic night with the transgressor, Nelli wishes she had asked him his name.

The Guru knows big names. These names belong to men and women who play Western Classical music, paint with oils on canvas, sing, dance, and write for a living. The Guru endorses some big names. He stands by those names which do not succumb to lifestyle encumbrances.

Life encumbrances are diverse from lifestyle encumbrances. Nominta's family is her encumbrance. She needs to learn a trade to earn a substantial sum of nine hundred rupees every month. This humble amount, the not-quite-thirteen-year old needs, to replenish the smokeless chulha in her hutment with foodgrains and pulses—bhath and daal too, to cook two meals and feed six mouths every day. If Nominta works hard, she can add two eggs and a succulent river maach on special occasions to the blackened cooking pots on the smokeless chulha. This chulha prevents Nominta's mother from inhaling toxic carbon dioxide while cooking; it has been installed two months ago in a ventilated corner of her hutment by Urmila Mahapatra.

***

Asha Paharia has not returned home for two days. Her mother and father, also grandmother, two younger brothers, and all the village elders are perplexed. Asha is a skilled worker, they say. She has been trained to assemble smokeless chulhas. These cooking ranges in the hutments of the Dalma Forests have considerably reduced the quantity of carbon dioxide the homemaker consumes while cooking, but Asha will not serve her people for money, the citizens of Thimri know. She, a loyal woman of the forest hamlet, believes in making the lives of others like her, healthy and less laborious. Within the hamlets buried in the Dalma Ranges, the woman is both homemaker and breadwinner during harvest time and off it.

It is harvest time, the rains have been kind this season. Men plough, women weed. Asha, who has left with the strangers, ploughed the fields in the absence of her brother who had been shot dead by the khaki-clad policemen only a few weeks ago.

Asha's brother had been absent from the fields for years. Ploughing the paddy fields during this season when the monsoon has smiled upon the Dalma Ranges, has been no difficult task for her, Asha's father says.

Asha has walked with the strangers for two whole days, and has seen deep layers of the Dalma Ranges she does not know exist. She does not mind longer than long walks, nor the toil in her fields. Briefly resting by the shade of a Sal tree, Asha is mindful of the fact that the khaki-clad strangers have offered her six thousand rupees every month to have the chulha in her hutment burning without a day's break in her brother's absence. The fields back home in Thimri fetch Asha a sum of thousand rupees on good months, and four hundred rupees during bad months. The bad months supersede the good months every year. On many nights, spanning almost eight months a year, Asha's father, mother and grandmother go to bed on empty stomachs. Her two younger brothers are fed one mouthful of jaggery each. For years, Asha's now dead brother who went away with the khaki-clad strangers, did not send any money home. On many Tuesdays, he borrowed an impossible-to-part-with sum of one hundred rupees from his large-hearted sister.

Where has all the money that Asha's brother had earned during his khaki-uniformed disappearance for six years in the thick of the Dalma Ranges, gone?

Inspector General Bawa has a lead. A Special Task Force, which will neither bend to the dark khaki-clad faction's pressure, nor the light khaki-clad faction's whim, will investigate the matter. The matter is not up for discussion at the Centre either. Inspector General Bawa's torn up list, contents of which are now tucked away in his conscious mind, includes suspects at the Centre. And no one is getting away with it.

IV

Perhaps, I will become a ray of sunshine to be embraced by your colours. I will paint myself on your canvas.

– Amrita Pritam

Swami Vishnu Prem Anand is getting away from the Vedic Vaishnav Ashram on a sojourn. The destination has not been announced to the members of the Ashram. It must remain a secret, and rest assured, it will. Even Nelli's Mentor Amrit who works closely with Swami Prem, will not know.

Amrit is livid.

Amrit, quite single-minded in his pursuit of suitable work for Nelli, is not acquainted with his Swami's Eclectic Disciples—they all look and sound alike, and seem so excessively disciplined! So, the nine well-toned, macho disciples do not utter a single word—in silence, they gear up to embark upon the sojourn with the haloed Prem Anand.

Gear up
To go
Where no one else dares.
Sum up
The sojourn
With song, dance
And a twist to Swami Vishnu Prem Anand's tale.

This is no tale.
This matter is serious.
Heads up.

I hold my head high, allowing the fast-appearing tears to stop short of their flow, and trickle back into my eyes.

I cannot get over being singled out of cheer. But his baby is very dear. I hold her smooth frame unto my bosom, and tell her that the journey will be just fine. My baby feels relaxed in my hold. I feel her warmth and remember her father from another day when he looked me in the eye. I catch the blue of his kurta in her eye, also in the sky outside the train window, and in the river which runs beneath the track, the sparkling waters flowing ferociously to merge with the river by his home. I see the man I love everywhere, but cannot find him.

I now see what I see.

I see what I love.

Nominta Debury's mother sees what she loves.

Nominta's mother finds her daughter in her dream. She wonders why her dream brings a premonition, her daughter is certainly not lost. She is in safe hands with her foster parents Urmila and Manohar Mahapatra.

Nominta Debury is not safe.

On the Sambhalpur Highway, hands tied, Urmila and Manohar Mahapatra are unable to free themselves. Their hands and legs have been bound together by three khaki-clad forms with shotguns and masks of sheer cloth. These social workers cum foster parents cannot scream out for help to drivers and passengers in passing vehicles on the highway—they have been gagged with rough jute strips which were once united to form a large bag to hold a yield of potatoes. And the driver of their closed jeep has gone missing.

From her window seat in the closed jeep, Nelli knows Nagaon is not far. A sudden fear grips her as the driver speeds to overtake a mud-laden lorry on National Highway 37. Nelli is neither afraid of speeding jeeps nor of mud-laden lorries. Nelli is afraid of her destination. Her heart is against her mind. Her body is against her work. Nelli feels faint.

Nelli has fainted.

In the Southern Capital with a Sea, Gowravva's heart skips a beat. But, the Central Jail in the Southern Capital is no place for the faint-hearted. The Lesser Known Goddess has a newly-acquired entourage of unreasonably imprisoned mothers. Headed by Gowravva, the entourage sings praises of its leader, the toothless Minnal who has embarked on a verbal massacre of the Minister of Accounting Affairs. Khakhi-clad women oppose the verbal massacre by showing the unreasonably imprisoned mothers 'lathi fright'. Lathi fright is much like eye fright. But the lathi is just a lifeless stick. Minnal and her entourage do not stop blurting verbal vengeance against Thiru Venkataraman.

It hurts the Lesser Known Goddess' heart

to call The Minister of Accounting Affairs a bluffing fart.

She secretly squirms in pain
each time the refrain
rises cold and angry over her warm motherly heart.

'Down, down, kandiri the mean Mandiri,' the mothers' plea.

'This Mandiri is the Minister of 'Discounting' Affairs!'

Amidst all the frenzy in the Southern Capital, Venkataraman is fast being discounted by Prasad Bharathi at the Centre. Venkataraman's Political Advisor Aandavan must detract the feisty uprising from further damage. Aandavan will visit the Central Jail in the Southern Capital—it is 'top' priority on his 'to-do' list which has especially been drawn up to quell Venkataraman's impending downfall.

Priorities switch quickly, especially when ministers in power come undone.

Venkataraman is now called the Minister of 'Discounting' Affairs—he has lost face with several members of his Party. Thick friends are now thicker foes, and they will not stand by their former comrade's side.

The Lesser Known Goddess is aware of the changing fortune in Thiru Venkataraman's lowly life. She and her entourage scream out loud…

'What goes up

Must come down.

Down, down, the Minister of Accounting Affairs!'

With this refrain, the Central Jail in the Southern Capital with a Sea resounds.

Gowravva's mind resounds with memories of Nelli in her womb.

In the brief quiet that reigns the huddle of women in the Central Jail, Gowravva remembers the day when all the farm hands of Kithapur, their wives, mothers, fathers, children, truant siblings included, shouted slogans against the landlords.

'Namagu hotte vuntu.

Namagu makkalu vuntu.'

We too, have stomachs.

We too, have children.

'Naavu dudida kaasannu thindavana paadu, haalu.' The man who swallowed the money the farmhands of Kithapur had earned by the sweat of their brows, will meet with a reversal of fate, they yell. Such is the law of karma, they loudly tell.

Fate had it that Gowravva take Nelli on this tirade. Influenced in the womb, Nelli was born a rebel.

Nelli rebels in ways unique to the feminine.

Rebellious feminine powers often arise from an abused woman's necessity to survive.

I survive the intense journey with his baby. I watch in smitten wonder as my baby relies on my fingers to stride the mighty streets of big city Bhubaneswar even as she unravels her feminine charm.

I exchange my thoughts via SMS with Herr Bauer—he understands feminine whim as would a wise man. He knows how to maintain the sanctity of parallel life tracks—he sustains his family ties on one track, and on the other, follows his passion to better the plight of female breadwinners, especially under-aged girls in India's poorest hamlets. His zwei töchter und liebe Frau have used their combined charm to keep Herr Bauer bound to the family, and to his documented roots in Der Bundesrepublik Deutschland. Herr Bauer does not know that together, his two daughters and lovely wife have, for years, hidden a certain cloth folder containing information pertinent to child trafficking in the Indian subcontinent. This folder, couriered to Herr Bauer by Zeta Rani's NGO, would send him running back to India, they knew. Frau Bauer, in a bid to keep her husband loyal to his documented roots, hid the folder, until it tumbled out of her cupboard one day, and landed on her husband's feet.

Herr Bauer has roots in the Indian subcontinent which cannot be severed. In Der Bundesrepublik Destuchland, the colour of his skin is considered an aberration. But with his command over die Muttersprache Deutsch in his Vaterland, his roots have not been questioned with appropriate seriousness.

Today, Herr Bauer calls me to discuss his mind, and breaks into a song for his Fatherland, Der Bundesrepublik Deutschland.

'Einigkeit und Recht und Freiheit
Für das Deutsche Vaterland!
Danach lasst uns alle streben
Brüderlich mit Herz und Hand!
Einigkeit und Recht und Freiheit
Sind des Glückes Unterpfand;
Blüh' im Glanze dieses Glückes,
Blühe, Deutsches Vaterland!'

Herr Bauer sings the anthem one more time, in English.

'Unity and Justice and Freedom
For the German Fatherland!
Let us all strive for this purpose
Brotherly with heart and hand!
Unity and Justice and Freedom
Are the Pledge of Happiness;
Bloom in the Glow of Happiness,
Bloom, German Fatherland!'

Playing the Deutsch National Anthem on his violin in his Vaterland, Herr Bauer often remembered his toothless mother from a distant day in his boyhood when he plucked weeds in the green paddy pastures of his Mutterland. Herr Bauer, citizen of Der Bundesrepublik Deutschland, now traces his roots in his Mutterland, India.

The Guru knows only too well that route, which connects Herr Hans Bauer to his mother.

Sridhar Haider D'Vaz must trace his route back to Dhauli.

Secrets have a natural way of sloppily tumbling out of their tightly shut closets in the Art College en route to the Buddha's Stupa. Together, D'Vaz and a certain mysterious Source, have discovered the secret behind the furore in the Art College. The student of art, who faced ire for his depiction of Radha and Lord Krishna, is the offspring of Thiru Venkataraman, the Minister of Accounting Affairs!

Un-named offspring often trigger the ire of societies sitting in uncalled-for judgement on all and sundry.

Must Venkataraman's artistic offspring face the ire of an angered mob of khaki-clad men of law? That too, for a decision made by his political father to have a third son outside the norms of wedlock!

Maestro D'Vaz knows the artistic son's mother from a remote hamlet in Keonjhar District, Orissa. The son faces the ire of two factions, the khaki-clad men of law and the khaki-clad people out of law, and both are up in arms against the woman who was forced into copulation with the Minister of Accounting Affairs. This is the same woman that Venkataraman took by force when she was just a newly-matured girl of fourteen. People read all about the son born out of this forced copulation on Page 1 of regional and national newspapers in Bhubaneswar and in the Southern Capital with a Sea even as night cracks into dawn. The news appears in the national section of at least twenty papers between pages 7 and 20, in the other 'not-so-pertinent-to-the-matter under contention' Indian states.

Browsing through the newspapers this morning, Zeta panics. The cat has been let out of the bag.

The silent cat, which appears when one least expects it, is viler than the Kalarpatra Bagha which strikes only when stirred in his secret lair.

Zeta knows it is time to hasten action on certain secrets comfortably sleeping in the cloth folder.

Action dictates destiny if one strikes while the perpetrator is seething hot.

Zeta makes a call to Herr Bauer. D'Vaz is consulted. The Guru decides to accompany the trio to the Art College by Dhauli in Bhubaneswar. I am already in Bhubaneswar, and his baby is with me. I am a member of the Guru's Special Force, and it is imperative for me to be present at the Art College for the sake of democracy. I will not leave his love's labour unguarded. Certainly not at this transitioning time. My baby will go with me.

The Vaishnav Ashram in Majuli is now unguarded.

Swami Vishnu Prem Anand has embarked upon his sojourn. He has left on a motorboat fuelled with kerosene from Kamalabari, the docking point of Majuli—he wears a saffron jhola upon his bare left shoulder. The destination of Prem Anand's sojourn will remain undisclosed. It has however been disclosed at the special morning satsang, that his band of Eclectic Disciples will also be away on a sojourn. Nobody will know for certain that Swami Prem Anand's Eclectic Disciples will be away with him. This indistinct force of nine, has always been forbidden from talking out of turn. The Eclectic Disciples mingle with the bhaktas at the Gurukul, albeit silently. They also mingle with the Mising in their hutments in Majuli. This combined force of nine becomes one with the devotees and the tribes of Majuli as and when it deems fit to do so.

The force of Eclectic Disciples knows for certain that Nelli is missing from her single-windowed room overlooking the mighty Brahmaputra in Majuli.

Aandavan knows that Venkataraman is in dire straits for ignoring the consequences of past actions. When the Mankadia girl, now mother of his artistic son was forced into copulation over thirty years ago in Keonjhar,

Aandavan had warned the Minister of its consequences. Hot blooded, Venkataraman who was but a novice in the Party under the guidance of Prasad Bharathi then, simply followed the uncouth path laid by his superiors.

Often, superiors perform inferior actions. They support the suppressed with money and hutments that are larger than the rest in their hamlets.

Venkataraman, as member of Prasad Bharathi's political party used his auspices with his superior to procure forest land to build a hutment for his 'keep'.

The creep!
He chose a 'keep'
to give birth to the meanderings of his manhood.
The 'keep' chose to mother the Minister's meanderings
and brought up their son
to follow his passion,
and become an artist.

Artists, unknown to their conscious minds, go on to cause shame to their fathers. The shame is detrimental, especially if their fathers happen to be ministers in the Cabinet of the most dangerous and greedy Prasad Bharathi.

The shame is worse when the father happens to be the Minister of Accounting Affairs, and is married to a woman who rules his vote bank by the sheer might of her ancestral wealth.

A politician scripts his self-ruin when all his actions feed his greed. When a girl is forced into womanhood in the prime of her play time, the perpetrator faces the consequences in the prime of his political career.

Prasad Bharathi is not so surreptitiously preparing the consequences of Venkataraman's past and present folly in consultation with the Cabinet of unscrupulous ministers at the Centre.

The political future of the Minister of Accounting Affairs is at stake, he has been scripted for ruin.

Minnal has often told her ten sons that ruin befalls those who choose to disrespect women. Today, Minnal's heart tells her that her son will come to see her soon. She smiles. It is a genuinely happy, toothless smile. Her entourage smiles with her. She weeps. Her entourage weeps, but there are no tears visible to the passing eye.

The Lesser Known Goddess hopes against hope that her son will not harm an ee.

But that is not to be.

He has not harmed an ee.

He has harmed the Feminine.

Child. Woman. Mother.

He will not face the wrath of the harmless fly.

He will face the wrath of all these feminine powers put together.

'Down, down, kandiri mandiri!' shouts the female entourage in the Central Jail.

Gowravva shouts above the rest in her own tongue.

She shouts until the female khaki-clad law-keepers come to take her away to a private cell to be questioned. Gowravva is a miscreant from the neighbouring state.

Gowravva, a miscreant?

What on earth is Gowravva doing with the slogan-shouting miscreants who do not speak her tongue?

***

Inspector General Tuffwinder Singh Bawa has heard from the Centre, he comprehends the 'political-vocabulary-intense' tongue as he does twelve other Indian languages, with ease. He has also heard from the Central Jail in the Southern Capital with a Sea. This hearsay is alarming. The amalgamation of the 'political lack of sentiment' with the 'tribal full on sentiment', along with the shocking disappearance of certain mothers of missing girl children, is a complex matter. It is actually very complex. The matter must be investigated with calm persistence. Inspector General Bawa is well-known for his calm persistence. He is also well-known for his ability to untangle the most complex criminal knots with the finesse of a seasoned conjuror.

After all, Inspector General Bawa wears khaki.

So do the strangers who are taking Asha Paharia deeper into the jungles tonight—they too, wear khaki.

Tonight, Asha will follow the 'not in tow with law' khaki-clad strangers. For these khaki-clad strangers, it is another Tuesday, no matter what month or year. This Tuesday will go down in history, Asha will send a note, bidding goodbye to her mother, father, paternal grandmother and two younger brothers when they are lost to the 'awakened world of the night', and deep in slumber.

Inspector General Bawa doesn't wear khaki to slumber at night. He wears khaki to keep his Peacekeeping Ambassadors well within sight. Major Ashok Riflewala and Lieutenant Colonel Hamid Iyer, the Special Armed Ambassadors for Peacekeeping on Inspector General Tuffwinder Singh Bawa's Mission, will secretly follow Asha Paharia into the 'awakened world of the night'. In the 'awakened world of the night', Asha Paharia and her ilk will make plans to retrieve what rightfully belongs to them, and their families, the fellow tribes of the Dalma.

Both Peacekeeping Ambassadors have the unique advantage of having scored the depth of the Dalma Ranges during earlier missions—they will sneak in on Asha Paharia's plans.

Inspector General Bawa will not have the blood of any innocent being on the hands of the Awakened Peacekeeping Ambassadors. There are other recruits to the thoughtfully formulated Mission Deconstruct the Cabinet to Reconstruct Feminine Power aka MDCRFP—their identities will be revealed at suitable junctures, if and when necessary.

For now, say the strangers, enter the Dalma Ranges.

Kadam badao.

Take a foot forward.

Mudke na dekho.

Do not look back.

Zindagi mein kuch kar dikhao.

Do something with your life.

Khaki pehano.

Wear khaki.

Banduk uthao.

Pick up the gun.

Jai Jungal bolo.

Praise the Jungle.

Praise the Dalma Ranges.

Praise all those densely tree-intense mountain ranges which, through their 'not-so-easy-to-access' terrain, connect the Maoxals to the dark secrets of the jungles, and also their tribes. Do not hesitate. Keep your identity secret. Cover your face. Let the world see your eyes alone. You are the gift of the jungle. You are the saviour of its tribes.

Asha Paharia has followed the khaki-clad strangers into the deepest layers of the jungle. She has taken an oath to save her people from the ineptitude of the elected democracy of India. The Munda, Santal, Gond, Kharia, Oraon, and all the other tribes of the Dalma Forests are as dear to this mountainous terrain as are its leopards, elephants, snakes, tigers, monkeys, mayouros and fireflies—they, man, woman, reptile and animal, all deserve to be respected.

***

Gowravva is neither afraid of snakes nor of humans who spew venom. She bravely counters the venom spewed by the khaki-clad officials in the Central Jail, in her own distinct tongue.

'Nanna magalannu parari madidha aa kanthri manthriyannu naanu nodade hinthiruvudilla.' Gowravva will not leave the Southern Capital with a Sea until she meets the mean Minister Venkataraman who is responsible for her absconding daughter, the khaki-clad officials are made to understand by a prison interpreter.

Minnal understands the plight of a heartbroken mother, she will ensure that Gowravva meets the scoundrel Venkataraman, and gets one step closer to her absconding daughter.

Nelli has been absconding for over twenty years, this news spreads like wildfire in the confines of the Central Jail. Gowravva has learnt from sources at the District Headquarters of Kithapur that her missing daughter has signed the Form of Consent. Nelli's uninformed act will make it near-impossible to prove that the Minister of Accounting Affairs is a black mark in the face of failed democracy.

Impossibilities are passé in Gowravva's world.

Gowravva's will is her way.

Just the way this single mother has made it to the Central Jail with Minnal, the woman whose sons perhaps do not deserve her love.

Facing those whom one has wronged is inevitable in this lifetime. Thiru Venkataraman will visit the ranting mothers at his suitably early convenience.

Amrit Kumar is perturbed by Nelli's fainting. He must rush her to the nearest hospital in Nagaon. Or, should he? Swami Vishnu Prem Anand is unaware of Nelli's trip to Nagaon. News travels at lightning speed from the wards of Nagaon's Government Hospital to the Vaishnav Ashram in Majuli. And Lord God Vishnu alone knows how the Swami gets wind of everything, even when he is on a sojourn. Amrit is in a fix.

Meanwhile, lying in the lone ward in Nagaon Government Hospital...

Faint and fainter as Nelli grows, Amrit Kumar will stand to lose fifty thousand rupees!

This grand sum, if only Nelli were well and working, will fill his coiffeurs, that too, in a single night.

Oh! The bloody Mentor Amrit's sad plight!

Nelli will receive all of fifty rupees from Amrit's coiffeurs if she works all night. This grand sum of fifty rupees means the world to her. She will have some additional money to place an STD call to the post office in Kithapur. Nelli must talk to Gowravva.

ASAP!

But Nelli is unable to open her eyes.

Swami Prem Anand's Force has wind of Nelli's whereabouts. The chase has begun.

***

Zeta Rani has begun her chase. She prays that this chase does not take her to a dead end like her previous four attempts have. Chances of this chase leading to victory are high given the four-member core team which is studying the clauses in the Forms of Consent. Zeta's will is stronger than her emotions—this rare quality always brings her face-to-face with victory, eventually, if not immediately. To Zeta, victory is all about reinforcing the word of God, and creating a suitable environment for women to be able to live by their will, like all humans should.

Who is human? I address this question in my reporter's notebook in red cursive:

The Kalarpatra Bagha
who courts danger, to survive.
Nominta Debury
who knows that danger is in the face of a man.
Nelli
who visits danger by night.
Susanthi Bodra
who looks danger in the eye.
Asha Paharia
who mingles with danger by day and by night.
Inspector General Tuffwinder Singh Bawa
along with Major Ashok Riflewala and Lieutenant Hamid Iyer
trespass the dangerous territory
in the lair of the Kalarpatra Bagha
to give danger a bad name.

When Zeta meets with the Guru, Herr Bauer, D'Vaz and me, she will unravel the truth about Nominta who knows danger in the face of a once proclaimed dead man.

I am aware of the emotional danger of coming face-to-face with the man who perpetually dons a blue kurta. There is danger. There is warmth too. I feel a tremor of warmth in his eye from the last time we met. The warmth still holds me in a ring of secure love as his daughter feels comforted on my lap.

Herr Hans Bauer felt secure until he found out that his roots did not render him an Aryan by birth. That night, hand upon his first love Greta Meier's hand, eyes fixed on the Hohensalzburg Fortress from a distant day in his teen years, ended in a final kiss. His sweetheart Greta Meier pointed out that Herr Bauer could never be her husband. He was as dark as the night which held the stars in the skies serenading the Hohensalzburg Fortress. Herr Bauer was not an Aryan. He looked Indian, with features resembling citizens from the country's southern side. In later years, Herr Bauer was to discover that his roots found their beginnings among the Katunayakan tribes in a southern Indian forest. Herr Bauer's bearings are in the same forest where the lissome Jasmine Creeper's ancestors took root, centuries ago. This is the same forest from where Minnal carries justice in her mother's bosom and takes the emotion all the way to the Central Jail with an address in the Southern Capital with a Sea.

There is no woman more just than a mother who can call her erring son a spade.

***

Naren Nayak hears a woman shriek. He wakes up to the crescendo of his own baritone snore which has leapt a few notes upwards on the treble cleft, scaling two octaves of the A Major range, making him sound like a shrieking woman. His open eyes look upwards, then sideways, and back until they come to rest upon a pile of abandoned travel bags. He rubs his eyes, scratches his uncombed head, lowers his gaze to the floor, and ponders until the butt of a rifle raises his downturned chin. Naren stares into the face of a khaki-clad law-keeper, who in broken Hindi, reveals that the traveller from Orissa has been untouched so far simply because he resembled a rucksack. Bah! Ah! Naren doesn't need to ponder anymore. He now knows that Platform No. 1 in the Central Railway Station is under curfew given the recent riots and mothers' uprising in the Southern Capital. Naren quietly follows the policeman to the waiting room where passengers from across the Indian subcontinent hover with trepidation. Naren's women platform mates have been rounded up and taken to the Central Jail, he is told by a kindly porter who speaks his tongue.

Maa Taarini! Naren has arrived at another dead end.

There's more information reaching me through my secret Source—Nominta Debury is feared dead. In the place where she belongs, it is best for a mother to know the worst. But Nominta's mother does not know the worst. She can only fear it.

Fear is worse than the actual truth. Fear shows you nightmares by daylight. Nominta's mother perceives these daydreams to be the truth. The absolute truth.

How is Nominta's mother to know the truth? Her second-born child's foster parents Urmila and Manohar Mahapatra cannot be reached on the mobile number they have written out in big bold hand in her daughter's double-ruled notebook. Nominta has left this notebook by the sacred photo of Maa Taarini; it contains information of her whereabouts along with details of her training schedule at the Sambhalpur Rozgaar Kendra. The photo of the Goddess occupies prime place above the smokeless chulha, the fire of which makes raw ingredients suitably edible for Nominta's family. Today, the mud-cooking range does not emanate carbon dioxide. Nominta's mother cannot locate the desire in her palpitating heart to cook for her sleeping children—this meagre meal for their day's survival. She hopes against despair that her second-born child, the future breadwinner of the family, Nominta Debury, has not slept forever. She shrieks a prayer to Maa Taarini.

The Uncrowned Head Prasad Bharathi shrieks in the inner rooms of the Maha Mantri Bhavan—the official palatial residence of the Prime Minister of India. Swami Prem Anand has subtly announced his divine presence to the security officials at Prasad Bharathi's official residence. The impact of the Swami's divine presence sends holy shivers down the spines of the uniformed guards' already wobbling knees. His Divine Holiness, Swami Vishnu Prem Anand must be received on a plush blood-red carpet. The shade of the carpet must be just right—blood-red. The carpet is at the dry-cleaners. After six washes, the dry-cleaners have not been able to match the appropriate blood-red shade. How can the Cabinet of plush blood-red carpet-owning ministers be so unprepared? The Uncrowned Head is uncontrollably chagrined.

Chagrin sets the stage for pandemonium at the Centre.

The Uncrowned Head addresses his ministers in the privacy of Maha Mantri Bhavan's Stately Auditorium where all important guests are received. He also translates his own speech on the go:

'Gayon aur bhaison

Cows and buffaloes

Is desh ke kameenon
This country's rascals
Mere Cabinet ke badnaam keede
My Cabinet's cursed worms...'
Prasad Bharathi speaks, his Cabinet squirms.

From his place at the security gate, Swami Prem Anand can see the goings on in the Auditorium—he blatantly squirms in return. Only, the Uncrowned Head and his Cabinet of 'cows, buffaloes and cursed worms'—all ministers in high offices, cannot see the returned squirm from their meeting place in the Stately Auditorium.

Prasad Bharathi continues to give his ministers a dressing down.

A team of high-profile decorators continue to give the Stately Auditorium a dressing up.

These high-profile decorators are hand in glove with the Swami, they plant secret cameras, some devices pointing upwards, others facing down.

Swami Vishnu Prem Anand can see and hear Prasad Bharathi's secret meeting on his iPhone 6, he does not frown. Especially when he is accoutred as he is, in his flowing white dhoti and sacred thread of three cotton strands—mark of brahminhood blatantly manifest from his right shoulder all the way down to his left waist. All his disciples at the Vedic Vaishnav Ashram wear similar tri-cotton stranded sacred threads in varying off-white hues to show off their singlehood, and more importantly, their 'upper-class Brahminhood'.

In the Southern Capital, Venkataraman wears the sacred thread, it comes united in nine separate slim cotton strands to indicate that this 'upper-class Brahmin' is married, and has fathered two sons to top his esteemed status. The Minister's wife does not know of the third son her husband has fathered. When Mrs Komalavalli Thiru Venkataraman learns of the existence of the third son who another mother has carried in her womb, brought into this world, and nurtured, all threads, sacred and otherwise, will come undone.

Meanwhile, Aandavan has masterminded a counter story to the damaging national news announcing the identity of the Minister of Accounting Affairs' third son. The Political Advisor is in cahoots with a certain land-hungry Political Reporter in the Southern Capital, he bribes him with an acre of property, and gets the scribe to twist 'facts' in the Minister's favour. People now read of the mother in Keonjhar, who, according to the Political Reporter, 'is pulling a fast one' for a quick buck and mention of her name on Page 1 in Bhubaneswar and in the Southern Capital with a Sea. The same news appears in the national pages of Left-wing and Right-wing media houses all over the country.

Here is a new twist to the story.

Venkataraman believes that this twist in the tale will save his marriage. He has married power in the name of Komalavalli. Venkataraman, upon being disowned by his legal wife, will need to return to his roots in the forest hamlet if he is divested of this powerful connection.

Deep down, the forest continues to lure Venkataraman. He travels to the deep forests of Keonjhar under the cover of his wandering mind to meet the mother who has birthed and bred the only son he is proud of, no matter that this 'out of wedlock' offspring has brought him ridicule. But the pride must remain in Venkataraman's mind. Any utterance of his pride is certain to cause a double flutter in his marriage and his political career.

I am proud of his daughter, she is so gutsy. This pride must remain in my mind. The mind has a way of recalling the person closest to your heart.

Nelli is proud of her mother. Gowravva is constantly on Nelli's mind. The words in her mind refuse to come out through her mouth. She cannot speak in her subconscious state. She lies faint in the hospital bed in Nagaon. The pride Nelli feels, has no choice but to stay firm in her mind.

Amrit Kumar has no choice but to cancel Nelli's appointment with the minister-cum-businessman who will make him richer by fifty thousand rupees for work performed on a single night.

Naren Nayak has no choice but to remain on Platform No.1 at the Central Station in the Southern Capital. Messages have invaded his Nokia 1100 throughout the duration of his slumber, filling his inbox to the brim while he snored oblivious to all sounds ranging from Minnal's loud shriek to the mellow beeps of his mobile phone. Naren is helpless. He cannot respond to the messages. He does not have any currency on his pre-paid SIM card. This basic instrument for communication—important and otherwise, has been given to him to receive crucial messages from the Special Force for the duration of his mission in the Southern Capital with a Sea.

Naren does what he utters best during helpless situations. He invokes the blessings of Maa Taarini—she, the Goddess who protects the deep, dark forests and its children.

It is prayer time at the Bochagora Government School. Domrudoru Baiga is unable to concentrate on the words that are sure to invoke the blessings of Maa Taarini.

Susanthi Bodra is unable to hold on to nature's call, which by this time, has trickled between her legs and all the way down unto the rubber-matted floor of the closed jeep. Susanthi turns red with shame. Tears trickle down from her button-sized eyes, slip between her lips, run over her chin, and slide over her neck. How can she be such a child? But Susanthi is still a child, she is not quite thirteen. Her foster parents from YUPAP become aware that the child has met danger in the thick of the Lantana shrubs that are growing wild by the highway.

Susanthi cannot speak of the danger to her foster parents. Only her best friend Domrudoru will understand this danger. How will the YUPAP volunteers understand that Susanthi Bodra has seen her dead biological father in flesh and blood? And, he had a shotgun.

Bandooko
Shotgun
Jhumko
Danger
Bhayo
Fear
Janyo manso aar rakto
Of human flesh and blood
When a dead man comes alive.

Susanthi does not know that a shotgun may not kill. But Susanthi does know that her father is alive.

Or, is he?

Susanthi is not a child. She must train other tribal girls who have lost their fathers to Mahua and shotguns to rear ducks which will lay golden eggs. She must not cry. Susanthi Bodra arrests her tears inside the convenient cover of her throat. She wipes the wetness under her eyes, also between her lips, and down her thighs beneath her pink frock.

Her foster parents from YUPAP watch Susanthi wipe her legs and her feet. Her feet are paranoid with bleeding bruises. Susanthi remains silent, tearless in the face of her internal and external pain. She will remain silent, and seek the blessings of Maa Taarini alone, until she meets her dark weather friend, Domrudoru.

***

The dark of the night carries a fair dream to Herr Hans Bauer. In die fairer traum, he meets his toothless mother. She tells him as a mother in a fair dream would, that he must protect his unfair brother from ruin. In die fairer traum, Herr Bauer sees the importance of calling his brother a spade. That unscrupulous spade which digs and plunders more than three hundred bank accounts in India, Europe and South East Asia.

Herr Bauer consults the Guru to get an educated handle on Venkataraman's bungles. The Guru reveals details of the misappropriated funds from memory. Playing the *Eine Kleine Nachtmusik* score from memory keeps facts hidden from files in view of the Guru's mind, long after the impact of the crime has passed on to its incident. It is much like the taxation system where the tribes who live off the jungles of Keonjhar and in the bosom of the Dalma Ranges, pay tax on commodities which have been weaned out of their own lands before they have been taken away to the city to be processed and packaged for consumption. For instance, Naren's wife Parbothi has paid an incidental tax on the purchase of the gold nose ring she wears as a symbol of her marital status. It is made of the same gold which has been winnowed from her ancestral lands. These are the same lands that hug the Kanjipani Mountains, this vast expanse nestling the gold of the Mankadia tribes of Keonjhar.

The mother who bore Venkataraman's artistic son belongs to the Mankadia tribe. She was married just once, to a tall thin man with sparkling eyes and a sharp nose. Right through her early childhood, up until she was twelve, she thought her husband to be very handsome. The man she was married off to, when she was still a girl of thirteen, belonged to the Munda tribe. She loved him until he disappeared, leaving her with their daughter and memories of their dead son. There is no evidence that this mother's Munda man is alive.

Inspector General Bawa and his Special Task Force of the Awakened Peacekeeping Mission have just gotten wind that the Mankadia woman's Munda man is alive.

Jhumur Jhumur
Jhumur Jhumur
Kothai jabo re,
More Swami?

The Mankadia mother who married the Munda man, never once consented to take Thiru Venkataraman as her Swami. Her only Swami is the Munda man, her legal husband—he is tall and thin, with sparking eyes and a sharp nose.

Where on earth is the Mankadia woman's Swami?

Where on earth is Asha Paharia?

She still resides in the forests of the Dalma, and there's a lot happening within its seemingly serene precincts.

Asha smells danger in the new lair which the khaki-clad strangers tell her, is now her home. This home does not have grandmothers, fathers, mothers, brothers and sisters. In this home, relationships are dead. And so are you, if you should step out of line. On the other side of this regimental line, is Asha's hunger-liberating kitchen in the far corner of the hutment where she first opened her eyes to the world. On that rain-fed night when her mother went into labour by the chulha, her grandmother and women from the neighbouring hutments formed a circle of life around her. This kitchen keeps Asha alive as long as she brings home grains, pulses and vegetables. When Asha has lands to grow the foodgrains and vegetables on, the kitchen waltzes. When her land disappears overnight under the shroud of a bulldozer and into the hook of an earth-digger, the kitchen abandons the coal fire. When the chulha rests, the kitchen remains dark long after the sun has trespassed into the night sky...

Far away from home, Asha feels lonely. The khaki-clad strangers promise eternal sun in Asha's new lair.

In the darkest depths of Dalma, the sun is playing truant.

In the darkest depths of Dalma, members of the Awakened Peacekeeping Mission are playing by ear.

Swami Vishnu Prem Anand is playing by instinct at the security check by the Maha Mantri Bhavan. His instincts tell him that Prasad Bharathi is merciless with fools. The Cabinet is full of fools. Swami Prem Anand has earlier divined an infallible method of luring the fools into the incense intense, alcohol-free chanting chambers of the Vedic Vaishnav Ashram. He will use his 'special divination' tools as and when required.

Nearly five hours ago, Minnal lent ear to the distressed, gave hand to the needy, and spewed advice of a sound kind to mothers missing their children on Platform No. 1. The mothers on their part understood Minnal's advice despite the fact that they all spoke in diverse tongues—the language of compassion needs no words. Minnal's 101 earth years have wisened her beyond her scanty grey hair, wrinkled skin, and all else the eye can meet. She had fast gathered followers, all women from here and there. Amazed by her simple supremacy, they joined the grand old lady in her strife for justice, hoping to find theirs too. The nation must be saved from men who do not care a farthing about women, the Lesser Known Goddess had indicated. They must all confront the Minister of Accounting Affairs. ASAP! Upon Minnal's advice, the women in tow, took the shortest cut to meeting the Minister—together, they created furore on Platform No. 1. Together, they were arrested.

Minnal is called the Lesser Known Goddess for good reason—she knows a thing or two about saying the darnedest things to the darnedest people to get what she wants. Minnal lures the khaki-clad fools in the Central Jail with her overt ability to call Thiru Venkataraman a spade. The law-keepers are falling like dazed ees into her trap, just the way they all toppled like drunken flies on Platform No.1 at the Central Railway Station. The khaki-clad men are dazed in the head by all that's being done and said, they concede. They will soon take Minnal and her entourage in the Big Police Bus fitted with iron doors and closely barred windows, and drive them all to the densely guarded stately abode of the very honourable Minister Venkataraman.

Gowravva is the leader of Minnal's entourage. She leads the entourage with the simple complexity endured by a wounded mother's complicated heart. But there is nothing simple about Gowravva's complex emotional state. When the entourage arrives at Venkataraman's stately abode, the planned explosion of feminine emotions promises to rock the core premise of this story.

There is wind of another explosion.

When we arrive at the Art College by Dhauli, the entourage of students will be ready to explode. D'Vaz has given us the heads up on the student uprising—the aroused members will not take the shame of their fellow artist lightly—they may be artistic, but they will certainly not be caught drawing doodles in the air! The aroused students might take on the shame by drawing an explosion of caricatures in the air, instead. But when the shame is two-fold, with both biological father and the norm-keepers of art denouncing the artist's identity as a non-issue, an impressionistic explosion of artistic perceptions is imperative.

His baby is impressionable, she is fettered by the impending explosion in the Art College—there's a tiny scratch on her face. I rub the scratch gently—my baby is traumatised by the upheaval in her father's life.

I hold onto a tender moment when, upon a moonlit night, standing side by side in his balcony, his unshaven cheek brushed mine. My mind is warmed, and I control the upheaval in my heart.

Hearts are in danger of being broken in Majuli. Moonlit nights in Majuli call for celebration. The oldest members of the Mising tribe, women included, empty earthen pots of inebriation-guaranteed rice toddy into their mouths. Bestowed with the colloquial intensity of the fresh moon over the macho waters of the Brahmaputra, the Mising lock their hands behind each other's waists, and dance to the never-ending circle of life, death and new breath.

Nelli, even in her absence, is the centre of their circle. She will not have the circle break. She must act fast. Amrit Kumar has been speaking to Mising girls, cajoling the poor innocent souls to sign the Form of Consent. ASAP. Fortunately, they can neither read, nor sign the document. When Nelli's piggy bank is full, she will pay the Mising girls handsomely in word and deed, to speak their minds at the Vedic Vaishnav Ashram. Swami Prem Anand holds the same powers that the Panchayat Mukhiya of Majuli does. Nelli does not have the power to open her eyes. But, lying in her subconscious state in the hospital bed not so far away from Majuli, in the town of Nagaon, Nelli has the power to sketch out the intricate details of her life's purpose.

The forests between Keonjhar and Dalma, have a new guest.

Nominta Debury has lost the power to scream. Mouth stuffed with an old piece of sheer cloth which was once a woman's odhni, Nominta will not allow any sound to emanate from her now petrified vocal cords.

Urmila and Manohar Mahapatra continue to be unable to emanate sounds loud enough to attract passersby. Their muffles continue to be faintly audible—but not loud enough to attract a possible pedestrian on the highway of dizzy motor-engine drones, the din punctuated by revving roars of overloaded trucks ferrying freshly mined iron ore. Urmila and Manohar are experienced in the ways of attracting help on highways. Their girl child rescue drives have attracted the admiration of the Awakened Peacekeeping Mission as well as the abuse of Prime Minister Prasad Bharathi, along with the combined chagrin of his Cabinet of ministers. The Uncrowned Head does not think highly of workers from non-governmental organisations butting into the affairs of people, especially the tribes who live in India's heartland. It is essential to leave the backward communities to their plight for his own Cabinet of ministers to make a buck, and more than survive. After all, the tribes of this region cast their votes without a noise, and make no demands for their right to land and Government schemes to benefit their well-being. If little girls from the region continue to be rescued and educated, they are sure to influence progress amidst their families and their communities. Progress in these tribal lands spells regress at the Centre. In Prasad Bharathi's head, there is no doubt that little girls must be curbed.

***

Today, Nominta Debury's mother knocks on Parbothi's door, weeping uncontrollably. No one has heard her weep or seen her tears hidden to the occasional passerby as she wears sadness under her sari pallu along the two-kilometre walk from her hutment to Parbothi's home. In these parts of Keonjhar, mothers who live in hutments buried in the secret abandons of the Kanjipani Mountains, cannot make a hue and cry about their missing daughters.

Sridhar Haider D'Vaz believes in making a hue and cry about matters which bring disgrace to the notion of self. He himself has faced the subtle ire of Prasad Bharathi for his explicit watercolour impression of the Kalarpatra Bagha—this conscientious artist fears the extinction of this exotic species of Indian leopards. The ire emanating from the Centre has been subtle. D'Vaz has been subtle about the distinct pride he takes in Indian mammals—they include the humans of the region and their four-legged counterparts in the Maoxal-intense belts of Keonjhar,

Balangir and Dalma. The Uncrowned Prasad Bharathi and his Cabinet of ministers fear the human mammals in these regions.

These mammals are special—they cannot be lured by the nasha of paisa—the intoxication of money will certainly not bring them to the big city.

The proud mammals of these regions
are rendered intoxicated by the heaving wet, red soil.
Also, the varying hues of forest green,
and sudden rushes of water risen unconsciously from distant springs.
They love the moo of the slim, perpetually hungry cow,
the slither of snakes meandering between paddy fields and forest lands.
Also, the smell of coal fires
cooking meals of daal, bhath and roti
ridge gourd and the frisky river maach, too.

The intoxication of money in the big city does not compare with the nasha of Mahua—this toddy freshly brewed from the spoils of its mother tree.

Even the four-legged mammals will not trade the intoxication of this paradise on earth for the caged freedom of the zoo. Let us not mention the caged confines of the moving circus, a restrictive treeless jungle which fortunately is almost passé. The Kalarpatra Bagha is a mammal. Some say he has two legs, others say he has four. No matter how many legs he sprints on, he cannot be confined, except within the artist's frame. It is the same frame which won D'Vaz his international accolade, and no award to document on the Indian soil. All thanks to the subtle ire of Prasad Bharathi and his Cabinet of ministers, any work of art involving dissent, does not merit a Government-endorsed national award.

Minister Thiru Venkataraman has been a major orchestrator of this subtle ire—he was bestowed prime position in the Cabinet when he showed Prasad Bharathi the unimaginable natural wealth that defines Keonjhar, Balangir and Dalma. The iron-rich land, the wood-endowed trees, the gold-smitten soil and mammals—two and four-legged creatures included, can bring unimaginable wealth to Prasad Bharathi's coiffeurs and the bank accounts of the Cabinet of ministers via a well-instituted committee of successful Indian industrialists.

Venkataraman has excited the 'greed spot' in Prasad Bharathi. Together, the Cabinet and Prasad Bharathi must own the mammals and the lands that are home and heaven to them.

In this heaven, the Maoxals were born. Asha Paharia is a Maoxal in her vision for a poverty-free life.

Inspector General Tuffwinder Singh Bawa is a mammal all the way. He believes in natural justice—the God-bestowed law which abides by the mammal's primeval urge to take that, and only that which is required for one's survival.

Is Prasad Bharathi fit to survive?

Is Venkataraman fit to serve Prasad Bharathi?

It doesn't matter which scoundrel minister is fit. The Guru is certainly fit. He knows exactly where the bungled accounts and Forms of Consent are masterfully elaborated and typed out with scant emphasis on the exact details. He will reveal the details to those who care about democracy when the time is appropriate.

Details are traitors—they tend to give away the unscrupulous intentions of greedy ministers.

Suddenly, I am greedy for chamomile tea. The nasha of this brew lifts me to a surreal paradise when the man in blue cups my small hands within his large palms. I rest my head upon his shoulder which I cannot reach unless I stand on tiptoe. Together, we walk towards the gushing waters of the freshly rain-fed River Shammakoi. I hold his baby tight, and I lose myself in my dream.

Susanthi Bodra is no baby. She is no adult either. Susanthi just does what adults do—she shoulders the responsibility of her family. She has family. She knows her mother is alive. Her father too, is alive. The child in Susanthi is alive. The child bursts into tears, choking uncontrollably under the constantly increasing weight of her responsibility. She has the responsibility of keeping her father's identity secret. In her adult experience, Susanthi knows that when a father covers his entire face with the exception of his sparkling eyes with an odhni and carries a shotgun, the khaki-clad force will uncover him. Susanthi finds solace in the sparkle of her father's eyes. They sparkle for freedom.

The Southern Capital is a big city with lots of money. Venkataraman owns most of its paisa and nearly all of its rupees. He also has bank accounts with euro in Der Bundesrepublik Deutschland, dirhams in Dubai, also dollars in the United States of America.

Venkataraman has fewer bank accounts than Prasad Bharathi.

The more bank accounts you have, greater the chances of claiming the throne of the Uncrowned Head.

Swami Prem Anand has a great chance of entering the accounting chambers in Prasad Bharathi's residence. The entry is a straightforward walk on the red carpet.

Leading Swami Prem Anand's straightforward entry to Prasad Bharathi's residence are four of his Eclectic Disciples, all accoutred in saffron dhotis to cover their lower limbs and sacred threads to show off on their upper bodies, which are otherwise bare. They carry a bronze kamandal each. These miniature jugs are equipped with supersonic voice-recorders, divined by Prem Anand. Three more Eclectic Disciples walk right behind their divine leader, they too are accoutred in saffron dhotis and sacred threads. They carry a jhola each. These jholas are equipped with supersonic video cameras, also divined by his truly, the one and only Swami Vishnu Prem Anand.

The remaining two of the nine Eclectic Disciples, both accoutred in matching white dhotis tailored to fit and 'just a tad loose, pot belly accentuating' shirts, are already inside Prasad Bharathi's residence. No one has noticed them slithering in—hat's off to two female cooks in the Uncrowned Head's master kitchen. These female cooks are Swami Vishnu Prem Anand's supremely secret disciples—they have managed to obscure the focus of the prying cameras in certain 'not-so-frequented' quarters of the ministerial home. In their turn, thin as pencils, the Eclectic Disciples, both experts in the art of slipping through gaps between doors, mostly windows, which the armed guards at Prasad Bharathi's official residence do not know exist, have made their way in.

Thiru Venkataraman does not exist in the Cabinet anymore. The Cabinet is full of backstabbers who have made their share of rupees, euro, dollars and dirhams to stash away in their own bank accounts. They also stash these currency notes in the accounts of their near and dear ones in remote banks across the latitude and longitude of the world.

Venkataraman has been their secret angel—he, an invisible guide through the process of this amassing of wealth. But his value has dwindled ever since the Cabinet has learnt of his artistic son born outside the norms of wedlock. The Cabinet cannot be bothered about their colleague's out-of-wedlock affairs. The Cabinet, however, is certainly bothered about their colleague's unwieldy artistic son who has the distinction of being a bastard, making insolent paintings of Gods and Goddesses to feed his own fancy for the unattainable exotic.

Bah!

***

Zeta Rani has the distinction of making incisive decisions, especially when a delicate situation is blown indelicately out of proportion.

The proportion of girls under duress is threefold.

Nominta Debury has gone missing.

Nelli is lying faint.

Susanthi Bodra is distressed under the duress of not being able to answer nature's call behind the Lantana shrubs on the Balangir-Sambhalpur Highway and allowing her uncontrollable excreta to flow in the jeep, instead.

Zeta Rani has decided that we will head out on a personal trip, external to the expedition of the Awakened Peacekeeping Mission to rescue these distressed girls. Herr Bauer, the Guru, D'Vaz and I receive SMSes from Zeta. We are immediately alert to Zeta's plan of jointly heading out from the Art College on our external mission. But we must arrive at the Art College by Dhauli in Bhubaneswar first. Our journey is not so personal after all.

Minnal and her entourage, with Gowravva at the helm, have just begun their journey. It is a long journey across the short distance from the Central Jail to Thiru Venkataraman's stately ancestral home in the Southern Capital. The journey is long despite the short ten-kilometre stretch.

Why pray?

Minnal has, at this opportune time, chosen to call the Minister of Accounting Affairs a fly, she spews a volley of 'ees' and other suitable abuses along with her entourage. The khaki-clad police find it suitable to stop the Big Police Bus every other minute to hush the Lesser Known Goddess and quell her hyper hallucinations of victory over vice.

So,

Shoo say the khaki people.

Ee says the Lesser Known Goddess.

Her entourage repeats—Ee, ee, ee, ee.

They all say ee in varying scales ranging from the lower octave sa to the higher sa, do to do, re, mi, fa, so, la and tee in between.

Shoo...say the khaki-clad law enforcers.

Minnal stares.

Her entourage also stares.

Big stare, bigger stare, biggest stare from Gowravva's really big eyes.

The khaki-clad law enforcers show their lathis.

The entourage of women make faces, some mothers, others paatis.

Grandmothers, also mothers, grab the lathis and attempt to yank the wooden sticks away from the strong grips of the khaki-clad people. Some mothers succeed, including Gowravva. She stands proud like the warrior queen Kittur Rani Chennavva, holding the law enforcer's stick high up in the air, and askance. Gowravva exudes the same flourish that the ancient Rani wielded centuries ago—the queen standing sword in hand as she led her people to victory. It is the same flourish with which the Statue of Liberty holds the torch that carries on it the message: 'Liberty Enlightening the World.' Gowravva has no idea that she resembles the 305 feet high Goddess of Liberty welcoming ships arriving at the tourist-smitten New York Harbour, but with an Indian twist accoutred as she is in her green sari.

Gowravva is indeed a grand sight for residents and tourists to behold in the Southern Capital with a Sea. News of chagrined mothers spreads faster than forest fire in the near treeless Southern Capital.

Naren Nayak has news about the revolting mothers from his newly-acquired coolie friend, he must escape the confines of the Central Railway Station to partake the grand sight. He is a law-abiding man. How will he break the norms of the curfew? Or, should he, just once? The khaki-clad law enforcers on watch at the Central Railway Station are keeping their beady eyes glued to him. He is the only prospective passenger on Platform No.1, who has not fled the railway station ahead of or behind the enlightened liberators aka mothers and grandmothers. These women are all strangers to each other, and the khaki-clad law enforcers simply cannot imagine why they have followed the toothless, ranting Minnal on the whim of an ee!

Strange women
are no longer strangers
when the consequences of motherhood,
their own children
are in danger of vanishing under the shadow of their own meanderings.

His baby is in danger of being hushed. She has not meandered. I am no stranger. I am her mother. I will not let her vanish.

Urmila and Manohar Mahapatra are livid. Their foster child Nominta Debury cannot vanish from right under their noses. They must use all the inner strength that is hidden beneath their already strong exteriors to abandon the prison of gags and ropes which bind them. They must find their foster child.

They must find her as soon as possible.

ASAP!

***

His team is at work—Inspector General Bawa has wind of a girl child from Keonjhar District, State of Orissa. She has been found in a Maoxal camp in the Dalma Ranges, State of Jharkhand. The Awakened Peacekeeping Mission is maintaining pace with this speedy wind they call the Source.

When the Source begins to enlighten awakened humans, all rural girls in duress are sure to meet happiness, sooner or later.

The girls of the forest are still in duress.

The man with sparkling eyes and a shotgun secured to his body with a sheer odhni, runs with the speed of the Kalarpatra Bagha, overriding the smell of food which carries its aroma in the wind, and travels through the cluster of Sal trees to reach the lair with his catch before the sun breaks its siesta. Close behind him, Major Ashok Riflewala and Lieutenant Colonel Hamid Iyer—the integral members of the Awakened Peacekeeping Force—both strict vegetarians with a cultivated taste for organic recipes, are alert to the smell of meat cooking in Maoxal lairs over coal fires. They are extremely alert to the sounds which accompany this distinct smell. They have heard muffled screams accompanying the man who runs with the speed of the Kalarpatra Bagha and has sparkling eyes. The muffles, they know from experience of rescuing underaged children from the deep dark forests of these regions, belong to a little girl no older than thirteen years of age.

Parbothi listens to Nominta's mother as the latter narrates her experience, intermittently letting the words sputter between her uncontrollable sobs. She has word from the Source—there's talk in Manipura that the hamlet's daughter Nominta Debury has gone with the wind. The Kalarpatra Bagha has crossed jungles unknown to the boundaries of her State with her second born, her future breadwinner, her own flesh and blood. Nominta's mother had refused to turn her second born over to the Source although the option promised instant monetary relief to her family. Masking her child from such impending jungle danger, she had sent the future breadwinner of her home away with her foster parents Urmila and Manohar Mahapatra, instead. They would enable her to earn a respectable living at the Sambhalpur Rozgaar Kendra. And when Nominta returned to Manipura, which seems like a difficult wish to make under the present circumstances, her mother imagined she would earn while she learnt her lessons by the light of the dibri.

Parbothi offers solace and assures Nominta's mother that her child will surely return, and unscathed at that.

Her mother is hopeful. 'When Nominta returns from Sambhalpur, she will rear golden ducks, and she will go to school in Manipura. Here, sitting in our hutment's backyard on a many-holed, weather-eaten charpoy with her younger siblings, Nominta will do her homework. This homework,' her mother sobs, holding her daughter's textbook tight.

This is the homework which Nominta Debury has brought back from school. This is the same Government school, where Naren teaches the tribal children of Keonjhar, Math, Oria, History, Science and the English alphabet. Every day, the tribal girls of Keonjhar walk the human-made path, which Naren and Parbothi have laboriously laid with stones and sticks over the slushy red, foot-grabbing mud. Nominta takes pride in this man-and-woman-made path.

One pluuss one bole toooh.
Toooh pluuss toooh bole phour.
Phour pluuss phour bole achto
Eight! Right ashche?

Beams Nominta as she counts the numbers her teacher Naren has taught her in the lingua franca of this nation and many others—English. Her classmates count the numbers along with her. Together, they cross their hands to show the plus sign, and wiggle a sashaying dance to represent the swirl of the number eight.

Nominta grins at this reverie despite her upside-down position in the Source's hands.

I pick up my notebook, and write in red cursive:

All is well with Nominta Debury.

But not quite.

All is not well with Nelli either.

When I was eight, Arti's mother made me realise that I want to walk the paddy fields of Kithapur. I wanted to walk across those same fields where Nelli, her eight-year-old maid wore a crown of tri-hued Lantana flowers. When I was eight,

I wanted to taste the bakri that Nelli's mother roasted over the coal fire. The bakri, fragrant and fresh over the coal fire, is the bread that the women of Gowravva's hamlet eat day after day when the fields are fertile with corn. In time, they grow strong. Nelli and I, we made a pact to meet one day, perhaps in the distant future, to go home to Kithapur by the lone train which stops at the station closest to the hamlet at half-past midnight. Years after I turned eight, the Guru and I travelled for twelve hours on a train from the city which nurtures Bangalore Blues, to arrive at Kithapur. I ate the bakri and shenga chutney made from the coal hearth of a mother who had lost her daughter to the big city when she was still eight. That day, I realised how Nelli must yearn for her mother's bakri—made from cornflour dough flattened on her palm, roasted over the coal fire.

Yeshtu chanda ee bakri
How tasty this bread of corn
Namma Nelli
Our Nelli
Nimma Nelli
Your Nelli
Yelli?
Where is she?

I close my notebook, I sigh.

Gowravva does not know where Nelli is. I do not send a message through Naren for fear of wounding a mother's heart. Gowravva's heart is strong with the knowledge that Nelli is far away, happy in another Lantana-besotted field, untouched by the vile desires of an unsuitable man.

The truth is, Nelli is far away. Is she happy? I cannot say. I do not tell Gowravva what I know from a friend I made when I was eight.

***

When Thiru Venkataraman masterminded the Form of Consent, he made not one friend, but many. These friends, all ministers in Prasad Bharathi's Cabinet, are now the decorators of the Stately Auditorium. Together, they have formed a High Power Welcome Committee to meet and greet Swami Vishnu Prem Anand and his force of Eclectic Disciples into the Uncrowned Head's residence. Together, they have decided to keep Venkataraman out of this committee.

Venkataraman's erstwhile friends have now turned foes—they change gratitude by the way the fortune blows. Prasad Bharathi's Cabinet of ministers are chameleons in human form.

There is regret,

Among members of the Cabinet.

Some want to touch Swami Vishnu Prem Anand's pedicured feet.

Others want to bite off his reliably Dettol disinfected clean big toe.

The Swami has stepped on many toes.

He has privately predicted to Prime Minister Prasad Bharathi, the Uncrowned Head,

That there is regret in the Cabinet.

Some, if not all existing members must go.

'Go where?' Prasad Bharathi had turned to the Swami for a suitable solution to the unsuitable situation.

'Worry not,' the Swami replied. 'My fiercely adept team of Eclectic Disciples will take care of your ministers' disappearance.'

Then, the most Honourable Prasad Bharathi can feast on all the foils, and take care of all their combined wealth.

'Ssshhh...' indicate the Eclectic Disciples—all nine holding their index fingers upon their pursed lips. 'Divine Swami Prem Anand has hatched this plan in stealth.'

The two Eclectic Disciples accoutred in matching white dhotis are inimitable plot-hatchers. They have informed Swami Prem Anand of the regret among the members of the Cabinet long before the almost blood-red carpet has been unrolled, spread stylishly, and brushed crease free.

Swami Vishnu Prem Anand is rich in his bearing, he does not carry a wallet. He does not need money. Wherever the Swami goes, wealth flows. He carries an iPhone 6 which he checks at the beep of a message. It is a special beep. It is called the Divine Beep composed by Simply Hare Rama—the country's foremost single-ponytailed classical-folk-jazz musician. In fact, Simply Hare Rama has exclusively composed the Divine Beep for the starkly accoutred, heart-stoppingly stylish force of Eclectic Disciples, and of course for Inspector General Tuffwinder Singh Bawa and the other members internal and external to MDCRFP.

Inspector General Bawa checks special beeps on his posh iPhone 6 plus. He is always on beep alert. Especially when it happens to be the Divine Beep, which transfers messages from all recruits of MDCRFP. In fact, the Inspector General promptly acts at the slightest beep of his iPhone 6 plus.

It is time to act.

Lights, camera, action.

Right, left, straight.

Stop.

Focus.

Shoot.

Wait!

The self-proclaimed Mentor Amrit Kumar cannot shoot a sleeping girl.

Not even a girl named Nelli.

Amrit has entered the general ward in the Nagoan Government Hospital to grab a video shot of the fainted Nelli. This shot is proof that the worker cannot carry out her 'official' duties given her sudden faint state. The important customer must be reconciled by this evidence. The important customer need not return unsatiated. Amrit will bring hot, new meat from Majuli to satiate this most important customer. They call this hot meat, a virgin Mising woman—she has pleaded that her identity be kept secret. She is, for all practical reasons, called the Mising Virgin.

Forget the Mising Virgin.

Nelli stirs.

Amrit leaps with relieved joy.

The lights come on.

The force of Eclectic Disciples can be in two places at once—they have access to supersonic jets, choppers, speedboats, race horses, and what not. While the Swami and his five other Eclectic Disciples keep the ministers engaged at Maha Mantri Bhavan, they have taken a supersonic ride to Nagaon to misguide the Mentor in his relief.

Amrit Kumar is neither in unshackled custody, nor in shackled captivity.

He is surrounded by a pair of Eclectic Disciples, both faces he has been acquainted with at the Vedic Vaishnav Ashram in Manjuli. He breathes a sigh of relief.

Relief!

Really?

The ungodly Political Advisor Aandavan Kangal's name translates as 'God's eyes'—he is relieved that Nelli is unwell.

The Minister of Accounting Affairs cannot feast on hot meat—certainly not now. In Venkataraman's hometown, the entourage of cursing women is bound to smell the scent of a maiden on him. These protesting mothers, they have experienced noses after all. No, Minister Thiru Venkataraman cannot afford to wear the scent of a maiden on his sleeve, the perfume of lust all over his white shirt and silken dhoti at this trying hour. Definitely not!

In the Southern Capital, Komalavalli aka Mrs Thiru Venkataraman is trying hard to distract the entourage of cursing women. All the cursing women are mothers, some wives, many widows, others minors shouting out slogans, tainting Venkataraman's scant-existent good reputation from the cover of their campaign carriage—the Big Police Bus.

They say,

'Poda

Hogo

Get lost, you son of a gun.

Sorry, you son of a toothless old woman!

They fondly call the Lesser Known Goddess.

But not until we have stripped you off your clean white attire

And exposed your unclean limbs

To the keepers of law.

What the hell is law?

Hahahahahahaha…'

Inspector General Bawa knows how best to enforce law, especially where there is acute disorder.

Watch out, Minister of Accounting Affairs. Watch out for the female entourage.

The Big Police Bus is berserk. It sways like an inebriated lion on four fat wheels. It misses light poles, potholes, also people walking the streets by mere luck. And then, it halts. All four tyres are sulking. Four thick nails have decided to flush the air out of their puffed-up bellies, the tyres are morose. Why? All four tyres, notices the female entourage, are punctured.

How?

Ask Venkataraman's wife Komalavalli if she will tell.

***

Susanthi Bodra will tell the YUPAP volunteers what she has seen behind the profusion of Lantana shrubs when the time is right. The woman who earns the bread and butter for her hutment is still a twelve-year-old child stepping on thirteen. She must first recover from the shock of coming eye-to-eye with the man who forced her into becoming the breadwinner of her hutment. She must first confide to her best friend Domrudoru Baiga who lives four hutments away from hers. Susanthi hopes that one day soon, her mother will return to their hutment. She misses her quiet presence, which is loud with endurance for the sake of her children, and their boisterous games. She misses the stench of bile which her mother inadvertently infused their hutment with, night after night, sometimes throughout the day.

How will Susanthi tell the YUPAP volunteers that she must return to Bochagora to meet her dearest friend Domrudoru at once? Breadwinning girls, under fourteen years of age from three districts of Orissa—Keonjhar, Boudh and Balangir are coming to train under her at the Sambhalpur Rozgaar Kendra. But, they must wait.

Why is Susanthi being so selfish and unreasonable?

Must Susanthi accede to her childish whim and return to Bochagora just to tell her dark weather friend that she is paranoid?

Yes, she must. There is great pride in being a woman, a breadwinner. But Susanthi must take pride in being a child. She is beginning to understand the importance of being a child.

Will the YUPAP volunteers understand?

The shock is stern on Susanthi's strong mind. It makes her stubborn. It gives a jolt to the child within her slender frame. If the YUPAP volunteers do not concede to take her back to Bochagora right now, she will flee. Barefooted, Susanthi Bodra will flee through the shortcut in the long jungle path running between the Sambhalpur Highway and the hamlet of Bochagora. She will run until her bruised feet go sore with numbness, and her body will no longer listen to her mind.

Susanthi is a strong girl born out of the bruised dreams of a man with sparkling eyes and a woman who has borne another child out of wedlock. Susanthi has a step-brother. She does not know of his existence. She has never met him.

Susanthi is restless—she has met the child in her near thirteen-year-old frame. Tears drench her face, she hears the child, a stranger to her, cry.

Inspector General Bawa hears his iPhone 6 plus ring the Divine Beep. He reads the message he has just received from Major Ashok Riflewala. He beams. He now knows who Susanthi's step-brother is. The Guru just happens to know everything. Always futuristic in his thoughts and communication applications, the Guru has been chatting with Major Ashok Riflewala via WhatsApp.

It is amazing how the Dalma stays connected, even deep in the secret lairs of the khaki-clad strangers who took Asha Paharia away just the other day.

Major Ashok Riflewala is close, very close to Asha's lair. The tall, thin man, with sparkling eyes, a sharp nose, a shotgun hanging loosely below his left waist and Nominta Debury dangling like freshly hunted deer below his right waist, is also close to Asha's lair. Very close.

Very strange are the ways of men and women with bruised dreams. Especially those men and women who dream of burning coal fires and kitchens stocked with foodgrains and fresh maach—fish from stagnant and running waters throughout the year.

Fish?

You wish!

It is that time of the year when the rains have failed. The rivers now run dry. The farmer is listless. The coal fire does not burn. The crops have failed. The elected democracy has failed to reach rations and medical care to the flood-devastated people. The industrialists have failed to create a medical insurance facility for the people they employ in their mines and brick kilns as daily wagers. The Maoxal leaders have failed to intervene with documented petitions to the elected democracy and to the mine-owning industrialists, they are up in arms instead.

When nature fails, humans follow suit—they act in odd ways.

The ducks in Bochagora are feeling odd. They have decided to stop laying golden eggs. How can they? They are perpetually hungry. Susanthi Bodra is not around to feed them.

When humans fail, nature follows suit.

Scoot!

An inner voice knocks at Susanthi's aching head... You are a woman. You cannot fail. Get back to Bochagora, Susanthi Bodra, your ducks need you. Domrudoru needs his friend in need. The woman who cannot fail, is a child. Susanthi must return to the Bochagora Bal Panchayat. Together, the children of Bochagora will shake Susanthi Bodra out of her newly-acquired shock.

***

Herr Hans Bauer is beyond shock. He has caught the scent of jasmine from a creeper, wise beyond her years. She has inherited the maturity of her mother, Minnal, the Lesser Known Goddess. This Jasmine Creeper seems to know what it takes to soothe the soul of a son grappling for identity, a fellow tribe tracing his way back to his roots.

Ich möchte eine tasse kaffee trinken.

I must drink a cup of coffee, brewed by my mother

Mutti, woher gehst du?

Mother, where have you gone to?

I visited our home and found my sister, the lissome Jasmine Creeper, taken after you... Herr Bauer writes in his black diary.

Herr Bauer will not be joining us at the Art College by Dhauli in Bhubaneswar. The Guru has turned him southwards, towards his roots. Herr Bauer has gone to look for his mother. The mother has, since the time he was taken away by his foster father, grown into a toothless riot, giving a certain irate Minister in the Southern Capital a run for his money, and a run away from his honey.

No matter how hard he tries, Thiru Venkataraman's past runs after him. In the past, he was paisa-less and happy. In the present, he is rupee-blessed and sad.

Money can make a man happy or sad, depending on how much he is attached to it.

The way he earns the money, makes Venkataraman a sad man. So sad, that his own mother will have none of him. She is out to expose his paisa-less past. And he, the well-informed politician, has no wind of it.

As Venkataraman alights the aircraft at the Grand International Airport in the Southern Capital, his white veshti blows in the wind. He is not too happy to have his hairy legs exposed at the parting of this white wraparound skirt, a garment designed for the macho Indian man.

God save this macho politician
from his very own wife
when she learns of his paisa-less past,
that too, from his very own toothless mother.
In effect, her mother-in-law
who, although people call her Minnal, has no name.
What's in a name?

When the thin frame of the Lesser Known Goddess has no qualms about calling her eldest born a spade.

It is only too obvious that Minnal simply cannot be bothered with names.

Don't bother. Action is the name of this game.

Achtung.

Beware the wrath of a toothless woman who does not give a damn about how long she lives.

'Long live the Lesser Known Goddess,' sounds the resonating refrain from behind the bars of the Big Punctured Police Bus full of trim and fit from toil, light as feather, and heavyweight mothers.

In the hamlet with the famous Vishnu Temple, Herr Bauer learns of his mother's escapade in the Southern

Capital. Her well-wishers from the hamlet will accompany Herr Bauer to meet and greet his long-parted mother. Herr Bauer head-counts the well-wishers to organise a line-up for the Big People Bus—riding this vehicle, they will all wear their roadside sunglasses, and arrive in style at the Southern Capital with a Sea. The line-up is long. It is long because every man, woman and child from every hutment, also the lone cement home in the hamlet, has turned up for the grand journey. Why not! Minnal is powerful. She is the mother of the Minister of Accounting Affairs!

Sigh!

Minnal is not so proud to be called the mother of the Minister of Accounting Affairs. But she will live with the 'proud mother' title. She has other sons, and particularly one, who has done her mother's title proud.

Who is this son that makes Minnal proud?

Ask the Guru!

***

Sridhar Haider D' Vaz always follows the Guru's advice. He has been advised to keep peace alive through art.

Art, subtle as it may seem, always stirs controversy, especially when the subject alludes to the conservation of rare species.

The tall, thin man with sparkling eyes and a sharp nose is a rare species.

He happens to be a Maoxal. He still loves his daughter Susanthi Bodra.

The khaki-clad gentleman who questioned Asha Paharia and let her off the handcuff is rare.

He happens to be the Inspector General of Police, Tuffwinder Singh Bawa.

The Kalarpatra Bagha is rare. This species is as rare as the Gonds, the Mundas, the Santals, the Mankadias, and all the other tribes who are lost in their own lands. Tall and abundantly leaved trees they have known since their grandmothers sang folksongs exposing the hideout of the Kalarpatra Bagha in their lairs, are missing. They have been felled for wood to make exquisite furniture in Prasad Bharathi's home. Lands upon which their grandfathers led the plough are not within their reach. They are caving under the pressure of bulldozers and metallic land diggers.

Worry not.

D'Vaz is out to bring the jhumurs back into the lives of these tribes. He has been exposing the ravage of land sharks through the feisty, sparkling eyes of the Kalarpatra Bagha, the 'manimal'.

The artistic son of Thiru Venkataraman is rare, just like the Kalarpatra Bagha.

The Kalarpatra Bagha is rare, just like the Lesser Known Goddess.

Minnal is strong at all times. Subtle, until she is stirred to action by her own flesh and blood.

The consequence of Minnal's actions are far reaching.

It reaches Nagoan, where Nelli still lies faint in the hospital bed. There is no Amrit Kumar to keep an eye on her, he seems to have disappeared after the appearance of the Eclectic Disciples. She does not care. There is no Gowravva to keep an eye on her baby. Nelli cares. Suddenly, in her subconscious mind, she reaches out to her mother and sees her marching proudly, head raised high, heart poised to find her lost child. Nelli knows her mother well. Gowravva will not fail.

Lieutenant Colonel Hamid Iyer cannot fail. He is keeping an eye on Nelli. Doctors and nurses at the Nagoan

Government Hospital do not know that members of MDCRFP are here—its recruits are known to work in secretive ways. They are well-networked and agile, they reach the scene of crime in no time.

How now? What is the modus operandi of the Force?

There are no shortcuts to the operandi here. It involves the lives of women who are held to work for Amrit Kumar by their own inadvertent endorsements on the Forms of Consent. The matter must be dealt with poise. Women are not easy to deal with. Especially when their femininity is being abused by the Cabinet and its vile members.

For now, demand the khaki-clad strangers, let us not skip the gun, please.

Shoot.

Asha Paharia fires at her first target with her newly acquired shotgun. She shudders. The strangers in khaki have entrusted her with a weapon within three days of her recruitment to their Society. Asha wonders why. She will learn by and by. The strangers, still unsure of why they hold weapons, tell their fresh recruit with certainty.

Swami Vishnu Prem Anand works with certainty, he makes the impossible possible.

Hail the Divine Master of the Vedic Vaishnav Ashram.

Touch his pedicured feet.

Kiss the almost-blood-red carpet he walks upon.

Prasad Bharathi is mesmerised—he follows all the instructions given by the Eclectic Disciples who accompany the Swami on the 'almost-blood-red carpet slow walk'.

Simultaneously, the Nagaon-returned pair of slick Eclectic Disciples in white give instructions to the ministers in the bedecked Stately Auditorium. The ministers are mesmerised, all the members of the Cabinet immediately lie flat on their stomachs, their noses kissing the cold cement floor, beside each other, behind each other, almost all over each other as Swami Prem Anand approaches the massive entrance to the Stately Auditorium.

The vile Cabinet is naïve.

The force of Eclectic Disciples is not naïve, its operations are monitored by the Divine Swami.

Inspector General Bawa hears the Divine Beep. He learns that the members of the Cabinet are all down on their stomachs. His lips extend to a satisfied smile for the first time since his special Awakened Peacekeeping officers and the Eclectic Disciples have scattered themselves in several parts of the country for the sake of MDCRFP.

Inspector General Bawa prefers long mission statements, there's nothing better than a self-explanatory call to action and imminent justice.

Zeta Rani's mission is not self-explanatory. She has explanations regarding the forests beyond the highways. She has gathered inputs while on her mission to enable working girls in India's poorest regions to earn while they learn.

It is a strong mission.

A long path.

The short of this mission is to enable the tribes of Orissa and Jharkhand to live by their lands.

The core ideal of this mission is to enable the virgin maidens of Majuli to copulate by choice, and choice alone.

The background of this mission is set in the paddy fields of Kithapur, close to the District Headquarters of Gulbarga where poverty is treated with the survivor's strength of the combined emotions of the Feminine Force.

Well Gowravva, you rock the soil you till!

***

The soul of the soil is determined by the hands that weed it.

Today, Nominta Debury's mother weeds the paddy fields, her soul lost to the cause. There is no news of her daughter, the child has vanished into the thickness of the forest. The forest is full of secrets which do not have the habit of coming out into the open by choice. Nominta's mother cannot keep her woe a secret.

She weeps.

She hollers.

She spits a curse to the heavens.

She wipes her tears.

They flow again, profusely.

She cries.

She simpers.

She whimpers.

The tears flow continuously.

Her face is salty.

Her eyes are red.

Her heart is weary.

She carries on with her day's work.

She has four mouths to feed back home.

Life must go on in Nominta's hutment until the future breadwinner returns home to Manipura.

Will Nominta Debury return home to her mother?

Ask Inspector General Bawa.

Rest assured that the mastermind behind the Awakened Peacekeeping Mission will not give secrets away—neither by personal will, nor by coercion. The only way to succeed in the explicitly stated MDCRFP, is to keep its agenda secret.

Prasad Bharathi is clueless about the enlightened agenda of MDCRFP. So are the ministers of the Cabinet. Also, Thiru Venkataraman is now external to the Cabinet. The Minister of Accounting Affairs believes that Aandavan Kangal is the sole controller of his fate—political, personal and otherwise.

Aandavan is ridiculously one-dimensional in his analysis of the goings-on at the Centre. He believes that the only foil in Venkataraman's political progress is Prasad Bharathi.

Venkataraman is blindly one-dimensional in his analysis of the controller of his fate. He believes that Aandavan knows everything about everything, in fact everything even about nothing.

Let us set the analysis straight.

Swami Vishnu Prem Anand is out to straighten the Centre.

Time out.

Just sit back and allow the analysis to unravel itself.

Naren Nayak allows the dormant norm-breaker in him to surface and overcome the curfew. He swoons. The khaki-clad police—several males and a couple of females—drop their lathis in an effort to revive him. Naren chooses to remain consciously unconscious, until he is brought outside the Central Railway Station on a stretcher of interlocked human hands. These are the same hands which wielded their lathis to check the norm-abider in Naren Nayak.

***

It is imperative to break norms and give destiny a shoulder.

Asha Paharia shoulders the destiny of her family from the safety of the shotgun. This safety can be short-lived. Asha does not care, so long as her family lives, one day, then another. She has shot a peacock, the bird king of the Dalma Ranges, and every other forest in India.

The bird of paradise
dies.
Its blue-green feathers...
They will be sold
in the market outside the Dalma Ranges.
Over the rivers,
across the seas.
in a foreign land.
In homes, in offices of brick and stone
where this peacock's feathers
will, for its medicinal qualities, ward off the languid lizard
from the wall it crawls on.

Asha Paharia will ward off lizards et al, to ensure that her grandmother, mother, father and two younger brothers have daal and bhath to keep them alive for another day, another month...until she receives her first pay. Six thousand rupees—this is a sum she has never counted at one go in her twenty-plus years of farming life. In fact, she has not even counted six hundred rupees at one go.

Sixty rupees, perhaps when Asha sold vegetables grown in her backyard at the Grand Nimdi Fair. When every man, woman and child from the cluster of hamlets was there.

Asha Paharia can never go back there. She has chosen to wield the shotgun to leave behind every worldly care. But she cares. For her mother, her father, her grandmother and her two younger brothers. She cares for the ducks in her backyard and the chicken in her front yard. Asha's desire to care, leads her to tears. The tears won't stop. She lets the tears roll silently in the darkness of her lair.

Major Ashok Riflewala is moved by Asha's tears. But he will not let the tears roll down his own bespectacled eyes.

Not yet.

Susanthi Bodra has no more tears to moisten her fears. She stares at the YUPAP volunteers, and wonders whether she must talk about her fears to her foster parents.

Not yet.

Zeta Rani is working hard to retrace the fears and check the tears of these young women aka girls aka near children.

Let the Force be with Zeta who has weighed the pros, cons and consequences of being trapped in a web of poverty in an elected democracy.

Inspector General Bawa hears another Divine Beep. He observes the recruits of the Awakened Peacekeeping Mission—they have tough exteriors and soft interiors. This is precisely the reason why Inspector General Bawa has appointed them as officers to aid MDCRFP.

***

MDCRFP has surfaced in Majuli. The Mising have been tipped off by a Source who wears the title of Lieutenant Colonel Hamid Iyer. Today, they celebrate the birth of another girl child in their hamlet of eight hutments. The central yard of the Mising Panchayat Mukhiya's home is overflowing with laughter. There is feminine laughter in the backyard of the masculine Brahmaputra. This is the same masculine river from the waters of which the Mising women have brought home rohu to cook and share with their fellow tribes to celebrate the birth of another girl child. There is more food to cook. The meat of fresh pink pork steadily turns brown over the hamlet's massive coal fire, and the mothers dance.

Ready for the celebration?

Steady.

Of course not.

The rice toddy cannot steady the happy Mising celebrating the birth of another girl child.

But how long can they be happy?

The Forms of Consent are on their way.

Their girls will go missing.

Nelli is missing.

Nelli, the saviour, who carries the DNA of Gowravva's blood.

She is brave in the face of controversy.

And she is missing.

But today, despite Nelli's absence, the Mising are happy to be happy.

Lieutenant Colonel Hamid Iyer, a core recruit to MDCRFP confirms that Nelli's heart continues to pound beneath the white sheet which keeps her almost warm.

The Mising are pleased.

They drink more rice toddy.

They eat more pig meat.

The new born Mising girl child is pleased.

She gurgles.

Dance some more.

More jebono bhalo re!

Life is good in the island of Majuli…

Or, is it?

The Guru has taken Herr Hans Bauer through the undercurrents of the Brahmaputra. When a motorboat fuelled with kerosene docks at Kamalabari, it brings along with it livestock and cooking salt for the customer. Amrit Kumar has accustomed the customer to the exotic island with Nelli's lure. But Nelli cannot be made to perform overtime. She is an exotic catch meant for celebration of victory in politics and trade. She is the queen of Kithapur, the girl who skipped through the paddy fields looking royal in a multi-hued Lantana crown. The Mentor will appease small political victories with fresh local flesh. Every new born Mising girl must preserve her flesh for Amrit's thriving trade.

Is Amrit still trading?

The answer is encoded in the Divine Beep.

How cheap!

The Mentor Amrit is a wandering creep.

Or, has he been captured?

Don't know.

Weiss nicht.

Theriyadhu.

Gothilla.

Gowravva does not know about Nelli's trade. Well, not quite yet.

***

All recruits to MDCRFP are not quite consistent.

'Consistency,' says the Guru, 'is the mark of a mediocre mind.'

There are no mediocre recruits to MDCRFP.

So, stay calm.

I am calm. I miss the Man in a Blue Kurta. But it does not imply that I cannot stay calm. Calmly, I talk to his baby about distant shores and my plans for her future. While my baby sleeps, I notice a storm rising over distant waters. The Guru insists we remain calm in the face of turbulence. It is the only way to get to the heart of missions which celebrate the Feminine Force. Such is the power to love sans the hope of reunion.

Hope is a carrot which dangles at the edge of every mission waiting to be accomplished.

Susanthi Bodra has never seen a carrot. Carrots do not grow in her backyard. Nor in Domrudoru Baiga's. The child takes over the woman, and Susanthi speaks. She tells the YUPAP volunteers that she must return to Bochagora.

At once!

Ami akhon ghoro jete chai.

I want to go home now.

Susanthi repeats her request.

The YUPAP volunteers are speechless.

Susanthi continues to speak.

Ami akhon ghoro jete chai.

The YUPAP volunteers cannot accede to her request.

At least, not right now.

There are prospective entrepreneurs waiting to be trained at the Sambhalpur Rozgaar Kendra. They are all under fourteen years of age, waiting to learn the art and science of rearing ducks from Susanthi Bodra. How can they displease so many children?

Isn't Susanthi a child?

Not anymore, they think.

Oh no! But she is. She is not quite thirteen years old.

They plead with her to complete her task.

Susanthi Bodra repeats:

Ami akhon ghoro jete chai.

She cannot tell the YUPAP volunteers why.

Not quite yet.

The YUPAP volunteers choose to buy time.

They insist on taking Susanthi to Maa Taarini Dhaba—they have just passed the eatery on the Balangir-Sambhalpur Highway. They can all have a meal there before they proceed.

The direction of their travel will be determined after the child's stomach is pleased.

Susanthi is not a child. She has stayed hungry for three days in a row when her father was considered dead.

But, Susanthi is a child. She must return home to Bochagora to her dearest Domrudoru at once.

She repeats firmly.

Ami akhon ghoro jete chai.

I want to go home now.

***

Home is an attachment. It lures even those who have broken ties with it.

Asha Paharia cries for the ties which lure her from here and there, from everywhere. Ties are crying for her in the air. She has heard from a fellow recruit that her grandmother is coughing blood. Her own blood boils, her forehead goes cold. Asha has made a vow never to return home to Thimri by daylight. It is the vow of the volunteers for self-enhancement, minus the intervention of the law-keepers. After all, the law-keepers have not always gone by the measure of equal punishment to all perpetrators of a proven crime irrespective of their caste, religion, profession and social status.

Will the Minister of Accounting Affairs get away from punishment if MDCRFP's recruits gather ample evidence in his disfavour?

Inspector General Tuffwinder Singh Bawa knows a thing or two about equality. He has never given or taken a bribe. Not even an emotional bribe. 'So, if you are on the wrong side of the law, just watch it. Tuffwinder Singh Bawa will get you.' That's exactly what Ashok Riflewala tells all the law abusers who are being interrogated by the prime recruits to MDCRFP.

Prasad Bharathi has no idea about the interrogation. The modus operandi of the Swami and his Eclectic Disciples is visible to Inspector General Bawa, but invisible to the Uncrowned Head. Swami Prem Anand does not believe in causing alarm, especially when the time is not yet ripe for the bells to go berserk.

When there are no alarm bells, the guilty continue to err.

The Force and the Eclectic Disciples continue to gather evidence, live and clear for all to see and hear.

The Uncrowned Head finds solace in the leader of the Disciples. Swami Vishnu Prem Anand lends a patient ear to all the erring committed day in and night out by the Prime Minister of the country.

To err is distinctly human.

Oh!

Who said the Uncrowned Head is human? The Uncrowned Head is the key abettor of the Form of Consent. Prime Minister Prasad Bharathi is no human, he is a fiend.

Swami Vishnu Prem Anand expresses dissent, but prescribes penance to Prasad Bharathi.

Prasad Bharathi expresses dread. And in penance, agrees to serve Swami Prem Anand blindly.

To serve is an awkward task for the supreme head of the nation. But penance is inevitable given Prasad Bharathi's nefarious record.

Mysterious are the ways of Swami Prem Anand, he makes evitable punishment inevitable.

The Cabinet is in the belly of the mystery. The Eclectic Disciples will take the ministers of the Cabinet on a mysterious mind tour. It is essential to hypnotise these ministers and trap them—they tamper with the daily lives of the underbelly of society. The ministers have no idea about their 'not-so-in-the-face' predicament.

The Cabinet of ministers faces a predicament. In the Stately Auditorium at the Maha Mantri Bhavan, the hypnotised ministers continue to lie on their bellies and kiss the floor upon which the Swami walks, his pedicured feet for all to touch and smell. When the divine Swami walks past their noses, and onwards to his throne in the Stately Auditorium, the ministers sit in a special yogic pose of poise and fasten thick strips of black cloth unto each other's eyes. They make signs at each other, until they ensure that nothing is visible to no one. The ministers of the Cabinet have all been instructed to blindfold each other. Blindfolded obeisance to Swami Vishnu Prem Anand will apparently fetch these ministers of the Cabinet the highest degree of punya—easy goodwill for their incredibly bad deeds.

Who said so?

The two Eclectic Disciples of course! Dressed in white, they are all over the place, even in dark impenetrable corners—they are Swami Prem Anand's most agile shishyas, all right!

Back in his office, a Divine Beep stirs Inspector General Bawa. The Centre is blind to punya, he learns. Good karma plays hide and seek with the ministers of the Cabinet. The other members of the force of Eclectic Disciples are positioned for the game. What a 'divine punya alluring' game this! Inspector General Tuffwinder Singh Bawa is pleased. Very pleased.

Prasad Bharathi is touched by the intense divinity and game-playing ability of Swami Prem Anand and his incredible Eclectic Disciples—they, all ten of them, are always on their 'never-say-stop' toes.

'Ahem!' says Inspector General Bawa, his iPhone 6 plus rings the Divine Beep. Evidently, the Centre is full of believers. Inspector General Bawa is doubly pleased.

***

Domrudoru Baiga is not pleased. Susanthi Bodra will not return to Bochagora soon. The Panchayat Mukhiya has told him so.

What does the Panchayat Mukhiya know of Susanthi's prevailing desire?

The now perturbed YUPAP volunteers are trying their best to divert the near thirteen-year-old child's yearning to return home. Susanthi is fast losing the will to convince her foster parents to take her home.

What do the YUPAP volunteers know about parenting a girl child who has just stared into the sparkling eyes of the same father she thought was dead?

Nothing!

Susanthi Bodra knows her instinct. Instinct tells her to find her own way home, as she often has from the wet paddy fields into which her ducks have waddled playfully every evening, after sunset.

The breadwinners of Keonjhar are alert, especially after sunset.

Nominta Debury opens her eyes wide after sunset. She has been too afraid to widen her glance until her emotions can be safely hidden in the crevice of her open eye, invisible in the darkening night. Her eyes are burning red with the fire to retrace the path she has carefully observed. She is burning with fever, the temperature rising from the shock of meeting the 'manimal' Kalarpatra Bagha's form. She has often seen the shadow of this Kalarpatra Bagha in the backyard of her hutment in Manipura. The human form all painted in leopard spots, counterpart to the same shadow, has now abducted her. No shock can win against the fire raging in the heart of a future breadwinner from Keonjhar's own hamlet. As Nominta's face dangles downwards—her waist held in the tight clasp of a man who knows the art of being a gentle father to a girl, she drops pieces of her broken orange bangle to remember the path.

Little girls like Nominta Debury do not leave chance of survival to destiny, they mark their own paths, and live by the law of the jungle.

Major Ashok Riflewala does not leave the safety of girls to destiny. He punches a message with renewed force. Inspector General Bawa receives a Divine Beep. He is aware that lost girls are preparing to retrace their paths, fearless in the fellowship of the jungle.

In the jungles adjoining the mountain ranges of Kanjipani and Dalma, the fellowship between its inhabitants is committed to survival. Humans and animals live to let live. They live by the law of nature. They do not step on each other's skin and kin.

In the Southern Capital with a Sea, humans are not accustomed to the ways of the jungle. How can they be? There is nothing natural about this Capital, or any other metropolitan city for that evitable matter. Given the brick, stone and mobile phone, silent communication remains a secret code between the humans and animals of the jungles. And the jungles alone.

***

Sridhar Haider D'Vaz and I share a secret code. The message in the code gives me a pertinent clue about the man I love. I find his likeness in his baby. She finds a likeness in me. We are similar. We both don't relish food—his baby and I, we both live on love and fresh air.

Love has a way of travelling realms that are supposedly out of reach and surprisingly within reach.

Zeta Rani is travelling to Bhubaneswar. So are we—D'Vaz, the Guru, his baby and I. There is love in the Art College by Dhauli, and fresh air to surround it. This air rendered fresh by the spirit of Samrat Ashoka, who almost twenty centuries ago, chose to denounce bloody war for the love of humans and animals, and for the sake of peace.

Peace is a word unique to those who have learnt to denounce footwear.

Swami Vishnu Prem Anand sits bare pedicured feet upon the mighty red throne in the Stately Auditorium of the Maha Mantri Bhavan. His feet breathe, he takes a sip of Mahua from the kamandal in his right hand, if you please. The Swami feels a deep sense of peace. In the thick of MDCRFP, Swami Prem Anand takes a secret vow. He will give up footwear even where there are no almost blood-red carpets to slow walk upon.

His Eclectic Disciples hover around—they engage in dialogue with the Swami in telepathic mode.

Point made.

For now, let us not deviate from MDCRFP please.

Point noted.

Swami Vishnu Prem Anand is alert to the blindness in the Stately Auditorium. He secretly wonders why the ministers need the façade of the black blindfold when they cannot see what they need to see anyway. These ministers with façades neither see the plight of near-thirteen-year-old girls striving to earn while they learn, nor hear the cries of their mothers struggling to make ends meet to give their children food, water and basic clothing.

Façades tend to discreetly uncover the explicitly stated, yet not-so-in-the-face missions. All right, let us focus on MDCRFP please.

Agreed.

The peace-intoxicated Swami Prem Anand remembers why the ministers of the Cabinet have been blindfolded. These blindfolds are imperative in the face of the complex MDCRFP. These hypnotised ministers will blindly lead the force of Eclectic Disciples, the Swami included, to the evidence which binds them to the crime. It is the crime of hogging the lands of the tribes. It is the crime of trading money for weapons from the East and the West, the North and the South of the nation, and mesmerising young girls to shoot peacocks and other birds, reptiles, mammals and animals in their new-found role as Maoxals. It is the crime of snatching virginity from girls who have life encumbrances, especially when they are not willing to give it all up to men they do not care about.

Inspector General Tuffwinder Singh Bawa has carefully drawn up the statement of MDCRFP based on this blind abuse of other peoples' bodies, namely feminine freedom in a 'democratic for over half a century'land.

Democracy is dead.
The Minister of Accounting Affairs thinks he is a king.
The Lesser Known Goddess is his dread.
Resurrect the dead.
Bring back democracy.
Down. Down. Kandiri Mandiri.
Up. Up. MDCRFP.

The Southern Capital with a Sea simmers with renewed Feminine Force. Minnal and her entourage in the Big Punctured Police Bus cannot be blown by a whimsical passing wind. Only the starched white veshti of Thiru Venkataraman cares to heed the whims of passing winds.

The winds of democratic change are blowing in the Southern Capital with a Sea. Thanks to the perpetually rejuvenated Feminine Force trapped in the Big Punctured Police Bus.

The Special Force headed by the Guru is all over the place—the winds whisper so.

Thanks to the Guru, the winds blowing over the Great Arabian Ocean carry a song which he often sang to bring relief from foreign bodies that pervaded his being, shaking the chemical balance within. I need balance—these lyrics of change tell me to hold on to the message in the wind. Change is about listening to your heart. My heart has another heart to meet. I have places to go, and attitudes to change.

Herr Hans Bauer has places to go. The first stop is by the Southern Capital with a Sea. Herr Bauer has a heart, it pounds fast. He is about to meet his mother. How does she look? He remembers her slender and tall frame. He yearns for her strong shoulders which carried firewood on one, and a boy child on the other, with ease.

Also, when Herr Bauer last saw his mother, she had teeth—all thirty-two of them, shining like the freshly installed tubelight at the head of their hamlet's lone main street.

Inspector General Tuffwinder Singh Bawa hears a Divine Beep. It is from a Source external to the Forces acting everywhere. This Source is a supernatural recruit, secret to the Force, planted by Inspector General Bawa in consultation with his well-tempered instinct.

The supernatural Source propounds that there is scope for human error, thanks to wavering emotions.

When humans err, hear the Guru stir.

Under no circumstances can MDCRFP deviate from success.

Recognisable success is imperative to MDCRFP if Indian democracy is to earn a good name.

Success is a relative term. Zeta Rani cannot be bothered by the gravitas of the mere seven letter word. She prefers to go by the time-tested approach of holistic intervention. The gravitas of this approach is far reaching. It reaches your still centre. It determines the rest of your life, right from the time you choose to walk away from your strife and put yourself into the eye of democracy.

***

Strife is just another six-letter word.

Access the Feminine Force to sock strife in the head.

Ask Gowravva how she wields her mental strength to harness her physical might.

Watch the brave mother from Kithapur hamlet, Gulbarga District, Karnataka State, break the iron bars of the Big Punctured Police Bus.

Minnal's entourage pioneered by Gowravva pours out of the Big Punctured Police Bus, leaving the iron door with steel bars agape.

The khaki-clad law-enforcers find stars in front of their jaded eyes—they just stand and gape at their mode of transport—they don't dare call the Big Police Bus, albeit punctured, theirs anymore.

Really!

This is no time to just stand and gape.

Action!

There is commotion in the Southern Capital with a Sea all over again.

Inspector General Bawa receives a Divine Beep again. He is extremely pleased with the message in this pandemonium-laced beep.

Pandemonium is an essential precursor to well-earned peace.

Stop, the end is not here—there is a lot to be witnessed between the precursor and the outcome.

Inspector General Bawa will continue to mastermind the outcome with his solitary weapon the iPhone 6 plus from the secrecy of his plush hideout equipped with high end computers, drone cameras, also a helipad if you please. The Guru will appear in the plush hideout every now and then. He will continue to operate discreetly, just the way he has acted so far.

There are discreet representatives of the Force acting for democracy in various pockets of the country.

Naren Nayak cannot be discreet about his altered level of consciousness any longer. He is no conscious stage actor. He acts for one cause, and that alone. Naren will ride on any train, sleep on any railway platform, and give up his aloo, daal, bhath and the occasional maach even when his stomach is feeling abandoned. He will stay for days, nights away from his beloved ardhangini Parbothi, and feign a swoon in his single-minded pursuit to ensure that the tribes of Keonjhar are not treated with contempt by blindfolded ministers and their ilk.

Naren will not take contempt against his tribes sitting down.

Naren sits up. There's panic in the hearts of the khaki-clad force which carries him. The stretcher of interlocked human hands disintegrates amidst 'ahhs' and 'hoos' from the female and male khaki-clad law-enforcers, respectively. This disintegration results in a thud. Naren has 'thud' landed on the tarred road, just outside the Central Railway Station in the Southern Capital with a Sea. No matter in which corner or centre of the Indian subcontinent he has landed, Naren is capable of extraordinary strength when the safety of a girl child from Manipura is at stake. Strength is on Naren's side—out of the blue, in broad dazzling daylight, he gains the prowess of his jungle's own Kalarpatra Bagha, leaps out of the circle of abashed khaki-clad law-enforcers, and disappears from their combined vision within the fraction of a second.

How did he do it?

Even Naren Nayak does not know. Extraordinary strength is a natural phenomenon, which accompanies those who do not care about spending days and nights without a bath on Platform No. 1 at the Central Railway Station.

***

It is natural for people who choose to kick strife in the butt to create a phenomenon. When the phenomenon is natural, the result inspires unnatural awe. The awestruck khaki-clad law-enforcers in the Southern Capital with a Sea are pell-mell.

Warum?

Yaake?

Yedhukku?

Kyun?

Keno?

Why? Why? Why...

Why on earth are the khaki-clad law-enforcers in the Southern Capital with a Sea running helter-skelter?

There is uprising everywhere. The perpetrators in the eyes of law are armed with the might of the Feminine Force. This weapon is intangible. It is unsurpassable in contrast with its tangible, hurtful, volatile, injury-generating counterparts—the lathi and the gun.

The Lesser Known Goddess and her entourage harness this weapon from within their own bodies and minds. Naren Nayak harnesses the power of the Feminine Force from the women he worships, their energies spanning diverse worlds from the omnipresent Maa Taarini to the absent Nominta Debury, the ever-present Parbothi, and other wives, mothers and girl children of the tribes of Keonjhar.

When I met Naren for the first time, he worshipped me too. Naren thinks no end of women. He is on the verge of meeting more. They are all mothers who scale miles, walking barefoot on roads and railway tracks, travelling outside the boundaries of their hamlets almost empty handed. They tread paths they were not told about during their growing years, break iron doors and shout slogans to counter the might of the irate Minister Venkataraman. They neither care about the Minister's lathi sporting people in khaki, nor his rifled bodyguards.

The retaliators—Venkataraman, khaki-clad law-enforcers et al, are together intimidated by the Feminine Force expanding beyond the boundaries of the Big Police Bus, exploding into the streets of the Southern Capital, their preposterous act of bravery for the sake of democracy, influencing the entire country which is watching them on news channels. The law-enforcers will not charge nor shoot this provoked mother's brigade.

Yet another Divine Beep applauds the prowess of this mothers' brigade. The early to bed and earlier to rise Inspector General Bawa abandons sleep over this Beep. He readies to accompany the prime recruits of MDCRFP from the discomfort of his not-so-plush chair. Inspector General Bawa is uncomfortable sitting down, even on plush chairs. He prefers to march—left, right, left right.

Read on, but stand at ease.

What is left on the right side of the masterplan?

To go for the kill minus the bloodshed, please.

Can bloodshed be avoided? Major Ashok Riflewala avoids bloodshed, but fires clean shots. When Major Riflewala shoots, the target can rest assured that the peg will touch the skin.

Ouch!

How is Asha Paharia to know of Major Riflewala's prowess with the gun? She does not even know that he lurks near her new-found lair. All Asha knows, is that she cannot meet her blood-spitting grandmother anytime soon. Or, can she?

***

Susanthi Bodra can do either of two things—listen to her foster parents or flee homewards to Bochagora. The adult in this child of near thirteen chooses to finish her meal of aloo, daal and bhath at the Maa Taarini Dhaba, first. Susanthi watches as the YUPAP volunteers finish their plates of bhath with daal and aloo. She repeats what she has said in the first place.

'Ami akhon ghore jete chai.'

'Na. Tumi Sambhalpuro Rozgaar Kendro jabe!'

No, say the YUPAP volunteers, Susanthi must go to the Sambhalpur Rozgaar Kendra.

'Naaa. Ami akhon ghore jete chai.'

'No. I want to go home now,' screams Susanthi.

Her foster parents have, until now, not heard the soft Susanthi Bodra speak louder than a whispering cricket, her controlled voice audible only in the still of the night. They are taken aback by the loudness—the YUPAP volunteers stop talking to Susanthi. They switch volume, and control their conversation to whispers, talking among themselves. They cannot outshout their foster child. It goes against the norms of selfless development work. They cannot return in their closed jeep to Bochagora without first completing the training at the Sambhalpur Rozgaar Kendra, they need to record progress to present to the donor agencies that support their NGO. They are helpless.

Helplessness is the precursor to untempered emotion.

Tempers rise, Susanthi and her foster parents, all turn red—there's synergy in diverging opinions.

The red on their faces—visible anger to the eye.

The controlled volume of their firm whispers—invisible anger to the ear.

Visibly, Susanthi quickly goes out of control. She moves her right leg forward, her left hand follows suit. Streamlined in the direction of the wind, Susanthi sprints, and almost immediately resembles a pink dot on the Sambhalpur

Highway. The YUPAP volunteers stop whispering, and gape after the vanishing spot of pink.

The YUPAP volunteers.

They blink.

They think.

For five whole minutes.

Then, they quickly leap into their closed jeep.

They should have leapt before they put their thinking caps on.

Alas! The girl is gone.

All right! Move on.

The driver revs the engine.

The spot of pink becomes invisible to the eye

In the fading evening sky.

The YUPAP volunteers sigh.

They die…

A million deaths

As fear gets the better of them.

They cannot afford to lose a girl child of the Munda tribe.

No, not so early in their YUPAP development careers!

They begin to pray, loud and clear for Maa Taarini to hear. The engine sputters to life. They drive in the direction of the vanished pink spot. This pink is from the frock which Susanthi wore on her journey to the Sambhalpur Rozgaar Kendra. This pink frock is among her favourite clothes to be worn outside the boundaries of Bochagora. The orange frock, which is her second favourite, neatly folded and kept in her cloth-bag, is driving along the Sambhalpur Highway with her stunned foster parents.

Susanthi is focussed on the Highway, until she arrives at the clearing by which grows the Lantana shrub bursting with purple flowers. She knows the way home from this clearing. Many moons ago, before Susanthi's father died, he brought his little pori—angel dressed in pink along this forest path, and showed her the maze of lights from small, medium and big motor vehicles disappearing into the night on the Sambhalpuro Highway. Susanthi has a vivid memory of the forest path her father brought her on. She still remembers the twists and turns, and also the lair where the coal fire burns along the jungle path to Bochagora.

Jhumur Jhumur
Jhumur Jhumur
Kothai jabo re?
Sambhalpuro?
Na.
Bochagoro jabo re.

Susanthi Bodra will go home to Bochagora—the near thirteen-year-old child has made up her mind.

***

It is pointless to pretend that Sridhar Haider D'Vaz has a home. He lives out of a suitcase. To every place he travels, he carries a refilled suitcase with freshly laundered suits. He carefully choses them from a cupboard where they are hung and stacked according to label and shade, back home in his colonial bungalow.

D'Vaz is a man of many bungalows. But these houses are just for the records. His real bungalows are the airports. Today, D'Vaz's bungalow is the Bhubaneswar Airport. He checks out and checks in to the upmarket cab service. He will be driven to the Art College by Dhauli by a uniformed chauffeur who steers Mercedes-class cabs—this service strictly exclusive to business-category travellers.

The Art College by Dhauli is ready to receive the much-travelled D'Vaz once more. He is travelling in the city of Bhubaneswar for two reasons, each interconnected to the other—to meet and set matters right for the tormented art student and, to make a round trip from the Keonjhar Highway to Sambhalpur, the Dalma Ranges in between, all the way out of the State of Orissa to Majuli in Assam, with a stopover at Nagaon, and back to his forever hometown, the city of Bangalore Blues. This is the outline of Zeta Rani's plan. I will accompany the duo with his baby in tow. I know the Guru is tagging along for reasons specific to the Form of Consent, and so is the man who occupies premium place in my heart.

The Guru is futuristic. A Divine Beep delivers the link to the masterplan. Inspector General Tuffwinder Singh Bawa is pleased with the recruits external to the internal Force.

The internal Force is in the loop.

What is the scoop?

There is a thin wire between life and death, confirms an internal member of the Force.

This wire connects the cylinder to the oxygen mask, elixir of breath.

We hope Nelli breathes.

Nelli is not dead.

No one is dead.

Or, so we think.

Lieutenant Colonel Hamid Iyer is in two places at once. He has one foot in Majuli by the hutments of the Mising virgins, and the other in Nagaon by Nelli's side, all thanks to the special chopper made available to him by Inspector General Bawa. He cannot give us hope, there is a thin wire in question. Lieutenant Iyer is a truthful recruit to the

Awakening Peacekeeping Mission, and its long purpose MDCRFP. He will not tell lies to hide the truth. He just will not tell out of turn.

So, wait.

Domrudoru Baiga has waited long enough for Susanthi Bodra. This long night is no time to expect young girls to scale the scary jungle path home to Bochagora. Who said the jungle is scary? Of course, it is. Susanthi is not certain that her hasty decision, born out of a stubborn desire to meet her dearest friend Domrudoru is the best way out of her inexplicable woe. The woe is explicable to Domrudoru alone—he stands by his friend Susanthi in the most troubled times. No one else can understand the travails of a near thirteen-year-old child who has lost her mother and found her dead father.

Please understand—Susanthi has spent the better part of her childhood losing and finding her parents.

***

Naren Nayak spends a great amount of time losing and finding his way on the confused streets of the Southern Capital with a Sea.

Who is confused?

Everybody!

Amma and Appa.

Mother and Father.

Paapa and Thatha.

Baby and Grandpa.

Also the khaki-clad law enforcers.

And, the sari-clad law detractors.

Everybody shouting slogans all over the streets of the Southern Capital with a Sea.

The slogans rise above the waves in the sea that lines the Southern Capital on one side.

Down. Down. Mandiri.

Hail Minnal, the Lesser Known Goddess on a mission to vanquish her own meandering, scoundrel son.

The Minister of Accounting Affairs will come undone.

The slogans rise above the waves.

Aandavan Kangal is livid.

Thiru Venkataraman is languid. Minnal will not berate her own son. Or, so he thinks.

Minnal thinks with her mind, loves with all her heart. When her eldest born emptied their neighbour's piggy bank and left its broken remains under the hamlet's oldest Mango tree, Minnal called the Panchayat representatives to deal her son a just punishment. The elders of the hamlet council in Mayavaram District, Tamil Nadu, let the boy scot free. What would he know, he was just a child, that too, a playful boy.

Playful indeed!

Displeased with the judgement, Minnal thought with her wise head, and took law in her stead. She watched her eldest born plough and weed the paddy field for an entire week, morning, afternoon and evening, into his playtime. In no time, he returned the money from the mud piggy bank to the boy he had stolen it from. In some time, he decided to leave the hamlet, which had caused him shame.

Is Minnal to blame?

Is Gowravva to blame?

Nelli has no time for this blame game.

She is overcome with feminine power. She derives this power from Gowravva, the mother who has no time for such pointless blame game.

This is certainly no time for guilt tripping. In fact, there is no reason for guilt. Minnal has only taught her son to give back what he takes. More so, what he takes unknown to the owner. Over the years, Venkataraman has taken a lot, that too by force—some known to the owner, others unknown. Not just money, but hearth and honey, too.

Honneyy

Darrlingg

Suweet chakkare kutti

Suweet sugar baby

Slurrrp!

Come to big daddy...

Burrrp!

The Minister of Accounting Affairs croons.

Come baby. Come now!

Yeeks!

Na!

Never again!

Nelli jumps out of her subconscious,

Shakes her faint head at the disgusting memory, and gives the oxygen mask the slip.

It is time for Nelli to embark on her trip.

Home beckons.

Homeward bound to Majuli.

Homeward inclined to Kithapur.

Home is where the heart belongs. Nelli's heart remembers the man whose name she does not know.

The iPhone 6 plus emanates another Divine Beep. Inspector General Bawa is happy to learn of Nelli's recovery. Lieutenant Colonel Hamid Iyer will continue to watch over Nelli, but from a distance.

Wide distance is essential to bridge narrow divides. I will walk the narrow, less-trodden path away from my life in the din of the big city for the man who takes pride in his much-darned blue kurta.

***

Parbothi walks the narrow path along the rain-drenched red soil of Manipura to the paddy fields yonder. Nominta Debury's mother watches the narrow path, her tears running in refrain with the pounding rain. Does Parbothi have word of her baby? Is the future breadwinner of her family alive?

Parbothi has heard from the breadwinner of her family. Naren Nayak is all out to bring Nominta back from the dead. That is, only if Nominta is dead.

Minister Venkataraman is sure to be dead.

The Feminine Force has taken the Southern Capital with a Sea by cyclone. There is a whirlwind of words stating the truth about the past and present, all of which is putting the Minister of Accounting Affairs to shame.

Shame shame Mandiri
Du bist eine kandiri.

Minister of Accounting Affairs! You are such a nasty guy.

No! Nominta will not sign the Form of Consent.

There is dissent at the Centre. In his blindfolded state, Prasad Bharathi learns of the furore in the Southern Capital with a Sea—Swami Prem Anand has deemed it pertinent to inform the Uncrowned Head, and win the former's trust completely.

'Why me?' screams Minister Venkataraman.

'Then who?' scream the mothers with renewed feminine power. 'You are so gross.'

Yes, that is what Minister Venkataraman is. He does not believe he is very gross, and also sly.

All this feminine rage must be a lie!

Aandavan Kangal, the all-observing Political Advisor asks Venkataraman to lie low. Another stone pelts the white Ambassador, the Government vehicle in which Venkataraman is driving home. Venkataraman's face is red from his white veshti-disgrace at the airport in the Southern Capital with a Sea.

Another stone misses Venkataraman's head.

There is dread.

The Southern Capital with a Sea is up in arms.

The khaki-clad law-enforcers are not certain whose side they must take.

Naren salutes the mothers who have given Feminine Power a grand name. He evokes the blessings of the omnipresent Maa Taarini.

Parbothi has word from her man, she is pleased.

Asha Paharia is displeased. Must she break all ties to keep the same ties alive?

Certainly not, feels Major Ashok Riflewala, intruding on her thoughts.

Rifle shots pierce the Dalma Forest air. The jungles come alive with the sound of confused birds. The birds have awoken from their mid-afternoon siesta. They hear Asha Paharia weep. She weeps for her grandmother, a firm Munda lady, who takes pride in being up and about. Her grandmother does not succumb to maintaining the pressures of the hearth. She prefers to go hungry than give up her identity as a farmer and resident of Thimri. She will neither migrate to the brick kiln in the big city, nor to the lair in the forest. She will stay in her own Munda home in the hamlet of Thimri, Rukdoo Block, State of Jharkhand, India. Asha has great admiration for her grandmother. She weeps some more.

Inspector General Bawa is deeply touched by the word weep in this Divine Beep.

***

Swami Vishnu Prem Anand is touched by the overt display of faith in the Stately Auditorium. There is something about its transient nature—faith moves each minister of the Cabinet by the measure of punya the divine Swami chooses to bestow upon him. It is imperative for the ministers to horde these blessings brimming with good karma to wipe out past sins and keep the repercussions of future sins at arms' length.

Swami Prem Anand lets out a karmic laugh. Even he knows that good karma cannot be transferred to a minister's being by the mere touch of his divine forefinger. This forefinger sports a ring with a miniature camera. But the cabinet is full of sinners. Sinners are fools. Swami Prem Anand cannot be fooled by sinners. Beneath his calm exterior, manifested at the centre of his forehead, he wears a razor sharp Third Eye. This eye-shaped remote-controlled spy camera has been sourced from Der Bundesrepublik Deutschland, especially for the sake of MDCRFP. From the corner of his Third Eye, the Swami spots one fool being, well, not so foolish. This prostrated minister of the Cabinet is trying to untie his black blindfold.

Does he have an ally?

Divine Beep. Mission alert. Inspector General Bawa sits up on his not-so-comfortable chair, and sends out the super alert message to all recruits internal and external to MDCRFP.

Watch it!

When Inspector General Bawa is alert, the Force dissolves into Swami Prem Anand's awakened Third Eye. His Eclectic Disciples fall into pairs, alert to the mechanically orchestrated blink of the awakened Third Eye. Three Eclectic Disciples clad in saffron dhotis take an integrated call when the divine glance of the Third Eye signals them to disintegrate into the three corners of the Stately Auditorium, from where, 'not so foolish' ministers can well escape.

Swami Prem Anand is divinely pleased.

This Divine Beep gets Inspector General Tuffwinder Singh Bawa on his toes.

Do not dare to step on Major Ashok Riflewala's toes, they are supremely sensitive to touch, especially feminine.

Asha Paharia sneaks out of her lair, and steps on something soft in the dark of the night. As a matter of upbringing, girls who grow into women in the hutments of the Dalma Ranges, do not scream when they step on something soft in the dark. Of course, Asha does not scream. She simply steps back and concentrates with her trained eye to seek out faces, features, even fingers and toes by the meagre light of the distant and sparkling stars. The spotlight brings Asha's gaze to focus on a man's bare feet.

Ouch!

Chamakthe tare!

Sparkling stars!

She has stepped on a man's toes!

Maoxal Recruit Asha Paharia has stepped on Major Ashok Riflewala's toes!

She looks beyond his toes.

The limbs of the man, master of the stepped upon toes, steadily sway to the rhythm of a snore.

Major Riflewala snores.

Jai Maa Taarini.

Thank Asha's sparkling stars.

But this is no matter to be thankful about. Asha is not within the boundaries of law. Major Riflewala minds the boundaries of law. In any case, he cannot sleep, especially under the distinct light of sparkling stars. Certainly not when he is on MDCRFP!

Divine Beep!

Cut the rhythmic snore.

Wake up.

Alert.

Stand up.

Stand at ease.

Stand in attention.

Major Riflewala has read Inspector General Bawa's new message, he regains attention. He looks for detail under the distinct light of distant sparkling stars. He needs to give Inspector General Bawa an informed update. All he has is a soothing recollection of a woman's soft foot treading upon his naked toes.

Divine!

Hang on! Was it just a dream?

This is no time to sleep. Remain alert.

I have received an SMS, I am alert tonight. His baby lies on my lap, and I recall our recent journey. The train sped through territories I might have never seen by daylight. Outside the window, and in the skies, the light from the distant sparkling stars brought me back to memories of the Man in a Blue Kurta.

Under the stars, one night, over two years ago, he held me close to his bare chest. I melted into his lingering embrace, and rode on sparkling stars in the distant skies. Months later, his baby came. She has a place in the firmament. Tonight, the stars have signed up to take her places—she will travel over the oceans, and across distant skies.

***

Nelli has signed up to give feminine power a good name. She will name the Mising virgins who are on Mentor Amrit Kumar's list one by one to save them from forced copulation with unknown men who call themselves ministers. But first, they must return to Majuli. Lieutenant Colonel Hamid Iyer agrees to take National Highway 37 from Nagaon into its winding offshoot—a stony path, to the docking point in Jorhat.

When stony roads lead into the deep waters of the life-giver River Brahmaputra, the homeward bound experience an inexplicable sense of peace.

Headed home, Nelli is feeling peaceful on the roof of the motorboat, which, as per the masterplan, chugs in well-practised, respectable momentum like a committed soldier on a peacekeeping mission towards Kamalabari. Lieutenant Iyer observes Nelli, he types out a message on his BlackBerry.

This new Divine Beep tells Inspector General Bawa that all is going as per plan. It is in effect, a masterplan. Thanks to the Guru who guides him in omnipresent ways.

Why is the Guru omnipresent?

Why is Maa Taarini omnipresent? Will she help the 'readily present wherever required' Naren Nayak in the Southern Capital with a Sea? Will she help Nominta Debury out of her quandary?

Nominta is not certain whether she must stay. Or, must she flee. For now, she cannot flee—Nominta lies still on the forest land drenched with dew. Her presence is a mystery to the dark Dalma night. In the dark of the forest, the tall, thin man, with sparkling eyes and a sharp nose, keeps the night patrol. He waits in watch as Nominta feigns shut eye, and Asha Paharia arrives to take control.

Nominta Debury is a new Maoxal recruit who will share the lair with Asha.

What? Most certainly not!

Major Ashok Riflewala has made up his mind. He is on watch near Asha's lair. He is waiting for a tiny loophole to surface in Nominta's abduction plan. And then, he will call the shots. He will resolve the crime and earn his place as a commendable officer, his accomplishment written in indelible ink and placed on Inspector General Bawa's table of most appreciated records.

For the record, this Divine Beep indicates that Nominta will return home—a little girl untouched by neither khaki-clad law enforcers nor khaki-clad law breakers. Major Riflewala must make peace with his own 'khakiness'—the rules the uniform subjects him to, are too extreme, and are bound to bring him to messy situations he does not want to be seen in.

Inspector General Bawa texts his reply to Major Riflewala on the iPhone 6 plus.

Major Riflewala receives the text message on his BlackBerry. It indicates that he might be suspended if he does not concentrate on the task at hand. The text slices the silence of the Dalma night. The message is loud. Everybody hears the Divine Beep—Nominta, Asha—even the tall, thin man with sparkling eyes and a sharp nose. Simply Hare Rama's composition of the high-profile Divine Beep is indeed alluring, everybody looks at everyone else. Except, they cannot see Major Riflewala—he is supposedly hanging out behind a tree with BlackBerry in his right hand and .22 'bang on target' rifle in the left.

Asha's heart misses a beat. She has not just seen him, but has also stepped upon his bare toes.

Of all the woes that can hinder MDCRFP
Love blossoms
Between two khaki-clad people.
One a law-enforcer
The other, a law-breaker.

The law-enforcer cannot seem to keep his emotions in check.

The law-breaker puts her pounding heart back in its place
And continues to go about her business.
She cannot be bothered by love.
No, not when she is the lone breadwinner.
And certainly not at this time of the night!
Asha Paharia has not signed up for love.
But she chooses to keep silent about her heart's discovery.

.22 in left hand, Major Riflewala is still hiding behind Dalma's much-matured Sal tree.

Phew! Major Riflewala will live to conclude MDCRFP! All thanks to Asha, the woman who has chosen to freeze the disease called love in her heart. Her mother, father, brothers and her beloved grandmother must all live—she must maintain her single status for the sake of their daal and bhath.

She must live well.

Asha's eyes well. Breadwinners who have chosen to work in the darkness of the Dalma Ranges cannot afford to spill tears, especially for family. They have all broken family ties to keep their kith and kiln alive, and their chulhas burning. They can only send them money, not love. And certainly, no tears.

No love?

Then die single!

Why is Nominta earning for her family when all they want to do is starve until they die because she has gone missing?

Ask the tall, thin man with sparkling eyes and a sharp nose—he moves from one lair to another in the thick of this forest cover. He, a replica of his animal counterpart, the Kalarpatra Bagha, brings young breadwinners under the regime of the Maoxal Society, home to one lair or the other.

Nominta recognises the Maoxal Society by the ability of its recruits to sever all ties with their respective families. She will not sever ties in the name of the gun. She is a child. The woman in her has only just begun to rise above her childish fear of the big world beyond Manipura.

Nothing can stop a child from returning home to her mother.

Nominta Debury will trace her way back home.

The time is almost ripe to leave this cold lair.

***

The time is here for Sridhar Haider D'Vaz to lead Thiru Venkataraman's artistic son towards freedom of speech and unrestrained expressions in watercolour, no matter which minister or khaki-clad force makes a hue and cry about his work.

The time is here for Zeta Rani to lead D'Vaz and me to the breadwinners of Keonjhar.

The time is here for me to meet the Man in a Blue Kurta.

Am I ready for the meeting?

Is Nelli ready to take on Amrit Kumar?

Amrit, who ensured that Nelli ate daal and bhath, also the weekly ration of deep-fried rohu flavoured with mustard and cooked with ridge gourd along with the world's hottest chilli, bhut jholokia. Amrit, who made her forget the taste of bakri and shenga chutney fresh from the groundnut fields of Kithapur.

Nelli has neither forgotten the pungent taste of shenga chutney nor crisp bakri, nor the spicy menshinkais of home. Neither has Nelli forgotten the woman who made a feast out of the lowest variety of jowar and groundnut to make her daughter feel like a princess. She, the princess who ran amok in the paddy fields of Kithapur. Nelli, the princess who showed-off her royal upbringing, scented with the feminine power of her tri-hued crown of freshly-harvested Lantana flowers.

This princess with a Lantana-flowered crown is now a queen. She bears resemblance to Kittur Rani Chennavva, the sword-weaning queen her mother Gowravva spoke proudly of summer night after monsoon night, even as she patted her first-born Nelli to sleep.

What happens when Queen Gowravva weans her sword?

Mentor Amrit Kumar is dead.

Stab!

No, not in flesh and blood—Amrit's body is warm.

His heart still beats inside his chest.

Lieutenant Colonel Hamid Iyer has put Amrit to test in the makeshift questioning chamber by the heaving waters of the motorboat-burdened Brahmaputra. Nelli has called Amrit a spade. He must now face the Panchayat of virgins from the Mising Feminine Force.

Will Amrit be slain?

God save Amrit. No, Lieutenant Iyer will. The Force will. According to Inspector General Bawa, death is an easy punishment.

So, no death by the Force please!

Minnal will not kill.

No, not even an ee!

'Thiru Venkataraman cannot harm an ee,' gloats Minnal, over and again, her voice loud and clear for all to hear.

Her entourage shouts along:

'Kandiri Mandiri,' loud and clear for all to hear, over and again.

'Baaro Manthri! Nanna magalannu haalumadida kolaku kanthri!'

Come here, you Minister. You dirty coward who ruined my daughter, booms Gowravva's voice in her native tongue, her curse rising above the rest. Minnal gloats some more about the vital ee. The Minister of Accounting Affairs is but a fly. He is sitting on a wall far away, and is rather high on imported Scotch whisky. The Feminine Force cannot be refrained, that too from stifling an ee!

This ee, the Minister of Accounting Affairs.

The ee, a fly sitting on high!

'Let him be! Ellarum yen purushana vudungo,' booms Venkataraman's wife—her husband is still perched on a high wall. They call this perch the prime balcony of Venkataraman's stately ancestral house. Aandavan Kangal has somehow managed to keep the pelted stones away from the Minister's head. He has even managed to bring him home from the airport to his master bed. Then, the mistress takes over. She yells once more: 'Let him be! Ellarum vudungo. What harm has the honourable Thiru Venkataraman done to all you respectable women—mothers, sisters et al?'

Et al, that's right!

He just has to get up to fight
If he thinks that he, indeed, is right.
But he is curled up in fright
Holding his pounding head
Lying mind boggled on his master bed

While his mistress Mrs Komalavalli Thiru Venkataraman takes on the Feminine Force.

The women in this Feminine Force they call 'et al', simply because the Minister of Accounting Affairs has emotionally screwed them all!

Really?

How?

Ask the mother, she will tell you how. But, only when the scooting minister shows his shamed face. Minnal knows only too well that her eldest born is a shocking disgrace.

What could her eldest born do? He did not have the Guru to guide him back to sensible track. Thiru Venkataraman does not believe in gurus who guide. He believes in Prasad Bharathi instead.

Prasad Bharathi is a magnet—he attracts deviant men to flourish in sin. The man who sins without respect for the Feminine Force, simply flourishes more. But he still yearns for his mother's pardon—he sees her strong hands cutting raw mangoes, seasoning pieces of the fruit with salt and red chilli powder. He just will not tell how much he yearns.

Minnal knows when a son of hers yearns for her pardon. Her other son, Herr Hans Bauer, kann nicht warten. He cannot wait to meet his mother. The Guru has guided him back home. Herr Bauer wonders why he fled the hamlet at the behest of his elder brother in the first place.

It cannot be helped.

Sons leave.

Sons return.

What can be helped though,

Is how they return.

Do they return with gratitude for Minnal's selfless love?

Or, do they spit feminine power in the face?

Minister Thiru Venkataraman is certainly a disgrace. Even his lawful wife is threatening to leave him. The Minister has wind of his legal wife's intent. Alone, he lies mind and body boggled in their master bed, and begins to sob. Aandavan has been forced to tell the truth about Venkataraman to all and sundry, standing on balcony edge at the Minister's bungalow. The Minister's wife does not like the truth. She is no less than the Feminine Force raging outside. Will Mrs Komalavalli Thiru Venkataraman decide to walk over to the other side?

God save Thiru Venkataraman.

'Maa Taarini, tumi Mahashakti,' Naren Nayak screams and beams from ear to ear in praise of the omnipresent Goddess standing in the driveway on the other side of the balcony in the Minister's home. Outside, the Feminine Force is relentless. The defied mothers will not return without sentencing the Minister of Accounting Affairs to befitting punishment. He must be put behind the same iron door with steel bars that they were imprisoned in just a few hours ago.

No bars for the Feminine Force in the Southern Capital with a Sea. No, not anymore.

Inspector General Bawa has a message from a Source in the Southern Capital. He is pleased with the outcome of the melee. A Source is part of the melee. I have met this Source in Keonjhar.

***

All is disturbingly quiet in Keonjhar. Nominta Debury's mother continues to cry, but the tears do not spill, and her voice does not quiver. Parbothi's voice is soothing and has solace to offer, she knows her husband is a Source. But she wonders in silence about Nominta's foster parents—Urmila and Manohar Mahapatra. There is no word from them. Their Nokia 1100s, both basic mobile phone models, must be switched off, she thinks.

Kano?

Why?

Amidst the melee in the Southern Capital with a Sea, approximately 1,412 kilometres away on National Highway 5, south of Keonjhar, Naren has news of Urmila and Manohar. Their Nokia 1100s do not ring. They are in dire straits.

There is no reason to panic.

The Force is at work. Maa Taarini is omnipresent. The Guru is everywhere. Inspector General Bawa hears the Divine Beep in reverb. It is a message from the netherworld. Everybody—Major Ashok Riflewala and Lieutenant Colonel Hamid Iyer; the Top Notch

Crime Busters (TNCB) including Swami Prem Anand and his nine Eclectic Disciples; the recruits external to MDCRFP, including D'Vaz, Herr Bauer, Zeta and I, with the aid of Prime Source Naren Nayak and the Guru, keep masterplanner Inspector General Bawa more than much informed. We cannot hold back any information. We do not have a choice in the matter. We have signed the Document of Extreme Commitment to the Mission. We are committed to report to him at every turn.

In the Art College by Dhauli, our plans take a new turn. The breadwinners of Balangir and Keonjhar—Susanthi Bodra and Nominta Debury, are both missing. The artistic student facing the ire of the khaki-clad law-enforcers is also missing. I am not certain I will meet D'Vaz's personally-mentored protégé anytime soon—he is reclusive. I think of the man I love, he is also reclusive. I hold his baby tight. She is the lure of every eye in the Art College by Dhauli. I am proud of her, she looks beautiful in her new wraparound. I am her parent, I know which wraps become her lissome frame.

Zeta Rani has information about the missing foster parents, both last seen on the highway to Sambhalpur. The cloth folder with essential information on the cunningly devised Form of Consent is waiting to be read. D'Vaz, Zeta Rani and I pour over the twisted content. It leaves us spellbound—the Minister of Accounting Affairs certainly has a cunning flair for all things natural and feminine. Spellbound, we realise we are almost eye-to-eye with a 'not to be missed' milestone. We will proceed towards this milestone, shortly. D'Vaz calls for a closed jeep, a crude violation of the upmarket Mercedes Benz he is so naturally inclined to travel in. But the hairpin bends of the Kanjipani Mountains are better meandered along in the pleasurable discomfort of a closed jeep. The closed jeep is a highway tease. It can hug the curves and run friction-perfect on the straight tarred roads defining the meandering Keonjhar-Sambhalpur Highway, with equal ease.

Jhumur Jhumur
Jhumur Jhumur
Kothai jabo re?
Manipuro?
Sambhalpuro?
Thimri?
Bochagoro?
Dalma ma jabo re?

Where would you like to go? Manipura? Sambhalpur? Thimri? Bochagora? The Dalma Ranges?

Na. Ami ghore jabo re.

No, I want to go home.

Majuli jabo re?

Home, to Majuli?

Moro ghore Keonjhoro mein.

My home is in Keonjhar.

His baby wonders about her destination, sitting on my lap, soaking in the virgin air of the densely elephant-inhabited terrain of the Kanjipani Mountains.

Jhumur Jhumur
Jhumur Jhumur
Kothai jabo re?

'Bochogoro! Ami akhon ghoro jete chai,' cries the voice of a child, a girl, a young woman from somewhere in the belly of the Kanjipani Mountains. D'Vaz looks at Zeta. She looks at me. We all look at each other.

Together, we panic.

Together, we yell. Stop!

The driver decelerates the engine. The closed jeep squeals and halts abruptly as the driver jams the ageing vehicle's 'not so easy to jam' breaks. In the thick of the night, with meagre illumination from the distant starlight, we look around to see where our search has stopped us. The milestone reads Balangir District, 100 kilometres.

A milestone?

Yes.

Yes.

Yes.

We reiterate one after the other.

Is it in the cloth folder?

Yes.

Yes.

Yes.

We reiterate.

Does the voice belong to a little girl from Bochagora?

Yes.

The little girl who has not signed the Form of Consent yet?

Yes.

Zeta, D' Vaz and I together affirm.

Wandering alone in the deep of the night, the little girl affirms from somewhere in the jungle.

Aloud: Ami akhon ghoro jete chai.

Louder: Domrudoru, amar bondhu.

Louder than loudest: Ami akhon ghoro jete chai.

I want to go home now. Now. My friend Domrudoru. I want to go home now.

Susanthi sobs. The near thirteen-year-old child sobs.

Susanthi sobs just the way Nominta Debury does.

Nominta's foster parents feel they can hear her. Urmila and Manohar Mahapatra smile for the first time since they have been made prisoners in their own closed jeep. They continue to be prisoners. This night is quiet. Their foster child sobs in the jungle. The hathi moi lurks in the dark, just as elephant mothers do in these parts. The Kalarpatra Bagha makes stealthy strides. Still, they have hope. They have heard another closed jeep make its presence felt in the dark. They have heard it squeal to a halt somewhere behind their own closed jeep. They have heard people speak. They seem like people who are here on MDCRFP.

Inspector General Bawa hears a Divine Beep.

It is magical how when forces external to the mission are awakened, all roads lead to the reconstruction of Feminine Power.

Really?

Certainly! The man with the iPhone 6 plus says so.

***

'Surround!', the man with the iPhone 6 says with utmost clarity.

The Force hears Swami Vishnu Prem Anand speak although His Divinity has not visibly opened his prominent mouth. He does not need to. He speaks with his feet as a TNCB head rightfully should, he is a man of action. Swami Prem Anand has indicated with two taps of his pedicured feet that it is time to take the Cabinet of ministers and Prasad Bharathi on a tour of their own secret stack of bungled files.

The secret stack is 'officed' in the Grand Meeting Room adjoining the Stately Auditorium in Maha Mantri Bhavan. The secret stack is pregnant with papers that have details on land handovers, accompanied by thumb impressions and occasional signatures. Makandias, Juangs, Mundas,

Santals, Gonds, Kharias, Paharias and Oraons, who have sat for at least six months in a Government school, can certainly sign in their native tongue, and occasionally in English. But they certainly cannot read an entire document of 'unofficially constructed official' words in Hindi, or in English.

The stack also has copies of the unofficially constructed official Forms of Consent. Female breadwinners under the age of sixteen have signed this official document with the hope of earning decent money by choosing a 'respectably' feminine trade. They cannot read the contents of the trade. The details of the respectable trade are buried in a code.

The code is blemished. Swami Vishnu Prem Anand and his nine TNCB gems, yes, the Eclectic Disciples have all read between the lines.

What do they see?

Not what we have read?

Not what Nelli has read.

Not what Susanthi Bodra has read.

Certainly not what Nominta Debury has been able to read.

Inspector General Bawa reads the code in the latest Divine Beep. He reads it once again to determine its accuracy. It is incredible how the Minister of Accounting Affairs has used his 'overfilled with numbers' brain to write a 'wordy code'.

The wordy code
Is unworthy.
Down Kandiri
The disgusting Mandiri.
You took my child away to distant Majuli
Gave her hope that she will be the princess of her own empire

A small business, which will fetch her golden eggs

And fish that taste like rohu.

She will sell the eggs.

She will eat the fish.

She will kuni with glee in a mooru-bannada Lantana hoovu crown…

Ayyo! And dance with glee in a tri-coloured Lantana flower crown with an entourage of flying veshti followers!

Only, she did not know that these followers are a Cabinet of frustrated ministers and their Uncrowned Head.

Nelli certainly takes no pleasure in bedding Prasad Bharathi.

Sleeping with Thiru Venkataraman is worse.

It is gross.

Gowravva is grossed out by Thiru Venkataraman—he has escaped the action of the Eclectic Disciples at the Centre, simply because Prasad Bharathi has not wanted him around ever since he has been named the father of an artistic son. But he has certainly not escaped the combined chagrin of mothers who have lost their daughters to the Forms of Consent—armed with disgust, they are all assembled in the Southern Capital with a Sea.

Jai Maa Taarini.

Hail feminine power.

So omnipresent, so in the face.

Hail the Lesser Known Goddess.

She has the power to give her own erring son a thrashing for his flying veshti.

Hail Kittur Rani Chennavva.

Hail Gowravva!

***

Here comes Her Highness Nelli, she is hale and hearty.

Hail her fitness!

Out of the Government hospital and in Nagaon, Nelli's entourage follows her to the banks of the Brahmaputra, all the way to Kamalabari, Majuli's receiving point for strangers, departing point for friends. Lieutenant Colonel Hamid Iyer has caught up with Nelli, and briefed her about MDCRFP, and she has promised to accompany him to bring the Mission to fruitful conclusion. The Mising tribes, especially the virgins who will speak against the vile Mentor Amrit Kumar, are visibly upset that Nelli, their dear leader and fellow resident of Majuli, is departing. They are invisibly happy, because Nelli has in secret, promised to return. When you recognise your own, you certainly make it a point to return home.

The Mising trust their own. Nelli trusts the banks of the Brahmaputra like the backyard of her childhood home in Kithapur. Nelli is Majuli's own child blossomed into a ravishing woman. But she must first meet her mother to learn all about how Gowravva finds the strength to respect her daughter like a queen, especially after she has learnt of her disrespectable trade.

Today, Nelli feels like Kittur Rani Chennavva, the brave and respected queen of her childhood dreams. She even has a trusted friend, they call her the Mising Virgin, and she will accompany her to the Court of Justice at the Centre. There, Nelli will speak of how she did not sign the Form of Consent, after all. She had, however, at the age of eight, cast her thumb impression under the guidance of Amrit Kumar on a printed document. Amrit had claimed that she was now legally bound to serve him for the rest of her life.

Indeed!

Nelli has only just rediscovered life, Amrit can kindly swallow his document alongside his pride and greed.

But Nelli has other virgins to save from the likes of the Mentor.

At the Centre, the Mising Virgin accompanying Nelli will speak of how she did not sign the Form of Consent. Nelli has alerted this Virgin to the misguidance of Amrit, who had promised the innocent girl discreet guidance.

Lieutenant Colonel Hamid Iyer has made suitable arrangements to accompany the princess of Kithapur turned queen Nelli of Majuli on her important journey.

Herr Hans Bauer is ready for the 'maha' grand journey to the Southern Capital with a Sea. Loaded with every man, woman and child from the hamlet with the Vishnu Temple in Mayavaram District, the Big People Bus is brimming with pride on either side. Pride spills over from the top of the Big People Bus, all the way down to its front door. The proud people of Mayavaram's hamlet Poothotum hang on to each other from head to toe, back door to front door of the Big People Bus. The long line of people from Minnal's hamlet will all arrive at the Southern Capital with a Sea—some on bus seat, others on bus top. This bus is big enough, anyway.

Herr Bauer's big heart gloats with pride. He holds a proud garland of jasmine flowers which his sister, the lissome Jasmine Creeper, has specially flowered overnight to adorn the neck of her toothless mother.

Thandane thaane naane na
Ammachi veetukku vaa
Come home, dear mother
Namma oorikku tirumbi vaa
Come back home to our hamlet
Von ponnu, von Malli Chedi, vonakaaga kaathirrukira.
Your daughter, your Jasmine Creeper, is waiting for you

Ammachi
Oye Hoi
Ammachi…

Sing the proud self-proclaimed musicians inside and outside, also on top of the Big People Bus in praise of their own Goddess, Minnal.

Meine Mutti
Oye Hoi
Meine Mutti
Ich komme heim. Wir treffen. Wirklich.

Sings Herr Bauer about how he has returned home to his mother.

Herr Bauer has no qualms about proclaiming his overflowing love for his mother. The Guru approves of this overt declaration of love by a long-lost son. Herr Bauer's brother, Thiru Venkataraman, would never approve of such an aberration. All affection in his profession as a politician, must be kept under wraps.

Who cares what the Minister thinks, let us wrap up this journey.

The Big People Bus explodes with the goodwill of its passengers.

Ammachi.
Vandhachi.

Here we come, Minnal, sing the proud men, women and children of Poothotum inside the Big People Bus and on top of it. They are unstoppable. They do not stop singing even when they arrive at the Southern Capital with a Sea. In the Capital, there are slogans in the air. They do not care. They sing above the melee as they head towards their Goddess.

The khaki-clad law-enforcers have given up all hope of curbing the melee. They join the rustic refrain instead, along with the others in the Big People Bus. The Southern Capital rocks with Ammachi, Herr Bauer's liebe Mutti. Ja, ja, aman, aman, yes, yes, Minnal is Herr Bauer's very own loving mother.

Amidst all this leibe, yes overflowing love for Ammachi, where can Venkataraman possibly flee?

***

Nominta Debury has decided to flee. She has spotted a loophole in the lair she has been assigned. This lair already has another new recruit, a twenty-something-year-old-near-woman from Thimri.

Asha Paharia's lair is a windowless hutment with a sole door. There are no other exits, except for the main bamboo door. So where is the loophole Nominta has spotted? In Asha's heart, of course. Matters of romantic love can remain unrequited. At least for the time being.

Nominta is Asha's new lairmate. The child recruit has started talking under Asha's 'unhindered by geographical boundary' care. They are from two different states—Orissa and Jharkhand. Yet, they speak the same language. It is the tongue of the breadwinners of the Kanjipani Mountains and the Dalma Ranges. Their tongues have long been tied—they have not spoken of their fears ever since the day they were born.

Where there is no money and your ancestral lands are under the combined unofficial properties of the Uncrowned Head and the Cabinet of ministers and leased out to mining companies for the highest financial bid, you have no right to speak.

'Kano na?'

'Why not,' asks Nominta.

'Kyun nahi?' reiterates Asha.

Major Ashok Riflewala overhears. He beams from ear to ear. He is pleased. He punches the good news on his BlackBerry.

This Divine Beep makes a suitable impact on Inspector General Bawa. The daughters of the Kanjipani Mountains and the Dalma Ranges will not stay back in the lair to die for what is already theirs. They will both flee. They will go back home to their respective families. Asha has been quick to change her mind about her destiny. Thanks to the enlightened child breadwinner from Manipura.

Special thanks to Naren Nayak, the man who believes in the supernatural powers of Maa Taarini and the natural prowess of the Feminine Force.

Zeta, D'Vaz and I feel powerless on the highway. We cannot trace the direction of the cry—Susanthi Bodra's plea to return home seems to be coming at us from everywhere, and yet nowhere. This girl child must simply return home, we all agree.

Susanthi must return home. She must remain physically unscratched and healthy, just the way the members of the Bochagora Bal Panchayat and the Mukhiya, including children and adults of the hamlet who had sent her off on the highway drive to Sambhalpur. But this child breadwinner of Balangir District is wounded from the shock of looking her dead father in his sparkling eyes.

The Sambhalpur Highway is no place for little breadwinners with homes in Maoxal-inhabited forests.

Urmila and Manohar Mahapatra look each other in the eye. Their eyes are the only channels to communicate with each other—their mouths are gagged, and hands bound tight. What a plight. They cannot wrong an innocent child. They cannot wrong Nominta Debury.

They struggle some more.

They lash out ferociously.

They wiggle.

They struggle more.

They kick with vengeance until the ropes which bind Urmila's legs come undone. She has no time to stop and be happy in her victory. Urmila kicks some more and pushes open the back door of the closed jeep with all her might.

We hear a pounding sound. We leap.

The Guru suggests we act; the pounding sound could well be made by the allies of MDCRFP.

How did the Guru, our ally suddenly arrive in these parts?

This is no time to ponder over arrivals and departures of all parties involved in MDCRFP.

We follow the sound of the pound.

Sound
Growing loud
Louder still
Fists pounding
Our hearts resounding
To the sound of the pound

Until we find ourselves nose-to-nose with a closed jeep.

This jeep is not ours!

It does not take too much effort to rescue two people, especially when we have the might of three. Yes, the Guru has arrived. But he has decided to stay back and take care of my treasure—the baby.

His baby is fragile, she must be handled with care.

Urmila and Manohar Mahapatra are relieved to be unbound. They are even more relieved to hear that Zeta,

D'Vaz and I are here to find the breadwinners of Balangir, Keonjhar and Dalma.

Our mission to find the breadwinners is common. Zeta has met the couple on a mission at a conference for development workers. The couple talk about the Form of Consent and its affiliation with the Sambhalpur Rozgaar Kendra. Urmila and Manohar Mahapatra are marginally shocked to learn that the Form of Consent, which encourages girls lesser than sixteen years of age to sign a 'legal' document, has been worded to suit the whims of Prasad Bharathi and his Cabinet of ministers at the Centre. The Form of Consent declares that once the girls—all aspiring breadwinners—are trained at the Rozgaar Kendras including the one in Sambhalpur, they are required to indulge in a 'suitable' trade prescribed by the Cabinet. In return, Prasad Bharathi and the Cabinet of ministers will use the breadwinners' bodies, brains and limbs as they please for further money generation. The trades include 'consensual' copulation and 'consensual' usage of life-taking weapons, especially shotguns at entry level, and AK 47s at advanced level.

Consensual indeed! What are girls under sixteen years of age, and living in forest hamlets to know either about copulation or about AK 47s? We all want to know!

Zeta Rani has studied the details of the Form of Consent, not once, but over five hundred times. She is aware of all the loops, the holes and the assholes who are involved in this crime of girl-child abuse. We are aghast. Urmila and Manohar are almost certain that Nominta's life is in danger. They are deeply concerned about life, especially in regions where sudden disappearance and ensuing death are perpetual possibilities.

Urmila and Manohar never waste time on shock, the impact marginal or otherwise—there is disappearance to contend with, and it cannot be brushed off as just another sad but true case of a lost girl child of the Kanjipani Mountains and Dalma Ranges.

Let's move.

The time is ripe to find the breadwinner, and 9 pm would be perfect. Leaving a small margin for delays, we all agree that three minutes past 9 pm would be the most appropriate time to enter the jungle. The interim wait leaving each of us with enough mind and body space to strategise our movements in the wild.

There are voices within—little girls in the thick of the jungle beckon us. They beckon whoever is there to rescue them. But ridden in their innocent beckoning is an innate confidence that they will continue to take onus of their own lives, even when they are straddling the wild dangers of the jungle and the horrors of the highway. These little girls are no cowards. After all, fate has not chosen the breadwinners of Keonjhar, Balangir, Dalma, Majuli and Kithapur to be responsible for the lives of their families, for cowardice!

The Guru messages an update. Inspector General Bawa's iPhone 6 plus rings the Divine Beep with renewed respect for the Feminine Force.

Major Ashok Riflewala's BlackBerry beeps with renewed respect for the Feminine Force. He watches from the loophole—this opening to the outside world unknown to Asha Paharia in her own hutment, and comes face-to-face with responsibility. Asha and Nominta are responsible for their own lives. They will flee.

Major Riflewala blinks.

Between the blink of the human eye

There is darkness,

And sudden light.

Major Ashok Riflewala sees within the starlight in Asha's temporary hutment, an empty space which until only a second ago, murmured with the ploy of two breadwinners to flee their bonded misery.

Major Riflewala is pleased. His heart feels warm. Warmer than that night when Asha first stepped on his bare toe. Major Riflewala is in love with Asha. Of course, that little girl Nominta Debury—she is brave too, for her tender age, he says in his newly punched emotional message. This sappy Divine Beep gives Inspector General Bawa an insight into the young Major's massive heart. He shakes his head from left to right, to indicate to Riflewala that there is more left in MDCRFP to right before the Major succumbs to his heart's escapade!

Fade.

Refocus.

Face reality.

Move it.

Major Ashok Riflewala takes off in the same direction as Asha and Nominta. The direction leads him deep into the Dalma Ranges from where the brave girls will take the secret narrow path to Keonjhar—Asha must ensure Nominta's safe return before she goes home to Thimri. This is the same path along which Nominta had dropped pieces of her broken orange bangle, observes the Major with genuine admiration for the near thirteen-year-old girl. From here, the girls will run nonstop, all the way to Nominta's home, under the shade of Asha's 'convenient' Maoxal status.

Phew!

These girls are fast.

See how they run.

They leap into the darkest corners of the night.

They embrace the jungles like the backyards of their own hutments!

Duh!

These jungles are the backyards of their hutments.

Nominta and Asha have family in this backyard—the hathi moi, the saanp, the mayouro, the pakshi—even the Kalarpatra Bagha.

Major Ashok Riflewala's heart brims with pride for the woman he has come to love overnight. All right, he is proud of the girl child Nominta, too.

The night is young, and we trespass the same jungles—these forests are home to the hathi moi, the saanp, the mayouro, the pakshi, the Kalarpatra Bagha, Asha Paharia, Nominta Debury and of course, Susanthi Bodra.

Where is Susanthi? What danger hovers over her near thirteen-year-old frame?

Our hearts pound with trepidation as we embark on our 'find-the-lost-breadwinners-overnight' expedition.

Trepidation.

Palpitation.

Fatigue.

Faith.

In MDCRFP.

In the girl child.

In the breadwinners of the Kanjipani Mountains and the Dalma Ranges.

We are running against the dark forces.

There is certainly a lot happening in the dark.

***

There is also a lot happening in the light. The divine light which defines Swami Vishnu Prem Anand's Third Eye is mesmerising. The blindfolded ministers of the Cabinet have been mesmerised to exit the Stately Auditorium at Maha Mantri Bhavan with the extremely focussed force of Eclectic Disciples.

When they exit, Prasad Bharathi will speak with Swami Prem Anand in private. Secrets pertinent to the unlawful escapades of the ministers of the Cabinet will be divulged, also in private. Swami Prem Anand will then rid the ministers of the Cabinet, off their sins—he will put an end to unlawful behaviour from every investigated angle. What the penance for unlawful ministers is, he will not divulge to Prasad Bharathi yet. Certainly not until all that he needs to know has been said by the street-smart Uncrowned Head.

But the street-smart Prime Minister Prasad Bharathi is certainly mesmerised by Swami Vishnu Prem Anand's divine route to ablution from sins, which he is well aware the Court of Justice will never pardon. Swami Prem Anand has won Prasad Bharathi's unwavering trust, he removes a pendulum from his cloth bag, and hypnotises the Prime Minister. Then, the Swami focusses his Third Eye on the Uncrowned Head and records all Prasad Bharathi must reveal about the misdoings of his Cabinet.

Eeeeks!

The sins of the Cabinet of geeks.

Freaks!

And unmentionable squeaks.

They sound horrible when they copulate with breadwinners others would like to woo and date.

For heaven's sake!

For Swami Vishnu Prem Anand's sake.

For the sake of MDCRFP.

Divest Prasad Bharathi of all power.

Delete the power to twist the context of the lives of breadwinners to feed the greed of the Cabinet, its ministers and their very own despicable Uncrowned Head.

Fie upon Prasad Bharathi!

They call him a leader?

Prasad Bharathi is a traitor—he is faithful to no one. Not even his Cabinet of ministers who report all that's hearsay directly to him—the Uncrowned Head!

Prasad Bharathi hears his ministers, says nothing in return, and uses all the information to feed his own greed.

Indeed!

Beware Uncrowned Head.

You are so dead

Once you have said

What Swami Prem Anand wants to hear you say.

Prasad Bharathi continues to speak without a care in the world, he is still under the holy influence of the Swami.

The Swami nods his head from side to side.

The Force is alerted.

The Swami's hiding force of Eclectic Disciples record Prasad Bharathi's truth from top, wide and every other unconceivable angle on high definition video phones.

Within minutes, Swami Prem Anand and his invisible force of Disciples have accomplished an incredible feat.

Unburdened in his head, Prasad Bharathi touches the Swami's feet.

And the Swami touches a button on his iPhone 6.

Oh, poor dear Uncrowned Head, you are so blessedly dead.

Well, almost.

Swami Prem Anand's iPhone 6 has delivered a video clipping—every news channel has received it. So has

Inspector General Bawa—he is immensely proud of this Divine Beep. All over the country, news channels have divine illusions of their primacy. Each network breaks what has been said by Prasad Bharathi, first.

Jeetey raho!

Stay alive and well, smiles Swami Vishnu Prem Anand.

Hahahahhaha!

The Uncrowned Head is so supremely dead.

About the death of the Cabinet of ministers, we shall certainly see. For immediate impact, the Swami's force of Eclectic Disciples has taken over the documents causing distress and taken off the black blindfolds from the beady eyes of the hypnotised Cabinet of ministers.

For the first time since the rage of the Feminine Force has knocked the bonkers out of the law-enforcers, Inspector General Bawa finds it apt to pat his own back, twice.

Pat. Pat.

MDCRFP is on its way to resolution, even though three breadwinners –Susanthi Bodra, Nominta Debury and Asha Paharia, share the secrets of the night with the creatures of the jungle, four-legged and otherwise.

***

Amidst all the melee in the Southern Capital with a Sea, Thiru Venkataraman's wife speaks otherwise. She has abandoned her despicable man to join the women on the other side. The Minister's wife is powerful, the Feminine Force has suddenly multiplied. It is evident that Venkataraman's faithful Political Advisor Aandavan has switched sides as well. He is on the side of the Minister's wife. The very macho Aandavan too, has joined the Feminine Force.

The Minister of Accounting Affairs is so dead, his closest aide Aandavan, is on the other side.

Down. Down.

Mandiri.

Nee oru Kandiri.

You are such a nasty guy.

You deserve to die! Repeats every man, woman and child on the streets of the Southern Capital with a Sea.

'Vendam,' says Minnal.

'Beda,' repeats Gowravva.

There is no need for him to die. Death is an easy punishment, the affected mothers believe.

The khaki-clad law-enforcers finally know whom to put behind bars.

Thank Maa Taarini for the relentless slogans of the women of might.

Thiru Venkataraman is gone—he is presently counting steel bars.

When one son goes, another arrives. Herr Hans Bauer meets his Mutti for the first time since he fled the hamlet of his birth, running behind the Ambassador car, which had taken his elder brother away. A minister with a long political career adopted Minnal's eldest born to replace the death of his own son. But he wanted only one son. So, he relegated the rest—sons number two to ten, who followed their eldest brother one after another into the metropolis, to the streets of the Southern Capital. Back then, the Guru was young, he worked for an advertising agency in the Southern Capital with a Sea. Taking a walk by the beach one morning, he found a boy who had forgotten all about his recent past. The Guru, a via media for all kinds of lost souls, found the boy a home. Herr Ferdinand Bauer, the Guru's friend, a musician travelling in India from Germany, was childless. He took the boy home to Der Bundesrepublik Deutschland. With all the recent goings on in the Southern Capital with a Sea, the Guru used his unusual presence to detect the roots the boy had forgotten. And Herr Bauer, named so by his foster father, has returned home to his Mutterland.

There is something about Herr Bauer's eyes. Minnal looks hard, and finds her missing son.

A celebration has begun in the Southern Capital with a Sea.

The Prime Source has been in touch with Lieutenant Colonel Hamid, he has also disclosed the whereabouts of Nelli.

Gowravva is headed to the Court of Justice.

The entourage led by Minnal will go along in the Big Police Bus, Komalavalli has had the punctured tyres fixed, and ready for the long drive.

The residents of Poothotum will all go along with Herr Bauer in the Big People Bus.

All Poothotum hamlet's people are to make a fuss for justice at the Capital!

Inspector General Bawa cannot get over the implications of the concluding drama at the Capital. He will be the masterplanner through to the grand finale.

But wait.

This is no time to plan the grand finale.

Where have all the breadwinners gone?

Ask the Kalarpatra Bagha. Ask the Munda—the tall, thin man, with sparkling eyes and a sharp nose.

***

We ask no questions, we enter the jungle. We wander the forests of the night, somewhere within the boundaries of the mining district of Keonjhar, away from the green-carpeted Dalma Ranges. The forest glows. His baby gapes in delight at the fireflies which dot the land and the skies of the night.

The night whispers a tune
To the gently awakening dawn
Just now
We cannot see beyond
A night smitten by fireflies
Lighting the path to freedom.

His baby is free.

The breadwinners of Bochagora, Keonjhar and Dalma must light their paths to freedom. Asha Paharia lights a match, and lets it glow. She has heard the grunt of a wild boar. She will shoot no more. From experience, Asha knows that the flicker from the match will keep the Banya Sikara, yes the Indian wild boar, at bay. Together, Asha and Nominta travel the narrow path between rocks, crevices and Sal trees, crossing deftly over tiny streams, also tributaries of the River Swarnarekha, this waterbody the life-giver which flows from the forest to the city, and through the industrial town of Tatanagar.

Major Ashok Riflewala follows quite happily, stopping for a moment to swing like a Bollywood star in love, hands askance, head up in the air, skipping around a century-old Sal tree.

Susanthi Bodra follows her intuition, she stops for a moment to examine a century-old Sal tree which she remembers from that walk through the jungle with her father. The Sal tree glows. Susanthi has only the light of the firefly by which to harness the dark precincts of the jungle. She whimpers, 'Ami akhon ghoro jete chai.' But, which narrow jungle path will take Susanthi Bodra home to Bochagora?

Ask the sleeping mayouro.

Ask the wandering hathi moi.

Check with the venomous snake if he is awake.

Or, simply trust the Kalarpatra Bagha.

The tall, thin man, with sparkling eyes and a sharp nose smells the presence of a child. It is a girl child. It is the same child that he took into his folded arms—a makeshift baby bed, and rocked her gently on the moonlit night when she was born. There was so much peace that night. He named her Susanthi which translates complete peace in his mother tongue. When his baby walked, he enrolled her at the Bochagora Government School at the behest of the YUPAP volunteers. He cast his thumb impression on documents which officially declared Susanthi admitted to school. Ever since, his baby is called Susanthi Bodra, his biologically begotten pori.

Susanthi whimpers.

The Kalarpatra Bagha stirs.

The Munda man, tall and thin with sparkling eyes and a sharp nose extends his arm all painted with the spots of the jungle leopard, and in the dark of the night, takes his baby's hand into his.

Susanthi trembles. She knows the touch of her father's hand—strong, gentle and protective, all three traits transmitted in the dark of the night, at once.

I clutch my baby in the dark and think of the time when I held her father's hand and walked through the jungles of the night, the air smitten with fireflies. I long to touch his hand again, I whisper a prayer to the universe. Suddenly,

I feel her father's hand—firm, artistic and playful, all three traits transmitted in the dark of the night, at once. There is another trait I detect in the dark—the man I love is tentative, he is uncertain of my response to his sudden touch.

I respond.

I try to break free.

But this is no reverie.

He holds my hand tight.

Susanthi attempts to loosen her little palm locked in the protective fold of her father's hand. She is unable to. This is no reverie. She is amidst irrevocable reality. Her father has decided to take Susanthi home to Bochagora.

The man I love has decided to take me home to Keonjhar. D'Vaz has a role to play in bringing us together—the Maestro leads the way.

***

Zeta Rani, Urmila and Manohar Mahapatra lead the way via a combination of unsafe shortcuts and safe long routes in the dark innards of the forest. They follow the path which the Man in a Blue Kurta has marked. He has known these jungles from the very day he was born. It is where his mother left him briefly, to be fed to the lurking Kalarpatra Bagha.

Really?

On the day she saw her new born baby boy, the mother was spontaneously disgusted about caring for the human result of a forced copulation. She was a proud Mankadia after all. She loved a man, her Munda man, the same man she had married as a child, two years before she started menstruating. By the time she had had her third period cycle, two men clad in white dhotis lifted her from the jungles at the edge of her hamlet while she had gone to answer nature's call in the wee hours of the morning. She was forced to copulate with a drooling minister of the Cabinet in a moving Ambassador car.

The man with sparkling eyes and a sharp nose—he is also thin and tall. This mother's heart is greater than a wife's anger. She took her son back home to her Munda man, she faced the risk of scorn and abandonment. The same Munda man she had married amidst 'nature Gods evoking' dance and freshly brewed Mahua in her Mankadia village. The same Munda man who took her back as wife, home to his hutment in the hamlet of Bochagora. He accepted his wife's son as his own, the baby boy who would turn artistic in later years. It was the same boy who was sired by Thiru Venkataraman—the one and only Minister of Accounting Affairs! The son loved his foster father and followed his jungle and farming ways. Until, he was told about his biological father by Aandavan Kangal—the Political Advisor who had decided it was 'career wise' to track Venkataraman's artistic son. His son's fame would bring the Minister name, he felt.

Some truths are better left unknown.

Chagrined and confused by his dual identity, he would now have none of his foster Baba's care. The Minister's illegally begotten son left home, also his biological mother and foster father whom he fondly called Baba. He drifted in the jungles where D'Vaz found him while trailing his internationally acclaimed masterpiece—the Kalarpatra Bagha. Almost twenty years later, Susanthi's mother went on to bear two more children, including the young breadwinner's older brother Tilka Bodra, who later died.

The tall and thin man with sparkling eyes and a sharp nose loved his wife and his foster son. By the laws of the jungle, biological parents are only in name. Children bring joy to every tribe in the forest land. They share the same sentiment as the four-legged inhabitants of the forests in the Kanjipani Mountains.

When Aandavan threatened to kill his foster son if he did not leave his wife and force her to return to bed Venkataraman, the Munda man took the hidden and 'secluded from community' path of the Kalarpatra Bagha and painted his body with the animal's spots to emulate the mammal's candour. The Munda man then lent his services to the Maoxal Society—he wanted to wipe out all atrocities committed against the tribes of the forest by industrialists, ministers and other perpetrators on the prowl.

***

The Munda man with sparkling eyes is unable to restrain himself from fatherly pride although he has committed to sever all ties, familial and otherwise to foster equality among his kind, as per the prescribed laws of the Maoxal Society. When he saw his biological daughter by the purple-flowered Lantana shrub on the Sambhalpur Highway once again, his heart instantly committed itself to regain lost familial ties.

Once she regained ties with the father she thought had long died, Susanthi Bodra reconciled to the fact that she was still a child.

Words do not come easy when one wants to reconcile oneself with severed ties, especially those which will help bridge the difficult mile back to an empty home, a hutment with the lingering stench of bile.

Silently, Susanthi allows the tall, thin Munda man with sparkling eyes and a sharp nose to lead her home to

Bochagora. She feels comforted by the strong yet gentle, protecting hands of a Munda man, her father.

At the end of a hard day, all roads back home seem rather long.

This walk through the jungle is rather long. Words do not flow when his touch is tentative. Steps falter when there are breadwinners prowling the dangerous jungle trek in search of home. I allow myself to relax in his touch, and hand-in-hand we wander homewards, to the place where my baby belongs.

But why is his touch tentative? Where has the man I love been, on the days, weeks, months he went comatose? He comes close, lowers his head and whispers into my ear. The secret he tells me will remain one, until I promise to keep it from Nelli.

Riding the waters of the mighty Brahmaputra on the reluctantly chugging much-used motorboat, Nelli remembers the man who stole her heart. It is the same man I love. They met briefly on the island of Majuli. He, a wandering artist in a blue kurta. She, a much-visited Maharani—Queen of Love. He promised to visit her that night in her room with a tiny window overlooking the bountiful River Brahmaputra. When the moon rose up in the sky that night, he took the last motorboat from Kamalabari back to Jorhat. From there, he returned home to Keonjhar.

All he could think of that night was his baby and me, he whispers. Will I stand by him? Will I go home to Keonjhar with his baby? Home, where his mother awaits our return in her hutment overlooking the monsoon-fed River Shammakoi in a hamlet of broken families?

I turn to the Guru for advice.

A shot in the dark disturbs my thoughts. It disturbs the entire entourage of searchers for the breadwinners of Keonjhar, Balangir and Dalma. We decide to rest by the swell of Shammakoi—the river of life in the ranges of Kanjipani, to ponder carefully about the implication of the shot.

***

Dancing around the Sal tree, Major Ashok Riflewala has let a shot escape from his .22 rifle in haste. He closes his own ears and hopes that the girls he is trailing do not turn around. He takes another long step with heightened haste.

When jungle paths lead homewards, haste is a virtue.

Nominta Debury and Asha Paharia are very close to Manipura, Keonjhar District, Major Riflewala hears them say. He knows there's no time to waste, especially when Inspector General Bawa insists that the Major lays off all matters concerning his sappy heart while still on MDCRFP.

Ditch it.

There is no time like now for romance.

Major Ashok Riflewala decides to hasten his steps, catch up with the girls on the run, and ask for Asha Paharia's hand in marriage. He beams, and makes his presence felt.

What better place to propose, decide and consent to romantic union in that order, than the jungles bridging the Dalma Ranges and the Kanjipani Mountains?

Asha hesitates to give in to Ashok Riflewala's mushy, 'down on his knees' proposal. The Major persists. Asha consents. For the first time, this breadwinner from the hamlet of Thimri lets her heart rule over her mind. Asha blushes and braves the overflowing emotion of love by extending her hand to her new-found lover. Major Ashok Riflewala does not hesitate to take Asha Paharia's hand into his own. Hand-in-hand they follow the path to Manipura, the hamlet with broken families in Keonjhar, along with the brave girl child Nominta Debury.

The trio, Manipura hamlet bound, scale the narrow jungle path until they halt.

But wait, what is Major Riflewala's identity?

Oh! Ho! The Major is faced with an identity crisis!

Asha's mind gets over the terrible mistake her heart has just made. She is a breadwinner after all and, cannot waste her precious working time on emotions like love, that too with a strange khaki-clad man who is neither Maoxal nor respectable farmer. But Major Ashok Riflewala cannot reveal his true self until MDCRFP has seen the light of day. He has been strictly divine-beeped by Inspector General Bawa to wait until MDCRFP has been accomplished to disclose his true identity to the woman who occupies his big, pounding heart.

Thud, thud.

Divine Beep.

Attention please.

Major Riflewala, Asha and Nominta have stopped by the swell of River Shammakoi to find out what the message in the Divine Beep is all about.

We have stopped. Urmila and Manohar Mahapatra light a fire to ward off the Kalarpatra Bagha. We have word that the YUPAP volunteers have stopped to light a fire in another part of the forest, hoping to find the near thirteen-year-old breadwinner of Bochagora. Susanthi Bodra and the tall, thin Munda man with sparkling eyes and a sharp nose have also stopped. They smell a fire. They see an unusual mix of people from the city and the hamlet walking together in the thick of the forest.

Susanthi speaks. She knows me from that day—the same day we said goodbye. 'We have a lot to discuss,' she tells her father. They decide to join our retreat to talk over matters pertinent to the lives of breadwinners.

Major Ashok Riflewala receives a Divine Beep—it is another instruction from Inspector General Bawa. The trio, including the Major himself, Asha and Nominta must join the retreat expanding with humans by the swell of Shammakoi—Kanjipani Mountains protecting the curve of this bulging river, the generous life-giver.

Life is all around.
Rhythmic beats engulf the retreating dark.
There is an enlightening tune.
Enlightened!
When the night whispers a tune
To the gently awakening dawn
And the stars surround the sun
Brilliance blinds our vision...

The Bal Panchayat of Bochagora is here. Domrudoru Baiga is here! The little boy and his friends have given the hamlet elders the slip and marched into the forests to look for the breadwinner of Bochagora. The breadwinner they fondly call Susanthi Bodra.

By the swell of River Shammakoi, we are ahead of MDCRFP!

But a question looms ahead of the Mission. How did Domrudoru know that his best friend is homeward bound, alone, the company of the Kalarpatra Bagha to keep pace with her?

Well, the Guru has written a message on the blackboard of the Bochagora Village School. This Guru, he acts in mysterious ways—unpredictable as always.

Inspector General Bawa is the mastermind as always. The Force is mysterious. Swami Vishnu Prem Anand is unpredictable.

The Force is at its mysterious best at the Centre.

The time is ripe to Deconstruct the Cabinet and Reconstruct Feminine Power.

How?

'Come to the Court of Justice,' signals the Divine Beep on multiple iPhone 6s, the brand's pluses and BlackBerrys in the most sophisticated language of Inspector General Bawa.

***

All roads to the Court of Justice are jammed. The Big Police Bus ferrying the toothless old grandmother and her entourage for this most important occasion, has been given a dressing up, a tri-coloured Indian national flag flutters on its roof. Right behind this vehicle, the Big People Bus sways from side to side, as Minnal, the Lesser Known Goddess' followers from her own hamlet Poothotum, her comrades from the Southern Capital with a Sea, kith and kin from other locations on the planet, dance in tune to their indigenous composition, 'Ammachi'.

Thandane thaane naane na
Ammachi
Vandachi
To the Centre
With her entourage and
With her 'Germany-returned' son, Herr Hans Bauer.

People all over the streets in the Centre are mighty impressed by this international reunion of the toothless paati—Minnal, the grandmother from Poothotum, a South

Indian hamlet in Mayavaram District with a long-lost and loving son from Der Bundesrepublik Deutschland.

Herr Hans Bauer is imperative because the Court of Justice wants him. Why?

Jhumur Jhumur
Jhumur Jhumur
Kothai jabo re?
Ami akhon Court of Justice e jete chai re.
Sings Susanthi Bodra
Sings every merry child of the Bal Panchayat of Bochagora
Sings Nominta Debury
Sings every parent who accompanies them
Sings Nominta Debury's mother
Sings Naren Nayak
Sings his dutiful ardhangini, Parbothi
Sings the Munda man!

The tall, thin man with sparkling eyes and a sharp nose is called Bisra Bodra—he is imperative because the Court of Justice wants him. Why?

Yay, yay, yay,
Country roads take us home
No, not home
Country roads take us to the Court of Justice
Where we belong
We sing this song
'Cause we belong
To every corner of our land

The man I love, Sridhar Haider D'Vaz, Zeta Rani and I, we all sing along. His baby chooses to listen.

We continue to sing.

We sing this song
'Cause we belong
To every corner of our land.

Croons Zeta confidently, in unison, then separately in a capella.

Zeta Rani is imperative because the Court of Justice wants her and her ilk. Why?

Yelli nanna Nelli?
Where is my Nelli?
Ninna thayiya hrudaya ninagaagi kaadide.
Your mother's heart beats for you.
Hogallo Manthri!
Get lost, you Minister!
Neenondu kanthri
You are cunning.

Sing Gowravva, Mrs Komalavalli Thiru Venkataraman, and the other mothers who accompany the khaki-clad law enforcers in the Big Police Bus. The puncture has been fixed, and the law-enforcers suitably ticked off by Thiru Venkataraman. They have permanently transferred their combined khaki loyalties to the other side. They sit on that side, which takes the fizz out of every minister who tampers with the childlike trust of the virgin breadwinner.

Hogallo Manthri
Neenondu kanthri

Sings Gowravva repeatedly, over the syncopation of voices in the Big Police Bus.

Gowravva is imperative because the Court of Justice wants her. Why?

Jazzz
Razzmatazz

Shrimmm
Hrimmm

Rings the Divine Beep, with its composer the pony-tailed Simply Hare Rama swaying to the rhythm.

Well, here comes the one and only Third Eye sporting Swami Vishnu Prem Anand!

Simultaneously, his Eclectic Disciples swish in with blinding psychedelic light emanating from their Rayban coolers. The enlightened Eclectic Disciples exercise extreme regime with the disillusioned Cabinet of ministers and the dejected Prasad Bharathi—the unscrupulous Uncrowned Head. The Minister of Accounting Affairs is included in this list; he is finally back with people of his kind, all soon to be ex-ministers counting the steel bars of the national prison.

Jazzz
Razzmatazz
Shrimmm
Hrimmm

Swami Vishnu Prem Anand is imperative because the Court of Justice wants him. Why?

Naanu akhon Court of Justice e jete hogabeku re…

Nelli sings in a confluence of words, ranging from the tongue of her 'princesshood', to the language of her 'queenhood'. She declares in her song that she must visit the Court of Justice. She must visit it now. Lieutenant Colonel Hamid Iyer agrees. He joins in the song. The Mising Virgin who prefers to keep her name a secret, tunefully hums along.

The Mising Virgin is imperative because the Court of Justice wants her. Why?

The Court of Justice resembles a place of worship, with an altar et al. The Guru, visible to the core recruits of MDCRFP alone, has special place on the altar alongside the Euterpe, his German piano—his spirit ready to tune into the composition of *Eine Kleine Nachtmusik*.

The Court looks dressed for a ceremony—a wedding perhaps? Major Ashok Riflewala walks hand-in-hand with Asha Paharia down the maroonish-red carpeted isle. 'You shameless Major,' whispers Inspector General Bawa under his deep breath. This disciplinarian simply cannot stand any digression from MDCRFP. Not even when it has been brought to near conclusion. Major Ashok Riflewala's sole intention is MDCRFP and the Mission alone.

Really?

We are precisely in the heart of Mission Deconstruct the Cabinet and Reconstruct Feminine Power, MDCRFP.

The Court of Justice has absolute power to declare the deconstruction of the Cabinet in a democratic country.

Here comes the declaration.

Deconstruct the present Cabinet of Ministers along with Prime Minister Prasad Bharathi, the self-proclaimed Uncrowned Head et al. All evidence is in disfavour of the ministers who have bungled during their elected tenure in office. All evidence favours the citizens of the country and outside the country who have shown absolute integrity and solidarity with the notion of democracy.

The country has a new head: Minnal, the Lesser Known Goddess.

Vandachi

Ammachi

The ambience in the Court of Justice is uproariously rambunctious as the most meticulous and honourable law-keeper of the nation Inspector General Tuffwinder Singh Bawa crowns the Ruling Head of the Sovereign Democratic Republic. Minnal is toothless and fragrant with the perfume of her Jasmine Creeper's flowers. The just Crowned Head beams a toothless smile, supremely in control of the aura she is emanating at the Court of Justice.

'Please note,' announces Inspector General Bawa, 'this crown is purely meant to adorn our new Prime Minister, Minnal. The country under no contention of law has been deemed autocratic. The Crowned Head will now work in tandem with a Ministry of Equals.'

Major Ashok Riflewala makes his useful presence felt. He announces:

'And the Equals are...

'Herr Hans Bauer—he, for choosing to return to his roots, and work for the cause of virgin breadwinners who have signed the Form of Consent by misguided intent.

'The tall, thin man with sparkling eyes and a sharp nose, the Munda Man aka Kalarpatra Bagha aka Bisra Bodra—he, for abandoning his own family for the safety of his foster, artistic son.

'Zeta Rani—she, for working with the tribes of the country, without making a shoo-sha of it. And since she has not made a verbose shoo-sha thus far, let us hear her speech on why the breadwinners of India's poorest States, Orissa, Jharkhand and Chhattisgarh included, as well as other Feminine Forces from across the country, need to be heard.'

Zeta Rani dutifully nods her head with 'matter of fact' grace, and walks up to the altar to enlighten members of the media and people from here, there, everywhere and other dignitaries present regarding the complexities of going to bed hungry.

'Hush, let us hear Zeta's shoo-sha,' mutters Ashok Riflewala under his loud breath to get formalities pertinent to the appointment of the Ministry of Equals over with, and move on to more important matters of the heart.

'Friends,' Zeta Rani's powerful voice puts a full stop to disparity and the hushes, before continuing her speech with clarity, 'I do not wish to make a shoo-sha of the deconstruction of the Cabinet of ministers to reconstruct feminine power with a Ministry of Equals. But, when elected ministers stop being the guardians of breadwinners, especially in the poorest pockets of India including Manipura, Bochagora, Thimri, Kithapur and Majuli among a vast expanse of poor regions in the nation, the affected people and their well-wishers begin to take matters of survival into their own hands. So, the shoo-sha is essential, especially at this power-packed gathering. Too verbose? Well, let's take a break and sing. Repeat after me:

'Tra la laa la laa
We citizens from near and far
Are just so glad that democracy isn't dying…'

The entire Court of Justice breaks into song, albeit in scales that Zeta has never heard before. Zeta patiently waits for the last voice to trail off, and continues with her speech.

'All right,' she says. 'Now listen to my shoo-sha, and don't fall asleep. Decades ago, in the late 1960s, the political party representing far-Left ideologies set foot on the least developed parts of the country to raise voice against the interpretation of land ceiling laws and exploitation of tribal lands for pharmaceutical and mining purposes. Thereafter, governments came and Cabinets of ministers changed, but the tribals—the Santals, Gonds, Kudmis, Mankadias, Mundas among others—continued to be given the cold shoulder, with their lands and their ancestral livelihoods biting the dust. Uncrowned heads came and went, some completing their five-year-long tenures not having raised a tiny finger towards the betterment of these tribals. Thus, leaving them in the dark for over six decades after India's independence, without electricity, sanitation facility, drinking water, nature ennobling sustainable livelihood initiatives, rail and road connectivity and of course, few schools with teachers, if any. I must digress here to praise Naren Nayak for his self-motivated efforts in making education accessible to the children of Keonjhar, especially to little breadwinners like Nominta Debury. Naren Nayak continues to be selfless, just like Urmila and Manohar Mahapatra. But, it has not been the same case with the elected democracy and members of the Maoxal Society. While the elected democracy largely continues to stay unmindful of sustainable development in the remote rural areas, members of the Maoxal Society who started out with the right foot over the Left idea of equitable development with their powerful voices, are now up in arms with their powerful weapons, instead.'

Zeta Rani takes a brief moment to straighten her spectacles, and catches Major Ashok Riflewala snoozing. 'Mr Soldier,' Zeta says sternly. Major Riflewala does not open his eyes. Inspector General Bawa taps him on the shoulder. Major Riflewala promptly opens his eyes and blurts out a series of whats: 'What, what, what what, what?' Zeta gives him a pointed stare and continues with her shoo-sha.

'The industrialists, largely owners of mining companies, believe they are the sole benefactors of the poorest. While the industrialists benefit, the poor toil. The poor continue to live a life of poverty because they lose their ancestral farming skills in lieu of laborious jobs. Now, these laborious jobs will stop providing them their daily wages as soon as their usurped farming lands, the natural habitat of the Kalarpatra Bagha, have been depleted off their natural wealth of minerals. Where power, money and weapons take precedence over sustainable development, the breadwinners need to take matters into their own, tiny hands. We, the democratically appointed Crowned Head and the Ministry of Equals, some names you already know of, others you will hear of soon after my shoo-sha, which, thankfully, is about to conclude with this oath... I repeat, we, the Crowned Head and the Ministry of Equals, will unabashedly stand by the breadwinners, especially little girls and women, both young and old, through thick, thin and all the die-hard din about squashing feminine power. That is all I have to say, thank you very much.'

Loud applause.

For some strange reason, Sridhar Haidar D'Vaz applauds the loudest.

Photo flashes.

Video coverages.

And SMSes lauding Zeta Rani's shoo-sha are received on Nokia 1100s, including Naren Nayak's phone. The message is WhatsApped and Divine Beeps ring on iPhone 6s and their plusses, Ashok Riflewala's BlackBerry included.

'This is certainly a matter of the heart, what a brave shoo-sha,' comments Major Ashok Riflewala under his breath, and continues. 'But the appointment ceremony must continue to its conclusion. Let's hear it for our next Equal in the Cabinet...

'Gowravva—she, for unabashedly loving her daughter even after Nelli sold her body for the sake of queenly aspirations at a very young age.

'Swami Vishnu Prem Anand—he, for carrying out the duties of the definitive force to deconstruct the Cabinet with subtle alacrity, pedicured feet, shirtless torso, sacred thread, see-through dhoti et al.

'The Mising Virgin—she, for refusing to sign the Form of Consent imposed on her by the now imprisoned Mentor Amrit Kumar that too, while she was on the verge of losing her family to death by hunger due to unimaginable poverty.

'With the appointment of these new representatives of the nation, the Cabinet has been deconstructed and in the process, feminine power reconstructed.'

Loud applause.

MDCRFP, yes Mission Deconstruct the Cabinet and Reconstruct Feminine Power has been accomplished!

Louder applause.

The Awakened Peacekeeping Force is duly dismissed from MDCRFP duty.

Sigh, but no sigh. It is time to reap the fruit of one's labour. Of course, love's labour cannot be lost.

Major Ashok Riflewala can now dance in peace with Asha Paharia. But his present dance partner and future bride will first serve a minor sentence as decreed by the Court of Justice. She has, albeit under duress, killed an innocent mayouro, the national bird of the Sovereign Socialist Secular Democratic Republic of India.

Asha might have killed a mayouro, but Prasad Bharathi and his Cabinet of ministers have killed and plundered, and taken everything that is not rightfully theirs, that too, by force. They will be imprisoned for years, until it is time for them to say goodbye to life due to illness or old age or both factors combined.

Nelli cannot say goodbye to the Mising, the rohu and the bhut jholokia. She will return to Majuli and continue to make love with life. She loves her life as Queen Nelli, where smitten customers sing royal praises to her by night. Her mother Gowravva approves of Her Majesty. Nelli has approval from her family—in Kithapur and in Majuli.

Susanthi Bodra and Nominta Debury will again bid goodbye to their families, but for a short time period. They will proceed to the Sambhalpur Rozgaar Kendra after the Court of Justice has been adjourned to get on with more important matters—their training in duck rearing.

'They can simply continue to earn, even while they learn,' decrees Zeta Rani. 'And yes, Domrudoru Baiga can go along. Why leave the future male breadwinners out of the duck-rearing learning curve?'

D'Vaz is rather impressed by the impeccably bred Rani. 'Zeta,' he calls her by her first name. She blushes.

I blush. The man I love holds my hand. I hold his hand, firmly. His hold is no longer tentative.

The Court of Justice has been adjourned.

The newly Crowned Head, Minnal, will proceed to Maha Mantri Bhavan in the prestigious company of her own Ministry of Equals. There is way too much mess to clean up. The work must begin as soon as possible.

ASAP!

Impossible!

There is more to learn.

As the Court of Justice empties, strains of *Eine Kleine Nachtmusik* fill the air. It is true that the Guru has been dead from the start of the story. He turns up in dreams when most needed, he acts in mysterious ways.

***

The story has only just begun. I sit in the rugged closed-topped jeep which left me and his baby behind not so long ago. I remember the day when the Man in a Blue Kurta left the labour of his love with me, and drove away—eyes lowered, his gaze no longer locked in mine. I hold his baby tight.

In the hutment enveloped by Lantana shrubs and vast expanses of land meeting the Kanjipani Mountains overlooking the hamlet where his mother lives, I unwrap his baby, a painting, and hang the likeness of my childhood friend Nelli on the mud wall.

Nelli was once the muse of the man I love. His baby, our baby, is like the princess in the oeuvre of Raja Ravi Varma, Leonardo da Vinci's 'Mona Lisa'. When the Man in a Blue Kurta came face-to-face with Nelli while crossing the Brahmaputra on the lone steamboat from Kamalabari to Majuli, he felt moved to capture her vivacious beauty in his artistic frame. And the painting of Nelli, became the artist's baby. The same baby has just won the Man in a Blue Kurta his first international award.

Sridhar Haider D'Vaz adjusts the unwrapped frame of the baby. Herr Hans Bauer looks on. The Guru has brought him to the home I have moved into. This frame has won the man I love the prestigious Budensrepublik Art Biennale award. Yes, the Man in a Blue Kurta is now a noted artist!

Our baby, the painting of Nelli, has places to go.

Go on.

The man I love signs on the frame. He has found his identity. The surname he never wrote, now reads Bodra. Artist of renown Mangal Bodra, the biological son of Thiru Venkataraman, has taken his foster father's surname.

Yes, the Munda man, the man of few words and careful emotions is now carefree—he smiles, and takes me in his arms, I write in the concluding page of my reporter's notebook.

Epilogue

As I give the finishing touches to the final pages of the novel, I find, resonant in the flesh of *Hunger's Daughters*, the faces of little girls from difficult backgrounds across India, in Kashmir, in Madhya Pradesh, in the alarm of the Kathua Rape Case, in the light or rather darkness of the series of rapes in orphanages in Bhopal.

There's emotional turmoil in the air.

Today, the twilight skies are clear, they add colour to the nascent soul. Apparently.

The soul, every little girl's to call her own. Justifiably.

The eyes, the limbs, the stomach, the face, the crowning glory et al, body parts to be remembered by. Inevitably.

And then, there's the mind. And free will. Thankfully.

So, around six years ago, when good friend Catherine (Cathy) Raja expressed the need for documentation material on the NGO Development Focus' projects in Orissa, Chhattisgarh and Jharkhand, I took a week off from my journalistic duties at *The Times of India*, Bangalore, and set out on a journey that inadvertently decided my future as a writer.

I followed Cathy through terrains I did not know existed on the Indian map. I met emotions I did not know would divest me of my deep-rooted beliefs that a girl bred in a city with easy access to 'quality' education develops. As a city girl, with no roots in rural India, I believed that life is equal and ours to mould by pursuing our dreams. I presumed that reservations were the foil of a non-democratic environment, as much as it provoked my ego to see young girls being pampered, having it easy in the city. Possibly because I started earning as a thirteen-year-old. My father who had plum assignments plummeted at his peak, and I, prodded by both my parents, took pride in earning while I learnt.

Years later, when I came face-to-face with the little girls of the hamlets of Boudh, Balangir and Keonjhar districts in one of India's poorest states, Orissa, I found myself documenting a programme called 'Earn While You Learn'. This initiative was helmed by Founding Trustee of Development Focus, Mr Thomas Paul, who, after spending a few years in the corporate sector, has dedicated his life to developmental work. The honorary assignment I had undertaken, was meant to raise awareness among possible donors to support the cause of enabling the children of these forest hamlets to thrive in their environment, and live off their own lands.

The road to these hamlets involved an overnight journey from Bhubaneswar. On my first visit, I clung on to the window by my seat on the rickety red Government bus to Keonjhar District—towns, forests, deep green mountains where the Naxals are camped, the gushing waterbodies and mining equipment swept my vision, and left my mind in a blur. And then I met the little girls of the deep forest hamlets, and particularly one child whose mother had gone missing on the day we arrived at her home. All this on my first visit to Orissa with Cathy.

On another trip, travelling alone to Paikmal, I wandered out of my 'safe' hotel room, and into the lodging's common dining area at the nearest big town, Balangir. Just one more table was occupied that night. Four 'rice' traders, all men dressed in printed shirts conversed in a mix of Telugu and Oriya. As I watched their gemstone-ringed fingers swoosh back and forth in that dimly-lit restaurant air, and their thick moustaches going soggy with the rum and Pepsi they sipped at more than regular intervals, I overheard them trading deals of not just rice, but 'flesh' from the mining district of Orissa. They were talking of trading little girls from this region, some as young as three. And their own relatives were involved in the exchange, thanks to the never-ending cycle of poverty that becomes a region where mining, legal or illegal, devastates the land, and its people. That night, I left my meal untouched, fled back to my hotel room, bolted the door, and prayed fervently for the safety of the little girls in the forest hamlets.

Travelling home the following day, I had no heart to leave the little girls—all playing, working, laughing, crying, taking care of their younger siblings in the distant hamlets of Orissa...

Back in the city, and many soul-searching conversations later, I sat by the French window at Bangalore's showcase café Koshy's Chillout, and began to write the story of *Hunger's Daughters.* I wrote every day for a month and a half, allowing my soul to take over my mind. Inspiration looked me in the face of the little girls I had met in Orissa, in the smile of an old woman I had met by a temple town in Tamil Nadu, in the mind of my Guru (late) Peter Colaco (renowned ad man, writer, documentarian), in the eyes of the artistic men in blue kurtas, in the hearts of the Knights of the Square Table at Bangalore's landmark restaurant Koshy's – Prem Koshy (renowned theatre person and owner of Koshy's), Darius Taraporvala aka Tuffy (renowned theatre person and head, NDTV South), Manohar Prabhu (engineer, musician, song writer, poet) thinkers and gyanis Nausheer Hameed, Sridhar DS and Ashok Krishnan.

Each day, as my mother sat on the washing stone in the open terrace of our home and wrote *Sreesamanya*, her Kannada novelette, I wrote *Hunger's Daughters* in Koshy's. Each day, Parmesh brought me several cups of tea, and two students of Communicative English—Yogita Dakshina and Mary Pascaline Radjou, sipping on hot chocolate, read the initial drafts of this novel, which I hoped would speak to the city students about the girls from India's most interior hamlets.

Acknowledgements

Hunger's Daughters found her share of first readers in writers Manohar Prabhu and mom Chandra Govindarajan, senior journalists Zahid H Javali and Jayanth Kodkani, renowned theatre person Ashish Chandra Sen, students of English, Engineering and Architecture—Sanskriti Pandey, Madhusree Narayan, Jerome R Manual and Ranjini Prabhu, and I felt encouraged to find her a home.

Hunger's Daughters has gone on to find a loving home in Om Books International. Special thanks to Publisher Ajay Mago for encouraging me to send the manuscript, and Senior Editor Ipshita Mitra for lovingly nurturing it.

Giving this novel her final dressing at the table by the picketed-fence in Bangalore's celebrated theatre space, Ranga Shankara, I thank Anju Aunty and Rohit Sudharshan for the soothing cups of black chai and conversations at their café, little Navyashree TR for modelling, theatre artist Lekha Naidu for the cover photos, interior designer Shilpa Ananthakrishnan for the author picture, IT man Vishal BS for fixing my laptop as it threatened to go kaput every now and then, and Dr Jampa Yonten for his body and mind-healing Tibetan medication. Also, Yogita Dakshina, Christina Daniels, Srividya Hangal, Manjari Ranasaria, Meghna Chaurasia, Tina Joseph, Catherine Raja, the Knights of the Square Table, and my extended family and friends for being there with me on this journey.

As I thank all the blessed people who have inspired this work, especially my mother Chandra Govindarajan who has not lived to see the release of *Hunger's Daughters*, my Guru Peter Colaco who passed on before I penned the first line of the novel, also my father who left this world over thirteen years ago, I feel their 'spirited' encouragement in my endeavour to spread this message of equitable living to the world.